# MURDER IN MANHATTAN

BOOKS BY STEVE ALLEN

BOP FABLES
FOURTEEN FOR TONIGHT
THE FUNNY MEN
WRY ON THE ROCKS
THE GIRLS ON THE TENTH FLOOR
THE QUESTION MAN
MARK IT AND STRIKE IT
NOT ALL OF YOUR LAUGHTER, NOT ALL OF YOUR TEARS
LETTER TO A CONSERVATIVE
THE GROUND IS OUR TABLE
BIGGER THAN A BREADBOX
A FLASH OF SWALLOWS
THE WAKE
PRINCESS SNIP-SNIP AND THE PUPPYKITTENS
CURSES!
WHAT TO SAY WHEN IT RAINS
SCHMOCK!-SCHMOCK!
MEETING OF MINDS
CHOPPED-UP CHINESE
RIPOFF: THE CORRUPTION THAT PLAGUES AMERICA
MEETING OF MINDS (SECOND SERIES)
EXPLAINING CHINA
FUNNY PEOPLE
THE TALK SHOW MURDERS
BELOVED SON: A STORY OF THE JESUS CULTS
MORE FUNNY PEOPLE
HOW TO MAKE A SPEECH
HOW TO BE FUNNY
MURDER ON THE GLITTER BOX
THE PASSIONATE NONSMOKER'S BILL OF RIGHTS (WITH
BILL ADLER JR.)
DUMBTH, AND 81 WAYS TO MAKE AMERICANS SMARTER
MEETING OF MINDS, SEASONS I–IV IN FOUR-VOLUME SET
THE PUBLIC HATING: A COLLECTION OF SHORT STORIES
MURDER IN MANHATTAN

# STEVE ALLEN

# MURDER IN MANHATTAN

ZEBRA BOOKS
KENSINGTON PUBLISHING CORP.

Zebra Books

are published by

Kensington Publishing Corp.
475 Park Avenue South
New York, NY 10016

First printing: July, 1990

Printed in the United States of America

# MURDER IN MANHATTAN

# chapter 1

**O**nce upon a midnight dreary, as I pondered weak and weary—

No, wait a minute, that's not how it started.

In the first place it wasn't midnight. It was about 9:45 A.M. and I was at the piano—the one in the living room—playing Jimmy Van Heusen's "But Beautiful," blissing out on that great composer's basic harmonics and also throwing in a few touches of Errol Garner's ballad technique, just to keep myself awake on this particular dreamy California morning when Jayne flounced—trounced?—breezed?—zoomed? across the screen of my consciousness.

Without lifting my hands from the keyboard, I stood up in a sort of Groucho-ish stoop and wiggled my head back and forth idiotically to attract her attention.

It worked.

I didn't have to explain that I was tape-recording a performance because Jayne was well trained to know that when I'm playing, she should under no circumstances make a grand first-act-Kaufman-and-Hart entrance talking at her top speed, which tops anybody else's speed in our part of town.

While Jayne is perfectly willing to permit me to play a modest role in our frequent conversations, she does not actually depend upon my participation. In fact, sometimes she will look upon a casual "No kidding?" or "Oh, really?" as an unseemly interruption. Be that as it may, and I'm not sure it is, in this instance she stopped, pantomimed an "Are you recording?" message, to which I nodded. I decided to end the performance

at the conclusion of the first chorus, turned the machine off, and
said, "What's up?"

"*Look* at my face," she said.

"I have been looking at it now, on and off, for thirty-five
years. Is there something new I'm supposed to notice?" She was
not amused.

"I'm not amused," she said, "but just *look* at my face."

"I dig it," I said.

"I don't know if I'm going to be able to stand much more
of this," she said, meaning life on planet earth, I suppose. "I'm
not getting nearly enough sleep, and I'm all bags and wrinkles."

"You are not. You look like that every morning."

"Thanks a lot," she said, dripping with sarcasm. And jewelry, too, now that I took a closer look.

"No," I said, "what I mean is you look the way everybody
does in the morning. Even babies look wrinkled and tired when
they first wake up. And I don't know why you're always worried
about your face. Everywhere I go people say, 'How's your beautiful wife?' 'Say hello to your beautiful wife.' You do know, don't
you, that you've got the face of a thirty-nine-year-old woman?"

"Yeah," she said, giving the line an I'm-doing-the-old-joke
reading, "and I'd better give it back because I'm getting it all
wrinkled. What time is your interview?" she said.

"What interview?"

"I don't know, it's your interview, not mine. But they called
from the office to say—"

"Oh, my God, you're right. Let me look in my appointment
book. I've got it right here."

And there it was. A fellow was coming from a local radio
station, with tape recorder, to interview me.

"Thanks for reminding me," I said, rising. "The guy's supposed to be here in about five minutes. Do you think he'll mind
interviewing me in my bathrobe?"

"Certainly not," Jayne said. And then, doing the Groucho
reading without which a good deal of communication among
professionally funny folk would apparently be impossible, "And
how the guy will *get* into your bathrobe, I'll *never* know."

I gave her the sound of a rim shot and looked out the front

window to see if the gates to the property were open. They were not, so I walked into the kitchen, hit the proper button, and watched as the large iron barriers swung back.

"What are you plugging this time?" Jayne said.

"Chiefly the new book."

"Which new book?

"I think he wants to talk about *Dumbth*," I said.

I poured myself a tall glass of freshly squeezed grapefruit juice from the refrigerator, threw in a few ice cubes, and drank it down in almost one gulp, being constantly in a state of at least moderate thirst.

"God, that's good," I said.

"I'm not God," Jayne said, "but I can understand your making a mistake like that."

Jayne switches from kidding to deadly serious in a millisecond, a transformation for which she seems to have a genetic gift. "And what is that?" she asked.

"Since my back is to you at this moment, I'm sure you'll understand my difficulty in interpreting the word *that*."

"Well, *look*," she said, kicking a foot-long black object across the floor in my general direction. "A wing-tip shoe."

"Wrong again, Jayne," I said, noting the exhibit that had just been introduced into evidence. "Wing Tip Shu was the prime minister of Cambodia before the coup of 'sixty-two."

Onstage Jayne is literally the best "straight man" in the comedy business, but at home she often will not deign to descend to my level. Perhaps, fortunately, at that moment an old station wagon with wooden panels pulled slowly through our open gates.

"Here he is," Jayne said. "Don't let him in till I've gone back down to my bedroom. I don't want him to see me without makeup."

She quickly poured herself some hot decaf, grabbed a banana and a bran muffin, put the collection on a tray, and hurried back to the bedroom wing of the house. I opened the front door. Our visitor turned out to be a young fellow with an affable but slightly dopey expression. "Mr. Allen?" he said.

Questions like that are automatically entered into what I

call the drowning-worms file. An illustrative instance concerns a fellow who, when he happened upon another man sitting at the end of a dock, holding a pole and line in the water, actually said to him, "Fishing?" To which came the prompt answer, "No, I'm drowning worms."

I thought of a number of interesting answers to my visitor's question. "No," I might have said, "I'm Jack the Ripper. Please step in and expose your throat." Or perhaps "No, but I do happen to be the winner of the recent Steve Allen look-alike contest."

What I actually said was, "Yeah, hi. Come on in and make yourself at home."

"I'm Jack Corning," he said.

"How do you do, Mr. Corning?"

"I do a deejay interview show here called *Corning in the Morning.*"

"*Corning in the Morning?* Is that right?" As we spoke I led the young fellow into the den, pointed to a wall plug for his recording unit, and nodded to a comfortable chair, in which he seated himself.

"Would you like something to drink?" I said.

"No" he said, "I don't drink."

"I wasn't referring to anything hard," I said. "I mean would you like some coffee, tea, orange juice?"

"No, thanks."

"Do you want to get right down to business?"

"Sure," he said.

I pulled another chair close to the mike he held in his hand and smiled expectantly.

"All righty," Corning said. "Now, let's see here. Mr. Allen, I'd like to ask—er—whatever happened to that wonderful old gang of yours?"

"Well," I said, "you'd have to specify which gang you mean. My first gang consisted of several intimate friends with whom I attended Visitation Parish School on the South Side of Chicago at the age of ten. Then I had another terrific gang in seventh and eighth grade when I moved to the Hyde Park neighborhood. The Broadway actor Richard Kiley was a member of that gang.

Then in Hyde Park High School itself there were Mel Tormé, Niles Lishness—"

"No," Mr. Corning said, "I mean the old gang from your prime-time comedy series."

"Ah," I said. "And you were asking what *happened* to them?"

"That's right."

"I see. Well, let's take them one by one. Have you ever heard of a famous American television comedian called Bob Newhart?"

"Yes, I have."

"Good," I said. "if you've watched his highly rated program for the last several years, you will have seen that it features, each and every week, one of our old group, Tom Poston by name. And I wonder if you've heard of a program that was enormously successful in its first run and has been in constant reruns ever since, called *The Andy Griffith Show.*"

"Oh, yes," he said. "That was always a favorite at our house."

"That's nice," I said. "Then you may recall the little nervous fellow who was Andy's sidekick? His name is Don Knotts, and he was a member of our man-on-the-street gang. He's had a remarkably successful career. As for Louis Nye, he is constantly performing in nightclubs and occasionally appears as a guest on sitcoms. And Pat Harrington, Jr., of course, was the costar of a terrific show called *One Day at a Time,* which ran for seven or eight years, I believe."

"Well, swell," Corning said in such a way that I knew he had retained absolutely none of the information I had just shared with him.

"All righty," he continued cheerfully, looking at a list of typed questions that I had not previously noticed. "Well, let's see here. You and Mrs. Allen have a reputation in the business as a very happily married couple—been married about thirty-five years and all that—but I imagine you must fight about something, don't you?"

"If we did, Mr. Corning," I said, "we'd be very unlikely to want to discuss it publicly, don't you think?"

"Well, swell," he said. "Let's see here, you have one son, right?"

"No," I said, "I have four sons, one with Jayne."

"Well, swell. That's five sons."

"Four," I corrected him.

"Yeah, four, five," he said with a sort of give-or-take-a-son-or-two shrug. "All righty. In case you've just tuned in, folks, this is *Corning in the Morning,* and our guest today is Steve Martin—er—Allen."

At that moment Jayne glided back into the room, having added lipstick and dark glasses.

"Well, look here," I said, this time addressing Corning's listeners rather than him. "Ladies and germs, my favorite actress, Jayne Meadows Allen, has just swept into the room. You may not know this, but she's one of the great sweepers in the housecleaning industry—"

"Oh," Corning said, "is Mrs. Allen actually a good home-maker?"

"Indeed she is," I said. "As a matter of fact, last night she made it home about four in the morning."

Corning looked as if he believed it.

"Hello, dear," Jayne said.

"I wonder," I said, "if we could slow Miss Meadows down long enough for her to join us here on the *Corning in the Morning* show?"

"Gee," Corning said, "that would be a neat idea."

"Neat?" I said. "Well, isn't that fortuitous? Because when it comes to neatness, Jayne is a real stickler. As a matter of fact, if people want neatness, they automatically send for Jayne, and she comes in and she stickles."

"She what?" said Corning, apparently honestly puzzled.

Pulling Jayne onto that portion of my lap unoccupied by my own stomach, I said to her, "Sweetheart, Mr. Corning would, I'm reasonably certain, like to put a question or two to you. Is that all right?"

"I'd be delighted to answer your questions, Mr. Corning," she said, "though I am in a dreadful hurry."

"Jayne was born in a hurry," I explained.

"Okay," Corning said. "Mrs. Allen, have you and Mr. Allen ever thought of divorce?"

"Divorce, no. Murder, yes," Jayne said.

For the first time Corning laughed. "That's very funny," he said.

"Indeed it is," Jayne said. "Unfortunately, it's not a line of ours. It was written by Jean Kerr for one of her very funny plays."

"Jeannie Carson, you say?"

"No," Jayne said, "Jeannie Carson *you* say. *I* say Jean Kerr."

"Well, swell," Corning said. "Tell me, how do you like our weather?"

Jayne seemed dumbfounded that the subject had been changed, however ineptly.

"If I may speak for my wife," I said to Corning, "which I am rarely permitted to do, we have lived here, in this very house, since 1959. It's unlikely, therefore, that our opinions about the southern California weather would be any different from your own, assuming that you, too, are a long-time resident."

"All righty. I see by the biography your secretary sent me that you were a visiting professor at Radford University not long ago. Is that right?"

"Yes. I lectured on philosophy and history."

"Why did they call you a visiting professor?"

"Because I was visiting some of the professors there."

"Well, swell," Corning said. "You're listening to *Corning in the Morning,* and our guests today have been two popular favorites, Steve Allen and his lovely wife, Jayne Meadows, who I'm sure you all remember from her happy years as Jackie Gleason's wife in *The Honeymooners.*"

Jayne's eyes crossed.

My legs crossed.

"At the risk of further confusing your listeners, Mr. Corning," I said, "it was not Jayne who worked with Jackie Gleason."

"It wasn't?" Corning said. "Then who was it?"

"It was Nadia Comaneci," I said. "You may remember the year she won the gold by jumping through that beloved old window, just to the right of the door through which Ed Norton used to enter, over near the sink and the icebox. Remember how she leapt in from the fire escape, jumped over the kitchen table, and hand-flipped right into the bedroom?"

"No," Corning said, "I'm a little on the young side. I don't remember that."

After the young man had packed up his equipment and left, Jayne said, "Good Lord, what exactly *do* young people today know about anything?"

"Actually," I said, "some of them know quite a lot."

"Oh, my God, I forgot to tell you that Irvin called."

"What did he want?" I said.

"What did who want?"

"Irvin, my agent, remember?"

"Oh, yes," she said. "I don't know what he wanted. He just said for you to call him."

It was April 1—a foolish day to take anything too seriously, I reminded myself. The sun was warm, but not too hot—the wind from the Pacific Ocean had swept away the smog and left everything feeling fresh and new. Jayne and I live in the rolling hills above the San Fernando Valley, where, in earthquake season, the hills do roll indeed, and while it is easy to make fun of southern California, there are still occasional days like these when you can faintly smell orange blossoms in the air and remember why all the people came here in the first place.

I suddenly realized I had spring fever. The sweet smell in the air carried half-forgotten thoughts of youth, love, travel, and adventure. I felt like telling Jayne to drop everything, pack our bags, and escape with me on the first flight out of town.

"Oh," she said, "I do remember now. He said that he had an offer for you."

In show-biz lingo that means an offer of employment. I thanked her, walked down the hall to my workroom, and picked up the phone, wondering what surprises Irvin had in store.

# chapter 2

"How'd you like to go to New York for a few weeks and earn a ton of money?" Irvin said when I got him on the line.

"Could I weigh it myself?" I said.

"What?" Irvin has never been the world's greatest straight man.

"Or if not that, could I weigh Marie, from the famous Italian song of the same name?"

Irvin was kind enough to give me an Ed McMahon laugh.

"But all seriousness aside," I said, "what's up?"

"Well, if I were in your shoes, I'd jump at the chance to work with La Volpa."

Hoping that I didn't sound too much like *Corning in the Morning,* I said, "La who?"

"You haven't heard of the woman who is Italy's top fashion model, now an actress, and they say she may soon do a rock album?"

"They say Nancy Reagan may soon do a rock album," I said. "She's got the rocks for it."

"Cut it out," Irvin said. "La Volpa is about nineteen or twenty and absolutely gorgeous. She's the biggest new star in Europe at the moment."

"Jeez," I said. "I go out of town for a week, and I miss all the news. How long has she been that?"

"What time is it now?" he said, using the stock Hollywood line which is accompanied with a glance at the wristwatch if the scene is being played out in person.

"I have the feeling you're leaving out part of the message," I said.

"Well, if you'll stop with the jokes," he said, "La Volpa is signed for the movie, and they want you to work in it, maybe in some scenes with her personally."

"Who are they?"

"The only one I know about," he said, "is Bernie Barnes—you know, Bernard L. Barnes. I think the picture has about a twenty-million-dollar budget, which is a hell of a lot to spend on a comedy, and I guess Barnes is figuring to get some of it back by using international stars. You know, people from Europe, some American movie names, some TV people like yourself."

Actually I was impressed by the offer. Most of us who have specialized in television over the last four decades—Johnny Carson, Jack Paar, Arthur Godfrey, David Frost, Phil Donahue—haven't done that much work in pictures.

Knowing Bernard L. Barnes by reputation only, I was surprised that he was aware of my work, since film people, generally speaking, inhabit one planet and TV people another. I knew he was one of the *auteur* types, a producer/director and to some extent writer who had made his reputation by producing rather bizarre, spectacular comedies. His work wasn't exactly to my own taste, but then I could say the same about some of God's work.

"How much of my time would be involved?"

"I don't know exactly, but at least a few weeks—which means it's a good part."

"What's the name of the picture?"

*"Murder in Manhattan,"* he said. "I haven't had time to read the script myself, but one of my guys here says it's a story about a group of rich New York socialites—you know the type, a lot of time on their hands—and they get pretty serious competing to win first prize at some big, lavish costume party."

The characters, I would soon learn, included matrons and mystics, houseboys and billionaire playboys, and even a French poodle with a trust fund—with one of these assorted socialites willing to commit murder in order to win at the climactic costume party. As for me, I was supposed to play a famous author whose writing days were mostly behind him and who now had an unquenchable passion to succeed in New York society.

"When do they want me?" I asked.

"Tomorrow."

"Tomorrow? What kind of production is this?"

"Look, Steve, I know this is sudden. It seems Barnes is a very creative sort of guy—changes the script all the time. The picture's been shooting for a few weeks now, and just last night Bernie got this sudden inspiration about you. It could be lots of fun. He really wants you."

"I'm flattered, but I don't understand. Why me?"

"This is the clincher," Irvin said. "It's the way you look, you see. It's your striking physical resemblance to somebody. Don't you get it? Remember, the plot revolves around a costume party. Can't you guess who Barnes wants you to be?"

"Do you mean . . ."

"Exactly," said Irvin. "You're supposed to come to the grand finale party as Clark Kent!"

I carried the phone closer to the mirror. One of the odd things about me is my uncanny resemblance to the mild-mannered reporter from Metropolis. In fact, it's been the point of many jokes over the years. Once, on one of my old television shows, the entire audience showed up as Clark Kent look-alikes, just to put me on. It's the glasses, I suppose, as well as the hint of granite underneath. I turned my profile to the mirror. I'm older now, but the resemblance is still there: Just a mild-mannered guy, but let me anywhere near a phone booth . . .

"Not only that," Irvin continued, "but in the middle of the costume party he takes off his glasses, sheds his fifties suit, and turns into . . ."

"Superman!" My voice was a whisper.

"You got it, baby. Red cape, blue tights, little booties—the works!"

"Do I get a big S on my chest?"

"The biggest."

"Well!" I puffed up my rib cage a little and posed before the mirror. I felt I could leap at least tall bungalows in a single bound.

"Irvin," I said, "this is all very nice, but that was over thirty years ago. I don't look like that anymore."

"That's what we told 'em last year when they wanted you for that Jerry Lee Lewis thing—*Great Balls of Fire.*"

He was right about that. The producers of the picture tried to cast a young, thirtyish actor to play me but couldn't find anybody so they finally asked me to play myself.

"But I can't see them using only long shots of me for three weeks in this deal," I said. "The Jerry Lee Lewis role was just a cameo."

"You did it," he said.

"You know my slogan: I'd walk a mile for a cameo. Anyway, I'll think it over and call you back."

"Okay," Irving said. "Remember, I can get you big bread—"

"To hell with bread," I said. "I want money."

"I can get you that too," he said.

An hour later I called Irvin back, this time from my office.

"Listen," I said, "I still don't know whether I'm going to like the script, or the part, or even if I can get a plane out of here in the morning to New York, but let's assume that all of that can happen. Where are they going to put me up if I get there?"

"Oh," he said, "didn't I tell you? The Plaza."

"Corner suite? Windows overlooking the park?"

"Why the hell not? If they need you, they need you."

"Can we get a piano in the suite?"

"You got it."

# chapter 3

**A**nd so on the morning after April Fools' Day, an auspicious day to begin any adventure, I boarded the silver bird from LAX to JFK—two of my favorite acronyms.

There was not a cloud in the upper sky from one coast to the other, and I was in an equally sublime mood. Spring fever had triumphed over reason—I was heading off into the bluest of horizons.

I sat in the first class section, compliments of Bernard L. Barnes, next to a delightful woman who told me all about her children. I am the sort of person people like to tell things to, I suppose. Stories of their lives. Perhaps it's my years as a TV talk show host.

A little later the flight attendant came by and then the captain, and they, too, friendlied it up. I felt quite at home. In fact, everything would have been dandy except for one small matter that occurred to me only when we were halfway across the country: I was about to act in a movie for which I had not seen a script with my role mentioned in it. What were my lines? I wondered. Shouldn't I be memorizing them already?

On the phone yesterday Irvin had given me a general outline of the story and the character I was to play—but I can't remember ever flying off across the country to do a project I knew less about. Of course, at 37,000 feet you tend to become fatalistic. I shrugged and hoped Bernie knew what he was doing.

The plane reached New York exactly on time, except for the fact that we had to circle the airport for two hours. New York, of course, is a very crowded place. Maybe we had to wait for a few people to either die, be rubbed out by the Mafia, or abscond before they would let us in. But what goes up must come down, and eventually we did, too, with a bounce and a jolt, upon the marshy fields of Idlewild.

Even if you've been there a million times, New York always comes as something of a shock. The moment I stepped off the jetway into the crowded waiting room, I had a sense of hectic motion and throbbing humanity. Ahead of me there was an advancing bottleneck of sisters, uncles, cousins, grandmothers, and boyfriends meeting people from the plane, behind me the crush and shove of passengers trying to get off. I was reminded of the first commandment of New York existence: To survive here, thou shalt be aggressive.

"Excuse me, please. May I get through?" I asked with my most mellow California smile. Apparently my manner did not contain the right degree of homicidal fury. Neither sisters, brothers, nor boyfriends budged an inch.

"Hey, doesn't that look like Steve Allen?" one girl said.

"Are you stupid? Steve Allen ain't that tall, and he's much older," said her pal.

The general noise level was deafening. An old foreign woman ran a baggage cart over my right foot. Everyone seemed to be speaking five different languages at once. In the middle of all this modified mayhem, a lean, middle-aged man in a wrinkled gray suit began waving his arms frantically at me from a dozen feet away. Using his elbows, he forced his way through an Iranian family reunion and plunged toward me as if he meant to run me over.

"Mr. Allen! Mr. Allen!" he cried. His eyes were a little wild; there was a cigarette dangling sloppily from a corner of his mouth. I wasn't certain if he was friend or foe.

"Jack Wolfe," he said, offering his hand. He seemed out of breath and haggard.

Whoever he would turn out to be, I had to quickly explain something that relates to a decision I'd made some years earlier, that no one would ever again blow tobacco smoke into my face.

"Jack," I said, "if you'll forgive me, I have a serious problem with smoke."

"Oh, sorry." He dropped the cigarette to the floor and

squashed it with his heel. "Anyway, I'm the unit publicist. Have a good flight? Gimme your claim stubs, and I'll get your bags. The limo's at the curb."

Jack looked as if he had been battling rush-hour crowds in the subway for a month without a break. He had an emaciated face topped off by an untidy thatch of brown hair that fell over his ears. His tie was expensive silk, but the knot was hanging loosely an inch below the open collar of his shirt.

"Come on, Mr. Allen. Let's get out of this hellhole."

Jack led the way, pushing aside assorted Pakistani, African, and Puerto Rican children and old women to make a path.

"Easy," I told him. "What's the rush?"

"Beat it!" he snarled at a Hindu holy man in an orange robe who tried to give him a purple-colored pamphlet.

I stood with him at the baggage carousel while the luggage came down the chute. Then we found a porter to wheel my bags out the sliding glass doors.

"Where's the goddamn limo?" he asked the universe. The goddamn limo, as he put it, was just where it was supposed to be, waiting at the curb—a black Cadillac stretch with a little radio/TV boomerang mounted on the back.

"Wanna drink?" Jack asked as we settled into the cavernous passenger compartment. Not only did this car have TV, it had a bar.

"No thanks."

The limo took off with a lurch, and immediately the driver had to slam on the brakes as an even more aggressive car—another limousine, longer than ours—cut in front of us.

"Goddamn creep!" screamed the chauffeur.

"Schmuck!" shouted Jack, lowering his window in order to get into the fray. "Get the fuck out of the way!"

The other chauffeur was a very large Korean, who stepped out of the car, slammed the door behind him, and began yelling at our driver. "You think you own the road, motherfucker? I'm gonna bust you in the jaw!"

Jack wisely raised our electric window at the threat of violence, but kept yelling from the safety of the car. "Jerk! Get out of the way!"

A traffic cop saw what was happening and came over, hop-ping mad, to have a three-way shouting match with the two chauffeurs.

Sure is fun to be back in the Big Apple, I thought.

# chapter 4

"**M**y agent said whoever came to the airport would have a script for me," I said to Jack as we sped along.

"Script?" said Jack in disbelief.

I smiled uneasily. "You know, at least my scenes."

I didn't like the way he was smiling. "We *had* a script," he admitted.

"What happened to it?"

"Well, B.B. likes to improvise. A genius like that, he doesn't like to feel confined by words on a page."

"Ah," I replied uncertainly. It's one thing to improvise in a small theater off Broadway—quite another to do so with a twenty-million-dollar film.

"If anyone can do it, B.B. can," said Jack loyally, apparently sensing my doubts.

"Absolutely," I concurred. After all, as part of this production myself now, I thought it wouldn't hurt to show some team spirit. "There is, I suppose, a writer?"

"The best!" claimed the unit publicist. "Clancy Donahue himself."

"Himself, is it?" I said with the hint of a brogue. "That's the novelist?"

"Yep. The best-selling author of *The Ravaged Rose.* The man who won the National Book Award before he became a ha—a screenwriter."

"Ah," I said again.

We were silent as the limousine thundered out of the Midtown Tunnel into Manhattan, fighting for each inch of roadway. We nearly ran down an elderly couple foolishly trying to cross in the middle of the block, but with less than an hour on the ground in New York I was beginning to take such close encounters of the worst kind as a matter of course.

"Tell me," I asked cautiously, "is the film . . . coming along okay?"

"Oh, fantastic!" said Jack with a bright but false smile. He looked suddenly like a windup toy. "I think we're going all the way with this one."

"All the way where?"

Jack Wolfe laughed. "No, honestly, you can rest easy about the picture. Why, La Volpa's walked off the set only three times, and the helicopter crash last week—that was nothing."

"Helicopter crash?"

"Oh, hardly anyone was hurt. Just one broken leg and a few shattered nerves. But B.B. likes those clever aerial shots."

"But a helicopter crash!" I protested. "I'm surprised I didn't read about it. How did it happen?"

Jack shrugged. "I shouldn't have mentioned it, really. B.B. wanted the shot to start so low to the ground that the rear rotor of the chopper clipped one of the dressing room trailers. A *very* minor accident, as I said. I was able to keep the whole thing out of the papers by paying off a few people."

"My goodness! Was anyone in the trailer when it happened?"

"Only B.B.'s wife, Mimi. She wasn't hurt . . . but angry? You should've heard her! She stormed out of that trailer screaming that Bernie was trying to murder her and someone should call the police."

"Well!" I sighed, hoping my sudden weariness was only the effects of jet lag. "I'm certainly glad the film's coming along so well."

We reached The Plaza on Fifth Avenue and 59th Street without mowing down any pedestrians, and Jack gave me the key to my suite. Apparently, the film company had reserved the entire ninth floor of the hotel, which seemed a fair extravagance even in this day of multimillion-dollar productions. They didn't pay going rates, needless to say. Hotels are quite happy to make concessions to studios or production companies in return for the publicity they get from being featured in a picture.

My accommodations were everything I had asked for—a lovely corner with a bedroom overlooking Central Park and sitting room looking out upon the small plaza with fountain for which the hotel is named. In the sitting room was a beautiful sight to see—a dazzling white piano, a Yamaha baby grand.

The hotel has always been one of my favorites. There are few in the world that exude this kind of old-time glamour. The Plaza always makes me think about Eloise, the little girl who lived there, in the children's books, in a gentle, aristocratic world that is, sad to say, long gone.

I would have been happy to linger in my suite, play piano, and relax for a few hours, but a small envelope stuffed with three different phone messages that had come in for me within the past hour was at that moment slipped under my door. They were all from Bernard L. Barnes. Each said basically the same thing:

"Welcome to New York! If you're not too tired, would you please come to the set *immediately?* We're filming in a penthouse only a few blocks from the hotel—on Fifth and 71st—the chauffeur who drove you from the airport will be waiting downstairs."

The tone was polite but imperious. I was being summoned, whether I liked it or not, by His Majesty, Mr. Barnes. Being tired, I briefly considered playing difficult and refusing to budge, but my curiosity got the better of me. I must admit I was dying to get a glimpse of the cast and crew of *Murder in Manhattan,* to see what I was in for.

I found cold orange juice in the fridge, changed quickly into another jacket, and left the hotel. The chauffeur was indeed waiting out front, but I told him I'd walk. I had already risked my life and blood pressure once that day in New York traffic and decided that self-transport would be vastly more relaxing.

And then, too, I'd later be able to tell Jayne that, yes, I did get my daily exercise.

# chapter 5

There were the usual telltale signs of a movie company in the neighborhood more than a block from the location on Fifth Avenue— trucks double-parked on the street, two police cars redirecting the curious, and a number of self-important-looking individuals milling about the sidewalk, some with clipboards or paper coffee cups in hand.

It was a cool spring evening. Although I had left Los Angeles bright and early for the five-hour flight, I had lost three hours along the way, and was surprised to notice it was nearly nine o'clock. Either *Murder in Manhattan* was working late or this was a night shoot. The windows of the residential buildings along Fifth Avenue glowed with an opulent warmth, and the muggers were probably beginning to stir in the park across the street. I walked slowly, enjoying the sights and sounds of the city. As far as I was concerned, Bernie Barnes could wait. I've always loved to walk in New York, and in a few other cities as well—London, Rome, most European capitals, in fact. It would never occur to me to walk, just for walking's sake, in Los Angeles—there we do it for exercise—but in New York it's a show a minute, although in recent years there's been somewhat less comedy and more tragedy. Nowhere else does the richest nation on earth parade its homeless so shamelessly.

There was a policeman standing next to the doorman in front of the building on 71st Street, as well as an energetic young man with a kind of thirties haircut—long and wispish in front but cut short on the back and sides. He was wearing loafers without socks, pants that were baggy in the middle but tight at the ankles, a white T-shirt upon which was written PRESSURE

MAKES DIAMONDS—and, to top off this strange sartorial combo of styles, a deep blue blazer with a discernible Ralph Lauren Polo insignia on the breast pocket. When did street attire in our country stop being clothing and become costume? Probably in the sixties, I think, when young people began wearing Tarzan headbands, Buffalo Bill jackets, cowboy pants, and hermit sandals. Cradled in this young man's arm was the semi-regulation clipboard, by which I gathered he was a member of the crew.

"Hey! You must be Mr. Allen!" said the youth.

"Yes, it *is* an obligation," I concurred.

"Too much!" he said, from which I gathered he was glad to make my acquaintance. "I'm Trip Johnson, third assistant director. It's really exciting to meet one of the great names of yesteryear!"

I arched an eyebrow at the yesteryear factor while Trip Johnson shook my hand in a most energetic manner. He was a friendly young man—a little too friendly, in my opinion.

"You just flew in today, huh? Listen, Steve, you need anything, you let me know, okay? I mean, that's what I'm here for, to make everyone happy."

"Mokay," I said. "As a matter of fact, Trip, you could guide me to the set."

"The set? Hey, no problem, dude. All we do is get in the elevator and go uppity, uppity, up."

Trip led the way into the marble lobby whose old-New-York smoked mirrors on the side walls showed about sixteen of each of us walking with Rockette precision. We stepped into an elevator and went uppity, up—clear to the penthouse. Trip kept grinning all the while, apparently regarding me with great interest. I judged him to be about nineteen years old. Assistant director, of course, sounds like a fairly glorious job, but by the time you get down to *third* assistant, what you have is your basic gofer, usually someone's relative, friend, or lover, who is being given an opportunity to learn the movie biz.

"So you want to be an actor? A director maybe?" I said.

Trip shrugged. "All I know at this point is I want to make tons of money."

"Ah, well," I said vaguely. It's always inspiring to meet a young idealist.

The elevator door opened onto a posh foyer with some French provincial furniture, the kind that appears too old and uncomfortable to actually use. Across the vestibule I could see a crowd of movie people, actors and crew, wandering around the living room. Thick electric cables were stretched across the carpets, snaking their way through the apartment toward the terrace.

Trip was still at my side, beaming.

"Like I said downstairs, Steve, anything you want in New York, *anything* at all, you come to me."

The second time around I was beginning to catch his drift. Trip dispensed the pharmaceuticals. If I wanted to get high, low, or sideways, he was the man to see.

"Could you get me tickets to the ballet?" I asked, all wide-eyed innocence.

He gazed at me a moment as if I were slow on the uptake, then saw I was putting him on.

"Hey, too hip for the room," he said with a wink.

It was not looking good. Not only was the nineteen-year-old yuppie third assistant director a drug pusher, but the other thirty or so crew members were standing around looking glum and bored, talking in low, conspiratorial whispers. Movie making is a strange thing to watch: At any given moment on a set it may seem as if nothing is happening. But the nothingness I was witnessing here seemed even more final, perhaps apocalyptic. To give you an example, I noticed a carpenter—tool belt on his waist—curled up on a Louis XIV sofa fast asleep.

"These cats are pretty burnt out," explained Trip. "Everybody's been working since eight-thirty this morning."

"You mean this isn't a night shoot?"

"This is overtime, babe," said Trip.

"Good God."

I looked at my watch. It was nearly nine-thirty, which meant the crew had been working for thirteen hours straight.

One thing you must understand about movie making is that once you're into production, it's like a taxi meter that's running all the time. The union wages for an average film crew—the cameramen, focus pullers, gaffers, makeup artists, etc.—as well as the rental costs of the lights and cameras, location costs, catering, just to name a few factors, come to as much as twenty to thirty thousand dollars *per hour,* and when you start getting into overtime and night shooting, you can double that figure easily.

I was adding up these staggering costs in my mind when I became aware of a disturbance at the far end of the room. Two attractive young women were shouting at each other.

"I think it's positively *barbaric* to wear the fur of a beautiful living creature!" came the angry voice of a rather lovely blonde.

"But, darling, thees leettle mink—she's-a dead a long time," said the other, who was dark and sultry. I had a feeling this could only be the infamous Victoria La Volpa, who at the moment was wearing a tan raincoat with a rich mink collar.

The blonde was spitting mad. "Those poor creatures died for your vanity!" she cried. "If you were a bit more clever, Victoria, you'd know this year all the *really* chic people are wearing fake fur."

"Who you call not clever? When's the last time a man give *you* a mink coat, darling? Somehow, I think never."

"No, I pay for my own clothes."

"Are you calling me a whore?" demanded an irate La Volpa.

It was looking bad. The two actresses were on the verge of a real cat fight, pulling hair and scratching, when Trip Johnson dashed from my side and managed to get himself between them.

"Hey, babes!" he announced. "What you two dolls need is a real man—like me!"

This was so patently absurd that both women turned their backs to each other and made a show of total indifference. In a moment I heard La Volpa asking the cameraman if American women were *really* as frigid as they appeared. I shook my head and wondered what the hell I had let myself in for.

I wandered through the room on my own, listening to the grumbling of the crew members, who generally know if a film is going to be a hit or a flop long before the producers or the

director. The living room of the penthouse was about sixty feet
long. I turned a corner and came out onto an open terrace that
was set up as a little garden, complete with trees, a patch of lawn,
and even a small fishpond. From over the edge of the terrace I
could hear the sounds of traffic on Fifth Avenue, as well as
whistles, laughter, and a few screams of people perhaps being
raped or mugged in Central Park.

Bernie Barnes was standing on the terrace, one arm resting
affectionately on a 35mm movie camera—a big old Mitchell,
blimped for sound, mounted on a dolly. I recognized him from
photographs. He was an enormous man, over six feet four in
height and probably weighing three hundred pounds.

"Look, I don't care what it costs," he was saying loudly to
a small, tidy man. "I've *got* to have that shot."

"Bernie, please, *not* another helicopter," pleaded the other
man, who was every bit as small as Barnes was big.

"Oh, yes, a helicopter shot!" Bernie shouted. There were
a few people standing around besides myself, but Bernie and his
associate paid no attention to any of us.

"Use your imagination, for chrissake!" Bernie said—and
there was a faraway look in his eye as he visualized the scene.
"The camera is in as close as we can get on La Volpa, and we
pull back slowly, slowly . . . first her face, then her figure, then
we see this terrace, and still the camera keeps pulling back, back,
to show the penthouse, the building, Fifth Avenue, the park, the
East Side, and finally *all of Manhattan!*"

The small man sighed piteously. "Why not show all of
North America?" he cried in despair. "Just think how much *that*
would cost, Bernie."

"Money! Jeez, that's all I ever hear from you, Nash. Money,
money, money!"

I thought the small man was about to get on his knees and
beg, but he merely brought his palms together in prayer.

"Yes, money," he said. "Are you crazy? We've been shooting only fifteen days, and we're already four million dollars over
budget."

"You gotta expand your horizons, Nash," Barnes said

grandly. "Better *Murder in Manhattan* than 'Death at the Box Office,' my friend."

I was definitely beginning to think I should have stayed in Los Angeles. I cleared my throat and Barnes turned my way. His face lit up with sheer pleasure.

"Thank God!" he cried. "Superman to the rescue!"

# chapter 6

Although I am six feet three inches tall and weigh 200 pounds, Bernard L. Barnes clasped me to his breast like a long-lost child and kissed the top of my head with a loud smack.

"And so we meet at last," he said, holding me by my shoulders and studying me like a sculptor regarding a piece of clay.

"You know, I had a dream about you, Steverino," he continued in a dramatic whisper. In the instant I understood part of the reason for Barnes's success: He had the natural gift of the born conman, the ability to manipulate others through a somewhat paradoxical combination of aggressiveness and charm. It was the same quality I had seen in a good many politicians, a few military men, some members of the clergy, salesmen of the old-fashioned type, and—oddly enough—very few actors. "I was sitting on this fantastic golden throne surrounded by beautiful half-naked women, and slaves, and groveling PR men—and all of them wanted something from me. Have you ever had a dream like that?"

"Well, actually, Bernie . . ."

"And then it was as if the sky parted and a big white bird came down from the heavens and sort of perched near my nose—it was a pigeon I think—and the pigeon opened its little beak and spoke. Can you imagine what he said?"

"Schmock! Schmock!?"

"No. The pigeon said, 'Send for Steve Allen.' Just like that! Can you believe it? I was able to understand it and everything: *'Send . . . for . . . Steve . . . Allen!'*"

"This was the word from the bird, was it?" I asked politely, beginning to fear the renowned director was more than a little mad.

"That was it," Bernie said. "Well, I woke up and the first thing I did was call Nash—at three o'clock in the morning—didn't I, Nash?"

The neatly dressed man with whom Bernie had been arguing rolled his eyes. "You sure did, Bernie. Three o'clock in the morning. By the way, I'm Nashville Stuart, the executive producer," he told me, offering his hand.

"Pleased to meet you," I said. Stuart did not look particularly pleased, but he was trying hard to be nice.

"And *what* did I tell you at three o'clock in the morning?" Bernie prodded.

"You told me to get Mr. Allen," said Nash wearily.

"That's right! My exact words were 'Get Steve Allen here on the first goddamn plane out of L.A, *whatever* the cost,' " said Bernie, beaming at me in a proprietary way. "And you see? Here you are. It's kismet, isn't it? Or kiss ass, or somethin' like that."

"Could be," I conceded.

"You comfy in your suite?" Bernie asked suddenly.

"Loved every moment of the three minutes spent there," I replied.

"And the piano's all right?" asked Nashville.

"The piano's grand," I told them.

Nashville Stuart was not really as small as he had seemed in my first impression, except in relation to Barnes. They were an odd pair all right. Barnes, a giant, had a flabby, strangely childlike face. Just so you wouldn't miss him in a crowd, he was dressed in a kind of iridescent jogging suit. Nashville Stuart, on the other hand, was a genteel, frail-looking gentleman dressed in an impeccable gray suit. He had an aesthetic, Leslie Howard sort of face—aristocratic and slightly pained by the coarseness of the life he had to endure. I had a feeling he would rather be listening to Mozart than to Barnes.

"Well," I said brightly, "I'm dying to see the script."

All the false conviviality went suddenly flat. Nashville licked his lower lip and looked embarrassed. Bernie's eyes went cold.

"Look, I have to run," Nash said quickly, glancing at his

Rolex. "Great meeting you, Mr. Allen. Let's get together for dinner one of these nights. You and your lovely wife."

"Good idea," I told him.

The lovely-wife line, of course, is one of the great clichés of show business. In my case it makes sense, given that Jayne is extremely attractive, but she could have looked like Ernest Borgnine in drag, and Stuart would still have referred to her, to my face, as "your lovely wife."

Nash ran, as promised, as quickly as he could from our sight. Bernie put a big gorilla arm around my shoulder.

"You know, Steve, we're going to make a great movie here," he confided. "I feel it deep down in my soul—a *great* motion picture."

"Bernie, about the script—"

"Only we gotta be constantly on the qui viverooni for all the jerks—know what I mean? People like Nash Stuart, who don't really believe in the healing power of motion pictures like *we* do, Steve. This is his *second* feature film, but he thinks he can tell old pros like you and me what to do. Just because the guy's chairman of some big oil company, he thinks he knows all about film making, for chrissake!"

"Where's my script, Bernie?" I asked mercilessly, though smiling.

"Script!" he cried. "Let me go one better than that, let me *tell* you about your part."

I knew I was in trouble: *There was no script.*

"What I have in mind for you to play, Steve, is a kind of cross between, well, Truman Capote and Gore Vidal, with a little bit of Jackie Collins thrown in—see what I mean?"

"No," I said in all honesty.

There was a dreamy look in Bernie's eyes. I had a feeling he was seeing his ideas magnified a hundred times, projected on a big screen. Or maybe he was even further along than that, seeing himself step up to the stage at the Oscars to accept an Academy Award.

"Just listen to this, Steve—you're playing a writer, actually a small-town fella who's made it big in New York, and your goal now is to be accepted by all the rich society snobs. Get the picture? Maybe these people are using you, trotting you out at their cocktail parties like some kind of trained monkey, but you don't even notice that anymore. You're a guy with talent, but at the moment all you truly care about is winning first prize at some dumb costume party."

"This is a comedy?" I asked.

"This is biting satire."

"And so I come to the party as Clark Kent?"

"Yes! You see how symbolic this is? Deep within the soul of a writer lurks a secret hero. It's Walter Mitty time! And the party itself, it's going to be *fabulous!* We're going to film an entire sequence on a hundred-and-fifty-foot yacht that's anchored on the East River. It's all going to be so deliciously decadent—we'll outtrump the Trumps. What I'm trying to show, of course, is the utter wastefulness of the flashy rich. Once this film is out, no one will *dare* be rich ever again."

"I see," I said slowly, thinking I was going to go back to the hotel and telephone Jayne and Irvin to say I was coming home.

"I'm going to vivisect New York society," he confided. "Cut it up into tiny bite-size pieces. God, do I hate some of these rich schmucks!" He shouted suddenly—not to me, but seemingly to all of Fifth Avenue at his feet. "Goddamn stuck-up bastards like Nash Stuart who don't know *anything* about the—the suffering it takes to be a true artist."

"Well, that's all very interesting, Bernie, but without a script—"

"Pussycat!" he cried suddenly. At first I thought he was talking to me, which seemed strange even for a mad genius, but then, turning, I saw a glamorous older woman come up from behind.

"Steve, do you know my wife, Mimi? In the film she plays Josephine Van Arndt, biggest gossip in New York—a wonderful part."

I knew, of course, who Mimi Day was—she'd been a respected film star during the early sixties. She had put on some weight since her glamour years, and there was a subtle aroma of scotch surrounding her like a shroud. Only her hair remained as it had been twenty years before—platinum blond and full of elaborate waves. I said hello and offered my hand.

"Hello, Mr. Allen," she said in a throaty voice, and then to her husband: "Darling, what have you been doing to dear little La Volpa? She seems terribly upset."

Instead of answering his wife, Bernie turned to me and said in a man-to-man voice, "Ah, these actresses . . . who knows? They think they're the center of the fucking universe."

I was embarrassed.

"Except for me," laughed Mimi. "I've learned my place— it's the director who's the center of the universe, isn't it, darling?"·

Swell. Blood on the carpet, right in front of me.

"You got it, pussycat," said Barnes with a grand grin. He put an arm around his wife, and they both tried to look like a couple of lovebirds. It was not a convincing show.

"We must have Steve over for dinner one of these nights," said Mimi.

"Absolutely," Bernie agreed. "Hell, you can make sushi, for chrissake."

"I'm still a beginner," Mimi said. She giggled modestly. "At making sushi, I mean. My seaweed rolls tend to come apart."

"Ah, well," I muttered vaguely. This was fast becoming a conversation that was all bubbles on the surface but flat underneath.

Just then La Volpa came onto the terrace and Bernie, obviously relieved, said, "Time to get back to work. God knows we can't waste Nashville's precious money."

He left me standing with his wife. We watched him greet La Volpa with a kiss on both cheeks and then take her dainty hands in his own and begin to speak in soft, soothing tones. La Volpa, I should mention, was a striking young creature. She had raven black hair, a tiny waist, lovely breasts, and disturbing hips. Her eyes seemed almost turquoise, I noticed, and her skin was as pale and smooth as Snow White's.

Bernie led her gently in front of the camera, almost as if it were an accident that they should end up at such a propitious place. La Volpa was pouting, but he kept working at her with soft-spoken words I couldn't quite hear. Eventually I saw a small smile cross her lips.

By my side, Mimi had unconsciously taken hold of my arm and was squeezing hard. Her eyes followed her husband and Italy's newest sex kitten.

"One of these days I'm going to kill that bastard," she told me tensely.

"Kill, er . . . your husband?"

"Cut his bloody throat!"

Mimi let go of my arm and drifted away. Yes, I thought glumly—*Murder in Manhattan* was certainly looking like loads of fun.

# chapter 7

**O**ut of curiosity I stood behind the camera for a time, between the script girl and a light stand, watching Bernie direct the next scene with Victoria La Volpa. As soon as the camera began to turn, he became a new person. Big as he was, he was suddenly graceful as a jungle cat—and probably every bit as predatory—pacing restlessly near the camera as though he could barely stand the excitement.

"Cut! Cut!" he cried to the crew, and sprang out upon La Volpa as though he meant to eat her alive.

"No, no, my dear," he said with strained patience. "That's not quite it. We'll have to try again."

The camera turned once more, and Bernie watched the young actress, a most intent expression on his face. The scene was simple—there wasn't even any dialogue. La Volpa merely had to wander out from the penthouse apartment, walk to the edge of the terrace, and peer wistfully into the New York night. Simple, yes—but La Volpa couldn't get it right. They filmed one take after another, with Bernie making a supreme effort not to pull his hair.

Finally, since they weren't shooting live sound, he tried to coax her through the scene from behind the camera: "Don't walk, my dear, *float*. That's right, float out onto the terrace. Remember how stifled you felt in there. Now you're free, you're by yourself, you can let your emotions show. . . . That's right! Now walk to the edge of the terrace and take a big breath. Okay . . . but not *too* much air—you're not a fuckin' balloon. . . . That's it, sweetheart. Now, just for a second, we think you're about to do something really crazy, like tear off your clothes . . . or jump off the terrace—*cut!*" He screamed the last word.

"Was eet all right, Bernardo?" asked La Volpa anxiously.

Bernie pranced from behind the camera and seemed to be all around her. "Close, but not quite, my dear," he said, taking her hand. "Let's try it again, and this time try not to look like you're a mannequin in a store window."

"But, Bernardo . . ."

"Just trust me, my little osso buco. You must let the feeling well up from inside you. Don't just put on an expression as if it's a mask."

And so they tried again. And again. And again. Unfortunately, beautiful as she was, La Volpa was only a model—not an actress. Bernie did everything but do the scene for her himself. He was endlessly patient and kind, and his voice became ever gentler as she continued to blow one take after another.

"We have all night, sweetheart. Don't let this worry you a teensy bit," said the fatherly director to the young would-be actress.

At last I saw Bernie summon Trip to his side. I happened to be standing close enough to hear what he said. "Go inside, stand right behind the bitch, and just as the scene is about to begin, pinch her hard on the ass."

This was scene 147, take 13, according to the clapper boy. He stifled a yawn as he slapped the stick in front of the lens.

"Rolling!" said the cameraman.

"Action!" cried Bernie.

From inside the penthouse we all heard a sharp cry as La Volpa got her bottom pinched by the third assistant. This wasn't the Stanislavsky "method," but for the first time all evening La Volpa came out onto the terrace with some dramatic flair in her movements. She looked suddenly like a young lady who could think of nothing except getting away from a very oppressive experience.

"Splendid, my little linguini," purred Bernie. "And now breathe in the night air, hug yourself a little—pretend you're in the clean, wonderful Alps instead of dirty old New York. . . . Now walk to the edge of the terrace. . . . Yes, my dear. Now look slowly down . . . down . . . to Fifth Avenue so far below. It looks so peaceful there, doesn't it? So dark and deep. You feel your whole body relax. . . ."

As he spoke, Bernie's voice became softer and softer, until it seemed to have all of us hypnotized. Suddenly, out of the softness, he screamed one horrifying word: *"JUMP!"*

The command came like a hurricane. I think we all jumped nearly out of our skins. As for La Volpa, the poor girl was standing at the edge of the terrace with only a waist-high railing to keep her from hurtling down the twenty floors to the street below. She lost her balance, lurched forward, and for a terrible moment I thought she was going to fall. Then she clasped the railing and saved herself. It was an Academy Award-winning impression of a young woman who had nearly committed suicide.

"Cut!" Bernie cried, this time in triumph. "That's a print!"

He rushed to the ashen-faced actress who was still staring at the avenue so far below.

"My God, that was sublime," Bernie said. "You see what a fine actress you can be? I absolutely *defy* the critics to say you're nothing but a big pair of—"

"But, Bernardo, I nearly fall to my death!"

"You must trust me." Bernie took her little-girl hands in his big paws and pulled her gently away from the edge. I saw her put her head against his shoulder and let out a small involuntary sob.

"There, there," he cooed. "Would I let my favorite little canellone get all squashed on nasty Fifth Avenue?"

# chapter 8

**T**rip Johnson tripped on over to tell me I had an appointment with Annie Locks, the costume designer. Still shaken from watching the near death of Victoria La Volpa, I followed him meekly.

"Is that the usual way Bernie directs a scene?" I asked.

"Hey, the guy's a genius," said Trip with a shrug of his shoulders. "What can I tell ya? We never know what to expect."

I was getting pretty tired of hearing what a genius Bernard L. Barnes was. Even if it were true, and I was not convinced that it was, there are still limits to what "genius" entitles you to do in a civilized society.

The third assistant led me down a long hallway to where a temporary wardrobe space had been set up in one of the bedrooms and disappeared, saying unfortunately he was too busy to keep me company during my fitting. I told him I'd somehow manage without him.

The room was a cozy clutter of material and sewing machines. Clothes of every description hung from temporary racks. Presiding over this happy chaos was a small but pretty woman with one of the most pleasant faces I have ever encountered. Annie Locks could not have been over five feet tall—she was like an elfin queen, with everything in miniature, and cute as she could be. She had blond hair that looked natural as sunshine, a round, smiling face, and big, childlike, china-blue eyes. The age of an attractive woman these days is more and more inscrutable, but if I were forced to take a guess about Annie's, I'd say near forty. She wore a smock whose many pockets were stuffed full of tape measures and other tools of her trade.

"Mr. Allen, welcome!" she said with a little laugh, shaking

hands shyly. "You're going to need your famous sense of humor on *this* production!"

"It's that bad?" I asked, laughing along with her. "At least I seem to have found one normal person in this crazy crew, Ms. Locks. I was beginning to despair."

"You must call me Annie."

"And you must call me Steve. I hope we're going to be friends."

I meant it too. What a relief it was to find one simple, everyday kind of person in this group of maniacs and kooks. I liked her immediately.

She stood me in front of a three-way mirror and began to take measurements from my ankles up, humming the Toreador Song from *Carmen* while she worked.

"Inseam thirty-two," I said, to save her embarrassment.

When she got to the upper part of my body, she had to climb on a small stepladder, which made me feel a little like Gulliver in the land of the Lilliputians.

"Oh, you're going to make a *lovely* Clark Kent," she said merrily.

"I hope so," I told her. "It does seem unusual, though, to be written into the script after the shooting has begun."

"Ye-es," she agreed, half singing. And then she added, almost in a motherly way: "Poor Clancy!"

"Clancy Donahue? The writer?"

"Himself. Poor man doesn't know whether he's coming or going. Bernie changes his mind all the time, you see. Sometimes he calls Clancy up at two, three o'clock in the morning with a totally new idea for the next day's shoot and expects the poor man to get out of bed and type up new dialogue—just like that!"

I made a clucking noise with my tongue. "That can't be easy."

"He's so sensitive too."

I knew I was encouraging Annie to gossip, which probably wasn't nice, but I was still trying to fathom the depths in which I would be swimming the next few weeks.

"Why do you think he puts up with it?" I asked casually. "Does he need the money?"

"Oh, it's not the money," she said in a low voice. "It's so he can be near *her!*"

"Ah!" I said. "Herself, is it?"

"And she doesn't care, of course. She hardly knows he's alive."

"When you say *she,* you mean . . ."

"La Volpa, of course! Have you met her yet? A sweet little thing, but, Lord, she totally devours the men! Has to have them all!"

"I couldn't help but notice," I mentioned, "that sweet little La Volpa and some blond girl were about to scratch each other's eyes out a short while ago."

"Oh, that must have been Suzanne Tracy," said Annie. "Such a lovely girl, and a very talented actress. Do you watch her in *Time and Tide?*"

"In what?"

"That's a soap, Steve. Very popular, as a matter of fact. Suzanne plays Alexandra de Milo, a Hollywood starlet who has only a few years to live and become famous before she dies of some rare disease."

"Hardly seems worth the trouble."

Annie chuckled. "Suzanne does a good job with it—but, of course, she studied with the Royal Academy in England for several years. She's a very serious young lady—an avid environmentalist. There's never been any love lost between Suzanne and La Volpa, as I'm sure you can understand."

Actually, I did not understand. Beyond the question of being pro-fur or anti-fur, I had no idea what the real problem was between Suzanne and Victoria. Moreover, I suddenly didn't want to know.

"Tell me something, Annie," I said impulsively. "I'm thinking of quitting this damn production and heading back to California. What do you think?"

Her blue eyes flashed at me in amusement. Generally I don't consult people I've just met about important decisions, but there was something about Annie that made you want to confide things to her. I was genuinely interested in her opinion.

"I'd give it a few days," she answered after some thought.

"I know Bernie can seem, well, abrasive. But he's not really such a bad man. You know how creative people can be—so obsessive about their work. Deep down inside I suspect Mr. Barnes is terribly afraid of failure."

"Deep down inside he almost drove La Volpa over the edge of the terrace to her death a few minutes ago! No matter what sort of genius Bernie may be, there's no excuse for *that!*"

"No," Annie said slowly. "I suppose not. It makes me sad to see what's happening on this production. You see, this is my third film with Bernie. Oh, we used to have such fun on location! He can be the most charming man you'd ever imagine . . . though that may be hard to imagine now."

"What made him change?"

"I think it's the pressure to keep making brilliant films. Recently he seems to be . . . well, falling apart."

Great! Just what I needed, a job with a director who's falling apart.

"Give it a few days, Steve. Won't you?" Annie said again. "And come to me, well . . . if there are any problems. There are things I know about Bernie—"

Annie stopped in midsentence and smiled ruefully. "I'm talking too much, aren't I? It's the curse of my profession."

"I bet everybody tells you their secrets."

"Oh, that they do. And I mean it about coming to me if you have problems with Bernie. There are . . . ways to deal with him. Why don't we just leave it at that?"

This was becoming a strange conversation, and yet I didn't doubt that little Annie Locks, in her own shy way, knew some powerful secrets indeed.

Humming softly, she searched through her racks and came up with a blue suit.

"Steve, do you mind trying this on? It's close to your measurements. It'll give me a better idea of how you're going to look."

I took the blue suit into a changing area behind a screen. I was out of my own clothes and stepping into the pants when I heard someone come in from the hall.

"Oh, my darling, what a *bloody* bore this film is," said a soft but strangely familiar male voice with a pronounced British accent. "Can't we get away somewhere for a few hours? Anywhere at all."

Well, well, I thought. Annie has a boyfriend!

"Guess who's here? Steve Allen!" Annie said quickly in a bright, unnatural voice. "He's trying on some clothes for me behind the screen."

"Steve Allen?" said the British voice.

"In the flesh, Jasper," I said, stepping out into the room. I had just succeeded in recognizing the voice and wished I hadn't. If possible, I would have disappeared on wings unseen out the door, but since I couldn't I put on a brave face and greeted Jasper North, the most famous of British actors, and my personal friend.

# chapter 9

Jasper looked splendid for a man his age—late sixties—a man who had been an institution in theater and films for a very long time. Perhaps his aristocratic bearing came from playing all those Shakespearean kings. The flesh now sagged a little, but he was still handsome, with distinguished-looking gray hair, ironic blue eyes, and a way about him that would always place him at center stage.

At the moment he was regarding me closely, I assume trying to decide if I had overheard his exchange with Annie. I pretended innocence.

"How's Jayne?" he asked.

"She's fine," I told him, and then added, more to the point, "and how's Emily?"—*his* wife, who happened to be one of my wife's best friends.

"Em stayed behind to take care of the garden. You know how she is—can't bear to be parted from her roses, though I hope she'll be joining me soon."

Jayne and I had stayed briefly with Jasper and Emily at their country manor in Sussex just a year earlier. A short time before that they had visited us in California. We had been exchanging occasional visits back and forth over the Atlantic for more than twenty years, but in all that time I had never had the slightest inkling that Jasper might be unfaithful to his wife. It seemed a little crazy. Looking from tall, decent Mr. North to sweet, elfish Annie Locks, I was beginning to think that maybe I had either imagined or misinterpreted those overheard remarks.

After that first painful moment Jasper started rolling out the charm in a way only a cultivated Englishman can. He insisted we have a bite together to catch up on old times. I tried to beg off, claiming jet lag, but he wouldn't hear it.

We met at eleven o'clock at Trader Vic's, which is more or less in the basement of The Plaza. Originally a restaurant, it was designed to make the casual diner feel as if he had just washed up on a Polynesian shore. Though they now serve only appetizers and drinks, they have kept the decor. The place is dark, and there are outrigger canoes hanging from the ceilings, and spears, shields, nets, and Polynesian lampshades. Jungle drums don't exactly beat in the distance, but you almost feel they might at any moment.

Jasper and I sat in a corner booth, each of us with gigantic pineapples set before us, straws sticking out of the top. The hors d'oeuvres at Trader Vic's are superb, and we decided on an assortment of prawns, wontons, and barbecued ribs—not the most healthful fare in the world, but, then, Jasper and I were away from home and feeling a little footloose.

We raised our pineapples in a salute—there was nonalcoholic juice inside, but I'm sure we both looked like dangerous beachcombers. We talked about old friends and old times for a while. One of our mutual friends on the London/L.A. axis is playwright Larry Gelbart, and we regaled each other with recollections of witty things Larry had said, but eventually the conversation came around to our present project in New York.

"Have you met Nash Stuart yet?" Jasper asked, waving a prawn.

"Briefly. He seemed nice—maybe not quite experienced enough to stand up to a bulldozer like Barnes."

"Ah! That's just my point," said Jasper. "Nash Stuart is a gentleman, but he doesn't know a thing about the entertainment industry. The man is CEO of an oil company, which took over a publishing company, which, in turn, took over a film company—this is the new kind of modern leapfrog, is it not? So our man Nash suddenly finds himself in the movie business, which he thinks he can run like he's pumping oil out of the ground, selling paperback novels, or building shopping malls. What he doesn't understand is that show business isn't so much a business as it is part magic and a dash of blind luck fueled by the desperation of a lot of crazy people with fragile egos hoping to become world famous."

I sipped on my pineapple. I am unable here to reproduce the resonance with which Jasper speaks the English language, the way he pauses and cajoles subtle varieties of meaning out of quite ordinary words. I could sit and listen to the fellow for hours.

"Bernie and Nash seem a fairly mismatched pair," I said.

Jasper smirked wickedly. "Mismatched! Ha! Bernie has that poor man running circles! Nash is supposed to be the executive producer, of course, but he can't even figure out where all the money is going!"

"The money *is* going, is it?"

"Going, going, gone," said Jasper. "I haven't seen anything so wasteful since *Cleopatra.*"

Jasper was referring, of course, to the film that caused a nearly bankrupt Twentieth Century Fox to sell off its back lot for what is now Century City—the city Elizabeth Taylor built, as the wags say.

"Well, is it worth it?" I asked. "Artistically speaking? Is Bernie making the masterpiece Nash is paying for?"

Jasper laughed unpleasantly. "Don't joke about art, Steve. You were on the set today. Bernie's a talented man, I won't deny him that, but he's a bit off his rocker. This film's become utter chaos. No one knows what the hell they're doing here. How can anything good come of that?"

This brought me to a question I had been hesitating to ask: I knew what *I* was doing here—I had had an unfortunate case of spring fever and answered the telephone at the wrong time. But what was a great actor like Jasper doing on this production?

"Jasper . . ."

"I know what you're thinking, old man. From *Hamlet* to Bernie Barnes—what a fall!"

"Well, I *was* wondering. Of course, film work's glamorous and all that—and there's nothing wrong with doing a light comedy now and then."

"*Light* comedy?" Jasper roared. (When Americans speak that loudly they tend to sound boorish. A Britisher, assuming he is either naturally cultured or has acquired the manner, merely sounds colorful at high volume.) "Listen, old boy. Last year I did a bloody telly commercial for Mitchum's underarm deodorant. What I wanted to say to the camera was that after I used the product I felt as if I smelled like Robert Mitchum, but of course I didn't change a word they'd written. And do you know why I did something in such questionable taste? I did it for the same bloody reason I'm doing this stupid picture." He cocked an eyebrow at me. "And if you're doing it for any other reason, I'm afraid I'll think less of you."

"Do you remember," I said, "back in the fifties and sixties, a lot of actors, particularly theater and film people, wouldn't do commercials? Said it was beneath their dignity. It turned out that all Madison Avenue had to do to get atop their dignity was up the ante."

"Right. As you Yanks say, up the ante—and up your auntie's husband as well."

Jasper was invariably witty, but now something unpleasant had crept into his voice. I tried to interrupt him, but he rolled right over me.

"Anyway, as for Murder in Bloody Manhattan, I did it for the lolly," he said, using his famous voice to come down hard on the cockney slang for money.

"Jasper, you're one of the most famous actors in the world. Your name is almost synonymous with good theater. And then, all those wonderful films you made . . ."

His voice became gravely quiet. "Steve, I don't want to bore you with this, but when I had the money, I spent it, and, quite honestly, Shakespeare never paid as handsomely as your average cops-and-robbers kiss-kiss bang-bang. So here I am, working for that pig Barnes, hustling a few coins so that Emily and the children won't be completely destitute when I've bought the small country garden."

Because Jasper was an old friend, I was trying to come up with some suitably cheerful reply when we were interrupted by a handsome couple coming over to the table to say hello. Unfortunately, this is the kind of thing that can easily happen in a place like Trader Vic's.

The handsome young people were Suzanne Tracy, whom I had last seen in a fur fight with Victoria La Volpa, and Zachary Holden—the year's most famous face on television. Apparently Zachary was attempting one of the more dangerous career moves, from TV star to film; he had a principal role in *Murder in Manhattan.*

"Oh, Jasper, just the man I need!" cried Suzanne, kissing Jasper on both cheeks.

While she had Jasper deep in conversation, I half stood up and shook hands with Zachary. Zach was nearly as tall as I was, rugged-looking with powerful shoulders. I judged him to be in his mid-thirties, a good time of life for a handsome, outdoor sort of man. He had a suave mustache, curly hair, and the kind of brown eyes I suppose women find appealing. In fact, at the moment every woman nearby was in the process of ogling him.

"Gosh, Mr. Allen," said Zachary in an unexpectedly boyish voice, "I've been a fan of yours ever since I was old enough to turn on a television set. I can't tell you what a kick it is to have a chance to work with you."

A nice young man—so nice I almost forgave him for reminding me of my age. I told him, truthfully enough, that I was a fan of his as well and occasionally watched his weekly TV cop show, *Bermuda P.D.,* in which almost every suspect was a beautiful woman and Holden's character solved cases with his shirt unbuttoned to the navel.

While Zachary and I were exchanging compliments, Suzanne was trying to enlist Jasper's help to save Antarctica—which seemed far enough away from our present Polynesian retreat.

"I tell you, it's an utter disgrace what's happening to the last virgin continent on planet earth," I heard her say. "This may come as shocking news, Jasper, but it's getting so the poor penguins can hardly find a place to mate anymore, what with all the oil exploration and scientists and tourists romping around!"

"God forbid!" said Jasper, stroking his chin. "Er, did you know this, Steve? About this serious problem with penguins?"

"I'm aware of many problems," I said. "But not this one."

Suzanne turned her hazel eyes my way, I guess trying to decide if I was friend or foe.

"Perhaps you'd like to get involved too, Mr. Allen," she said. "Quite a number of media personalities are working to protect Antarctic wildlife from the ravages of civilization."

The other women in the room were still staring at Zachary. Only Suzanne seemed to be paying him no attention.

"We're having a meeting this Sunday at the Museum of Natural History," she told me. "Perhaps you'd like to come. We call ourselves FOP."

"Friends of Penguins," Zach quickly explained.

"Tell you what," I said. "Why don't you send me your literature, and I'll study it."

"I'd appreciate that, Mr. Allen. Nice meeting you." Suzanne offered me a hearty handshake. "Come on, Zach. If we're going to have something to eat, we'd better get to it."

Zachary Holden, enormous TV star though he was, followed Suzanne to their table, looking meek as a puppy.

"Ah, to be young and healthy," said Jasper with an envious sigh.

"And have a hit TV series."

"But *no* sense of humor!" Jasper wagged his head sadly. "Ah, Steve, Shaw was right, youth is wasted on the young."

Jasper had looked quite merry for a moment, laughing with Suzanne over the sex customs of penguins, but now a deep melancholy seemed to come over him. He laid his hand on my wrist. "I had to bribe a doctor to pass me for my last physical," he said quietly. "Paid the bugger fifteen thousand quid, or I wouldn't have been able to be hired for this bloody film."

"Well, what do doctors know?"

"It's the ticker. Could stop ticking any moment. Had a close call in North Africa last year—fortunately I was able to hush it up. It's ironic, isn't it? A respected actor having to bribe a doctor in order to do a Bernie Barnes comedy!"

Given that some major stars are in their sixties and seventies, though they invariably look much younger, stories of this sort aren't that rare. About a year ago, at a birthday party for George Burns, Burt Lancaster told me about the heart condition

that unfortunately had forced him to pass up the lead in the film
*Old Gringo,* which consequently went to Gregory Peck. Many
virile-seeming actors are, in reality, not the macho types they
play on screen, but Burt, a true athlete, looks so healthy and
strong to this day that it was hard to believe the report of his
condition.

I now tried to conceal my shock. "Jasper," I said, "perhaps
if you really are in . . . well, in frail condition, you should be back
in England helping Emily with the rose garden. There are worse
things, you know."

"Ah, yes, *far* worse things." His eyes got a faraway look.
"But besides the money, which I need, it was a way to see Annie
one last time."

I had just about convinced myself there was some entirely
innocent explanation to the conversation I had overheard between Annie and Jasper, and now he had forced me to see the
reality.

"Oh, look who's there," he said with a twinkle in those old
blue eyes. "This should be interesting."

Jasper was pointing across the room at Bernie Barnes and
Victoria La Volpa, who were being seated at a table nearly opposite us. La Volpa had managed to make a very grand entrance,
refusing to relinquish her floor-length white sable coat and
swishing it around her as she came gliding through the room.
As for Bernie, he looked like a fat little boy who had just found
himself a new toy.

"Steve, let me explain about Annie and me," Jasper continued.

"You don't really have to."

"No, let an old man confess. As a matter of fact, Annie and
I go back nearly twenty-five years. A long time to keep a secret."

I played with a wonton I couldn't quite eat, unable to meet
Jasper's eyes.

"You have to understand, we met in some god-awful desert
in Egypt, where I was making one of those biblical epics that
used to be so popular. We were stuck on that shoot for nearly
five months—can you imagine? Annie was just a seamstress
then, but she was wonderful to talk with. Four months in the

bloody desert is a long time. Gradually, very gradually, we began to . . . have an affair, and over the years, we've—"

"Well, she seems like a very nice person," I interrupted. Ever since Jasper had told me about his bad heart, I'd had visions of him keeling over dead into the sweet-and-sour sauce in a fit of remorse.

"I never was able to tell Emily."

"I should think not, unless you were telling her it was over."

"You won't mention this to Jayne? She'd hate me for it."

"Of course not. But she's an understanding person, Jasper—and so am I. Listen, I think we should both just relax and enjoy this little film. Why take it so seriously? It's going to be fun having a few weeks together in New York!"

"You think so?" Jasper's doomed look brightened slightly.

"Absolutely."

At just that moment Suzanne Tracy walked slowly, purposefully, across the restaurant to where Bernie and Victoria were sitting. She trailed a long, filmy shawl behind her and moved with such deliberate dignity I had a feeling there was about to be trouble.

"Uh-oh," Jasper said, obviously thinking the same.

"Well, good evening, Bernard," we heard Suzanne say, her trained voice projecting across the room.

"How ya doin'?" Barnes said.

"Fine," Suzanne answered, then turned on the fur-draped sex goddess. "So, Victoria, when you walk down the street in that coat in Italy, do people shout at you and call you a murderer the way they did outside on the street a little while ago?"

This was one of the peak periods in the ongoing strife between the natural fur industry and its customers and those who think it a crime to kill animals—endangered species or not—for the purpose of keeping wealthy women warm and fashionable. Apparently Suzanne had witnessed a sidewalk encounter between the young Italian actress and a group of protesters.

"Meenk ees not endangered species!" Victoria shouted.

"But why should *any* animal be killed because of your vanity?" Suzanne responded, equally as shrill.

Victoria half rose from her seat, eyes blazing, and said, "I no murder the animals, but I murder you eef you don't get away from me."

"Nothing would give me greater pleasure," Suzanne replied. She stalked out, Zachary following obediently, his head low in embarrassment.

To my great surprise, Bernie suddenly roared with guttural laughter, shook his head, and said to the room, "Talk about crazy broads."

# chapter 10

"'m quitting," I told Jayne on the telephone. "I'm coming back to California."

"Steve, don't you think you should sleep on it?"

"I did."

It was the morning following my dinner with Jasper North. I was sitting up in bed with a glass of freshly squeezed grapefruit juice in one hand and the telephone in the other. Jayne was playing the voice of reason.

"Darling, you've never walked off a film in your life," she reminded me.

"I haven't *made* that many that they've been there to walk off of—or from." That was klutzy syntax, but the ice-cold juice had not as yet reached my brain cells.

"Besides," I told her, "I miss you."

"I'm flattered, darling, but what's so bad about *Murder in Manhattan?*"

"Bad? There's nothing good about it."

"Are you eating well?"

"Sure," I said. "Except for one brief fall from grace last night at Trader Vic's."

"What are you having for breakfast?" asked the diet police.

"Fresh grapefruit juice at the moment," I semi-lied, setting my glass on the tray with the still-covered corned beef hash.

"Ste-eve!" Jayne seemed to smell the deceit—or hash—from across the continent.

"All right, my diet's gone to hell—but I'm depressed. This whole production is crazy. People having affairs with other people . . ."

"Such as?"

"Never mind, but from what I've seen I wouldn't be surprised if someone ends up murdered."

"Steve!"

"I mean it. A gang like this would be at home in a nuthouse."

"Who did you go to Trader Vic's with last night?" Jayne asked suspiciously.

"Jasper North. He has a part in this insanity too."

"Jasper? Oh, how nice! You two can go to the theater and do all kinds of New Yorky things. Is Emily with him?"

"No, she's at home with the roses," I said. Under no circumstances would I have told Jayne about Jasper's sad, twenty-five-year-old secret, since it would have upset her terribly. Neither of us are Victorians, but Jayne and Emily have been friends for a long time. The realities were disturbing.

"Would it help if I came to New York? I could be there in two days."

"It would help," I admitted. "But I still think the best thing would be for me to get out of this nightmare as fast as I can."

"Darling, of course you must decide what's best. But it's really not like you to not finish something you start."

I sighed. Jayne was right, as she generally is.

"Just pretend you're away at summer camp," said Jayne helpfully.

"Poor Irish kids from Chicago didn't go to summer camp."

At this moment there was a knock on my door.

"Excuse me a second," I said. "I think it's the waiter for the breakfast table."

I left the phone dangling on the bed, tied a robe around me, and walked barefooted through the suite from bedroom to sitting room. I opened the door, but instead of a waiter I was surprised to see Suzanne Tracy peering into my room, dressed in jeans, sweatshirt, and dark glasses.

"Oh, Mr. Allen, can I talk with you? I mean, I'm terribly sorry to just barge in like this, but your phone was busy and I knew you were just down the hall . . . it's really, *really* important."

Suzanne Tracy seemed a little out of breath. I wasn't in the mood for company, but the young lady seemed upset, and I find it difficult to turn down a damsel in distress.

"Come on in, Suzanne. I won't be a moment."

I left her in the sitting room and went back into the bedroom to pick up the phone.

"Was that the waiter?" asked Jayne.

"No, just a dish," I assured her. "Just kidding—actually it's only a blond, twenty-year-old starlet dying to have a word with me alone."

"Steve, maybe you *should* come home."

I laughed. "I'm sure it's business, but I'll call you back later and tell you what it's all about."

# chapter 11

**S**uzanne Tracy sat at my white Yamaha baby grand playing a Bach French Suite and waited while I got dressed in the next room.

I listened to her for a moment from the bedroom. She played fairly well, but mechanically, like someone who had never quite survived her obligatory piano lessons as a child. There was nothing in her playing, for example, of the passion with which she had verbally assaulted La Volpa about her furs. Put *that* into your playing, my dear, I thought, and you might have something.

When the music stopped, I entered the sitting room, clapping enthusiastically.

Suzanne stood up, picking up a manila envelope I now remembered seeing in her hand when she first entered the suite. She gazed at me oddly, apparently trying to size me up. I smiled in my most mild-mannered way.

"Would you like some coffee?" I offered. "Tea? Grapefruit juice?"

She shook her head. "Probably it's a mistake coming here."

"Well, I suppose we won't know that until you tell me what this is about."

I realize I haven't described Suzanne Tracy very well, except to say she was blond, about twenty years old, and an actress. But she was more than that—or less, depending on your point of view—an attractive girl, certainly, but no Victoria La Volpa. Her face was a little too sharp, her eyes hawklike, predatory. Angry. These are the words that came to mind. I had the feeling this was a girl hiding behind the glamour of blond hair and a perfect Hollywood body. There was something a bit unattractive underneath, something that would no doubt become more dominant as she grew older.

"Mr. Allen—"

"You might as well call me Steve," I said. "After all, the third assistant director does."

She didn't seem to know what to make of me. Sometimes I have trouble communicating with people who have no sense of humor; it's as if we speak a different language. Without further preamble she thrust toward me the manila envelope she was clutching.

"Here, take this, please. Will you read it? Tell me what you really think of it?"

"What have we here?" I said.

"It's part of the first chapter and fragments of chapters ten and eleven," she told me a little dreamily. *"Busted in Babylon—* it's going to be the greatest American novel ever, Mr. Allen . . . Steve."

"My goodness, you play the piano, you're an actress, and now I learn you're writing a novel."

"Oh, it's not *my* novel! You don't understand—this is the work of . . . well, someone very special to me. A man I care about a great deal."

"Ah," I said. "Zachary Holden is certainly a lucky man— and I never would have suspected that beneath all that good-looking brawn there lurked a secret writer."

To my surprise Suzanne laughed—unpleasantly. "Oh, gosh! *Not* Zachary! Honestly, his idea of heavy literature is *TV Guide.*"

"I'm sorry. I assumed last night . . ."

"Steve, he's after me day and night to have dinner with him. He hounds me to go out to movies and all kinds of dull parties and things. Every once in a while I feel sorry for him and give in. The poor guy has a real thing for me. Probably because I'm the only woman he's ever met who's turned him down—which is not exactly a solid foundation for a *real* relationship."

"Well, he seems exceptionally nice," I put in on his behalf. "For a big star he doesn't seem at all stuck on himself."

"Oh, yeah, he's definitely *nice,*" said Suzanne Tracy with a shrug of total indifference.

I was beginning to wish my visitor would come to the point. I regarded the manila envelope in my lap.

"So this novel, then . . ."

"It's Clancy's. The long-awaited sequel to *The Ravaged Rose,* and he would *kill* me if he knew I was showing this . . . to anybody!"

"Then, as a writer myself, I'd better give it back," I said quickly. But Suzanne put her hands behind her and refused to take the damned thing. I was beginning to regret my early morning hospitality.

"Steve, please listen to me. Clancy Donahue is a genius who's wasting his talents, killing himself by working for Hollywood. I've come to you because you're known as sort of a problem solver, with your book *Dumbth* and all. Clancy respects you, and I thought you might be able to influence him. Once you've read this, I know you'll want to encourage him to get back to some serious writing."

"Well, I'm not sure about that. In my experience most people listen politely to the advice you give them and then go out and do exactly as they please."

"But this is a desperate situation, Steve—life or death! That fat bastard can't stand it that there's someone more talented than he is. He has to humiliate Clancy, belittle him, in front of everyone. No wonder Clancy drinks. His spirit is being destroyed! Read the manuscript, Steve. You'll realize what a crime it is for someone like Clancy Donahue to be forced to waste his time on trivia."

"I see. Just out of curiosity, do you know how much Clancy is being paid for this waste of time?" I asked.

"Ten thousand a week."

"Well, that's not all that trivial, is it?"

"But it's terrible, Steve! If the money were less, Clancy might have a chance to walk away. But no, it's ten thousand a week to sell your soul! A devil's bargain if there ever was one."

"Suzanne, there are some starving writers who'd cheerfully commit murder to trade places with Clancy Donahue, so if he's not getting what he wants, he really has only himself to blame."

Suzanne wasn't listening to me. I had the feeling I was irrelevant to her monologue.

"And do you know *why* Clancy needs the money?" she cried. "It's all because of her!"

"Her?"

"La Volpa! Can you believe it? How can a man of Clancy's talent be interested in a woman like that? Do you think *she* cares for literature? All she cares about are clothes, and jewelry, and, quite frankly, using her sex appeal to enslave every man in sight."

"Oh, dear!" I said. "I'm glad you warned me."

"What I don't understand is why Clancy isn't interested in me. I mean, I adore fine literature, I care about all the things he cares about—the environment, important social issues. I'm the total support unit he needs."

There wasn't much I could say to Suzanne about why a man might prefer a glamorous young beauty to a total support unit. The best I could offer was a weak "Oh, he'll probably get tired of La Volpa when he discovers how shallow she is. I'd give it a little time, Suzanne."

"I've been giving it time," she admitted gloomily. "And time isn't helping one bit."

"Clancy and La Volpa are still a hot item, then?"

"No!" Suzanne looked at me as if I were some kind of idiot. "That's the irony of it all. La Volpa gives him the cold shoulder—though naturally she's ready enough to accept the expensive gifts he sends her in the mail. Can you believe the nerve of that woman? She wears his jewelry and then won't have a thing to do with him, but that doesn't seem to discourage Clancy a bit. He's turned her into a kind of terrible obsession!"

I was beginning to understand, at least, why Suzanne had it in for La Volpa.

"Let me get this straight," I said. "Zachary is in love with you, you're in love with Clancy, and Clancy is in love with Victoria La Volpa. So who's La Volpa in love with?"

"Herself," said Suzanne, and then added, "the bitch!"

This was the kind of love quadrangle that makes a man of

my years glad he is no longer young and foolish.

"Suzanne, if I can offer some advice . . . First of all, you must understand that Clancy Donahue is the only person who can help Clancy Donahue. *He* has to walk away from the ten thousand a week and the nineteen-year-old Italian sex goddess who doesn't want him. From what I hear, he could also use some help for his drinking problem."

"But *I* can help him! If only he'd let me! Will you read the manuscript? Please? Someone has to encourage that poor, tortured man to write again—and I don't mean writing the garbage he does for Barnes."

*"Busted in Babylon,"* I sighed.

"You'll do this, won't you?"

"May I interject one more bit of advice? As someone old enough to be your father and then some, I'd like to point out that Zachary Holden really is an awfully nice young man—good-looking, healthy, rugged. All that and the guy even has a hit TV series. Don't you think it would be better if you—"

"You can't be serious! My God, Zach would probably marry me, set me up in a nice little house with a garden in the Valley. Probably we'd play tennis every day and drink fruit juice around the pool, and have boring children!"

"Where I come from that's called the American dream."

"For those who want it, yes, but it's not for me. I want love to roll over me like a . . . a tornado! And there's really only one man in the world who can do that—"

Thinking that perhaps it might help if I could make her laugh, I said, "Well, thank you, dear, but I'm already spoken for."

Far from laughing, Suzanne suddenly looked as sober as Jesse Helms speaking out for God, country, and the death-dealing tobacco industry. "I'm sorry," she said. "I can see it was a mistake coming here this morning. Please excuse me."

Gathering as much dignity as a woman can who's just admitted she's in love with someone who doesn't give a fig for her, Suzanne Tracy huffed out of my room.

I was left with a ruined morning. I was also left, I noticed, with a manuscript I didn't at all want, Clancy Donahue's unfinished masterpiece, *Busted in Babylon.*

I opened the door and looked down the hall, hoping to give the damned thing back, but Suzanne Tracy was nowhere in sight. My first morning in New York had gotten off to a dreadful start.

# chapter 12

**L**ater that morning I was to film my first scene, which was taking place at the carousel in Central Park. Since it was another gorgeous spring day, I once again told the limousine driver he could go on without me—I'd walk.

Central Park, on a spring day like this one, could make a New Yorker out of anyone. The trees were bursting with new green growth. Ducks floated lazily on the pond near 59th Street. The gently twisting paths were full of lovers and mothers with small children and old women feeding pigeons. There were break dancers and young people on roller skates, ladies in ankle-length fur coats walking elaborately coiffured poodles—as well as beggars, derelicts, entire homeless families, several obviously insane souls, pickpockets, prostitutes, and—well, this was New York à la carte—the rich and poor side by side, a tapestry of beauty and despair, gentle and brutal all at the same time. Always fascinating.

My call time to be on the set was eleven o'clock. I arrived at the carousel thirty minutes early, passed through the makeup trailer and wardrobe to emerge with a slightly orange tan and wearing a tweedy sports coat and brown trousers.

I was now decadent southern novelist Toots Gable, who resembled an aging Clark Kent and was hoping to cash in on this similarity to win first place at a costume ball.

In the scene I was about to play, Toots was having a secret rendezvous on the carousel with socialite Josephine Van Arndt to learn what the other guests would be wearing. At least this was the summary of the action I was able to gather from a distracted Barnes, who talked as fast as a tobacco auctioneer for exactly two and a half minutes when I first arrived. He said, in effect, not to worry—Clancy Donahue was about to arrive "any goddamn second" with the actual dialogue. I worried anyway.

The crew seemed far from ready to shoot. There was a trailer where I could wait, but because it was such a nice day I decided to sit in a sunny spot on an old green park bench on which countless lovers had etched their names or initials. I stretched out between "Manuel loves Marie" and "For terrific sex call 555-9871." Waited . . . and waited.

The carousel in Central Park, as you may know, is a romantic and gentle corner of the city. Under the round pavilion there are, of course, colored wooden horses on gleaming brass poles galloping in circles to the music of an old-fashioned calliope. Barnes seemed to be planning the most expensive and difficult way to film a scene: a camera car on a curved wooden track would circle the carousel in one single seamless shot, keeping pace with me and Mrs. Van Arndt—Barnes's wife, Mimi—as we rode on the horses. Very arty, of course, but the company carpenters were still trying to get the track level. Two bored-looking stand-ins were sitting on the carousel horses in place of Mimi and me. So I remained quite comfortably on the park bench, my face tilted to the warming sun, reading Isaiah Berlin's *Against the Current* and watching the crew at work. I had a feeling they wouldn't be ready for a long time. It had naturally occurred to me to wonder why Barnes didn't just position a camera on the carousel in front of us, but I decided not to butt in.

Not far from where I sat, Bernie was bullying everyone in sight, telling the carpenters how to hammer nails, shouting at the electricians. As I watched, I saw an aging derelict wearing a rumpled suit pass through the police lines and approach Bernie. The old fellow had a bottle sticking out of his side pocket, his nose was red, his hair wild and touched with gray, his shoulders stooped. I was expecting one of the assistant directors to send him quickly on his way, but Bernie turned to face him.

"Well, here's our *writer,*" he said sarcastically. "Do you have any brilliant dialogue for us today, or shall we just let our actors improvise?"

"You can let the actors commit sodomy on those painted

ponies for all I care," said the man with the red nose. "In fact, you yourself can join them, Mr. Barnes."

"Oh-ho!" cried Bernie. "We're feeling a little rebellious, are we? Perhaps remembering the days of fame and fortune so very long ago?"

The wrinkled suit shrugged, took the bottle from the side pocket, and raised it to his lips. I had the uncomfortable feeling that this wreck of a man must be Clancy Donahue. Himself. On a closer look, I could see that beneath the disreputable clothes and unshaved stubble, Donahue had once been a ruggedly good-looking man, and might be still after a hot bath and change of clothes.

"Well, do you have the goddamn pages or don't you?" asked Bernie.

Without a word the writer reached inside an inner coat pocket and pulled out a few folded sheets.

"Yuck! Did you blow your nose on them? You're disgusting!"

"If I've succeeded in disgusting you," Clancy said with a fatalistic shrug, "I have not lived in vain."

Barnes collared Trip Johnson and thrust the crumpled pages in the young man's hands. "Here—*you* rewrite this, why don't you? Whatever you come up with couldn't be worse than what this old hack's giving me. Get rid of the four-letter words and anything that sounds even vaguely Irish, then make copies for everyone—quick."

Clancy seemed resigned to abuse. He shuffled off to a nearby park bench, where he sat down with a long, tired sigh and looked prepared to spend the night. It was difficult for me to imagine that *this* was the creature for which Suzanne Tracy felt such glorious passion—but, then, who can understand a woman's heart? Or anybody's.

"I turn my back one second," Barnes was screaming at the carpenters, "and everybody's jerking off! Hurry up! I'd *like* to shoot this scene sometime this decade . . . *comprenez-vous*, schmuckolas?"

"One of these days he's going to go too far," said a soft, sad voice over my left shoulder. I turned to see Mimi Day standing near my bench. She looked as if she had come in a time warp from 1962—everybody's favorite blonde preserved in formaldehyde. Without a word she sat down next to me and lit a cigarette.

"Mimi, dear," I said, "if you don't mind, I'll have to get upwind of you now that you've lighted up."

"Oh, sorry," she said, more in annoyance than contrition.

Mimi was in full makeup, though it could hardly disguise the cruelty of time.

"I'll bet you're wondering why I stay with him," she said, nodding at her husband a dozen feet away.

"That's not what I was wondering at all," I assured her. "Why, I bet Bernie's absolutely charming when he's away from the pressures of work."

"Charming?" Mimi turned toward me in disbelief.

"How about interesting?" I tried. "Amusing?"

For a second I almost felt I had coaxed a smile out of her, but that was wishful thinking.

"Let me tell you something about that man you think is so charming and amusing. He cheats on me, he makes me feel ugly as a witch. And you know what I do in return? I give him money. I tell him he's the most wonderful person in the world."

"Why?" I asked reasonably. "Why do you put up with him?"

"Because he's strong," she told me. "And I'm weak."

"I'm sure you're not being fair to yourself."

"Oh, I used to be a very important actress," she said. "But not anymore. Now *he's* the famous one, and oh, how he lords it over me!"

"I loved your pictures," I mentioned. "All those zany comedies!"

"A million years ago," she said, "I was young and weak, and I let men walk all over me. Now I'm old and weak, and it's still happening."

"At least you're consistent."

"In public we appear such a happy couple, but I hate him," she told me. "I hate him so much, you know what I do? I bake him chocolate cakes with pounds of butter, cakes dripping with gooey frosting."

"This is hate?"

"And I make him apple pies and veal with sour cream and mushrooms, and broccoli with extra-rich hollandaise sauce—I'm a fantastic cook, Steve—that's one thing I've learned to do for all the men who've walked over me."

"You're making me hungry."

"And you know, he's gained twenty-five pounds in the last six months alone." She stared at Bernie, who was now ranting at the camera crew. "Do you know what his cholesterol level is? Two hundred and sixty-five."

"Whew!" I said. "He'd better watch out."

"Tonight I've ordered strawberry shortcake with real whipped cream—his favorite."

I watched a slow and nasty smile spread across Mimi Day's aging but still handsome face.

"They'll never be able to convict me, Steve, but *I'll* know how he died," she confided. "Clever, isn't it? Murder by cholesterol!"

# chapter 13

This is the dialogue young Trip Johnson delivered to my park bench about twenty minutes later:

Toots Gable and Josephine Van Arndt are side by side on two carousel horses in motion, popping up and down, urging their wooden mounts onward as if they are having a race. Occasionally throughout the scene Toots will kick his horse with his heels as if he needs to go faster to win.

TOOTS: I've heard Jimmy Dorsett is coming to the party in drag, dah-ling, as Marie Antoinette. Isn't that *too* much?

JOSEPHINE: Are you worried he'll beat you to the prize, Toots?

TOOTS: You can't be serious! Jimmy will make such an impossible Marie Antoinette, I'm sure the judges will faint dead away. No, dah-ling, it's Froggy Johnson I'm worried about—*he's* the only one with the *slightest* bit of imagination in this entire bor-ring city! I'd give anything to know what he's going to wear.

JOSEPHINE: That's easy. I'll tell you. But first you must pay with some absolutely wicked piece of gossip. You know everything nasty that goes on in this town, Toots.

TOOTS: (*thinks briefly*) How about *this* little tidbit? Katherine Kensington, the ex-wife of billionaire takeover mogul Donald Kensington, has sex with her chauffeur.

JOSEPHINE: *Every*one knows that, dah-ling! Tell me something new.

TOOTS: (*whispers*) Her chauffeur's a young woman.

JOSEPHINE: No! That's delicious!

TOOTS: Now tell me about Froggy.

JOSEPHINE: All right. He's coming as Mick Jagger. He's having a plastic surgeon put collagen in his lips.

TOOTS: *(looking worried)* Damn! That's not bad! *(A look of sheer malice crosses his face.)* I do believe, dah-ling, that Froggy is going to have a small but serious accident before the party!

And that was it—too many "dah-lings" for my taste, and I doubt if anyone's had a name like Froggy Johnson since the Roaring Twenties. Or Toots Gable, for that matter. Still, my real worry was not artistic but practical—how the hell was I supposed to instantly memorize a page and a half of dialogue? I may be a trooper, but I'm not suicidal. I took my small section of script over to where Barnes was peering at the carousel through a lens that dangled from a small silver chain around his neck.

"Bernie," I said. "This is impossible. You can't expect us to memorize this much dialogue five minutes before we shoot."

"Sweetheart!" cried Bernie in consolation. "Don't worry your cute little head over this! It doesn't have to be perfect, believe me. Just look it over, get the general idea, and improvise if you have to. You're Mr. Ad Lib, aren't you?"

Bernie went on to say that I certainly didn't memorize lines when I interviewed a guest on my TV talk shows, so what was so different about this? There was a big difference, of course, but he wouldn't hear it.

"Trust me, Steve," he said with a sloppy smile, as if he were my favorite uncle and he would *never* lead me astray. "If worse comes to worst, we'll dub in some lines afterward."

I was not convinced, but he was the director—God help us all. I took the sheet of dialogue into my trailer so I could concentrate and began to work. It was a good thing the crew was taking such a long time setting up the shot. For the next hour I went over my lines, aided by my ever-present pocket tape recorder and, rather to my surprise, got them down—or close enough for jazz. Of course with dialogue like this, if I changed a few words here and there, it might be an improvement.

It was midafternoon by the time they were ready for me. Despite my misgivings about the entire project, I have to admit it was exciting to mount my wooden horse and have the camera and all the big arc lights trained my way. I was on the outside horse, with Mimi on the pony to my left. I could tell she was nervous from the way she kept blinking at me. The faint odor of booze surrounded her more persistently than when we had talked earlier on the bench.

A sound man pinned small cordless microphones to our lapels; the director of photography held a light meter to our faces for a final check.

"Camera!" came a voice, followed by the response: "Speed! . . . Sound! . . . Rolling! . . . *Action!*"

The clapper boy held the little blackboard before the lens. *"Murder in Manhattan,* scene fifty-seven, take one," he said quickly—clapped the stick so that later on the editor would be able to use this mark to synchronize picture and sound—and then we were off, Mimi and I, on our high wooden horses, bobbing up and down to the frolicking music of the calliope.

I must tell you something about film making if you are to understand what happened next. Normally a scene such as the one Mimi and I were about to do would be broken up into a number of short takes—generally a wide master shot, a few close-ups, possibly a reverse angle or two—and then, later on, in the cutting room, the editor will splice all these bits of celluloid together, like a tailor making a suit of clothes.

This is the way it is usually done, but this was *not* what Barnes had in mind. The camera, as I have mentioned, was mounted on a small battery-powered car that was to circle the entire circumference of the carousel, keeping exact pace with Mimi and me on our horses, capturing the entire scene in one single *unbroken* shot. I emphasize this point because it turned out to be not at all easy.

On the first take, Mimi and I were doing splendidly. We got halfway through the scene—I was being deliciously nasty as Toots Gable, and she was being very snobbish as Josephine Van Arndt—when the sound man riding on the circling camera car cried "Cut! We're going to have to do something about those damned drums."

The drums he referred to were part of the calliope. After

some discussion with the man who ran the carousel, it was agreed that the music would be turned off for the shot, then added later so that the sound man could record our dialogue properly.

We were ready for take two. This time Mimi and I started off even better than before, but the cameraman called "Cut!" before we had managed four lines. The problem was either the carousel was going too fast, or the camera truck too slow—there was some discussion as to which. Whatever it was, for the shot to work the camera car had to be traveling at a significantly faster speed than the carousel in order for it to remain *exactly* along-side. This was beginning to resemble a problem in celestial navigation. Finding just the right relative speed of the camera car to the carousel ruined takes three, four, five, six, and seven. By this time Mimi and I were beginning to feel a little frazzled.

"I have to go to the bathroom," Mimi announced, swinging off her horse.

"Darling, couldn't you have thought to go to the bathroom *before* we started filming?" asked her director-husband with mock patience.

"That was an hour ago," said Mimi.

Nothing would dissuade her. She went to the honey wagon—as it is strangely called on film sets—and left the rest of us waiting for about ten minutes. When she returned, I could smell the aroma of scotch even more strongly than before. It took three crew members to lift Mimi back upon her horse, and when she was finally in the saddle, she gazed at me helplessly with slightly glazed blue eyes.

"Help me through this, darling," she whispered, "and I'll love you forever." I squeezed her hand. I was, after all, seated upon a big white horse.

"It's going to be oodles of fun, sweetheart, give or take an oodle or two," I whispered back, giving her a kindly kiss on the cheek. I was wrong. Now that the technical problems were solved, Mimi started blowing her lines.

On take number eight she didn't get past her first line— "Are you worried, Toots?" Mimi's version sounded more like, "Are you flurried, Shtoots?"

"Are you *what?*" screamed Bernie. "Cut! Cut!" He came hurrying over to the carousel. "What are you, getting senile or something? Can't you remember your goddamn lines?"

"I'm tired, Bernie. Can't we take a little breakie-pooh?"

"No, we *can't* take a breakie-pooh, sweetheart. Not until you get this goddamn scene right. Then we'll all break our brains out."

Bernie's attitude was unfair. After all, the first seven takes had been ruined because of technical factors that were theoretically his domain.

"Look, Bernie," I said reasonably. "This *is* the eighth take—Mimi has a right to be a little tired, don't you think?"

The beady eyes gave me a cold stare. "Listen," he said, doing me the favor of at least keeping his voice down, "I'm hip that some of you comics like to run the show, but there'll be only one director here at the moment, okay?"

"Of course. I only . . ."

"Then why don't we get on with it?"

Fine with me. On with it and *over* with it was what I had in mind. On take number nine Mimi seemed to regain her concentration. The horses went round and round accompanied by the camera car—at just the right speed—and Mimi and I played our respective parts. I think everyone on the crew gave a sigh of relief. It looked as if we were really going to do it this time, until Mimi came to her very last line. She made quite a simple mistake, changing "He's coming as Mick Jagger" to "He's coming as *Bianca* Jagger." This in itself need not have been a disaster. But as soon as she made her slip, Mimi broke character. "Oh, crap!" she said, and turned toward the camera car. "I'm sorry, Beebs. Honestly I am."

This time Bernie didn't shout. He didn't come over. His elaborate unconcern seemed worse. "This is what comes from hiring your wife," he said, too loudly, to the focus puller. "Well, let's try it again, shall we?"

And so we tried it. Again. And again. The shot seemed jinxed. Sometimes Mimi flubbed at the beginning, sometimes in the middle—and every now and then, just as the entire crew was crossing its fingers and holding its breath, she screwed up at the very end. Take fifteen looked as if it were going to be a winner, except that an armada of fire trucks happened to roar down nearby Fifth Avenue with sirens going full blast. The sound man tore off his earphones in disgust.

Take sixteen *I* flubbed. Have you ever tried to say something over and over again? After a while it can start to become gibberish. Barnes, meanwhile, had become uncharacteristically silent, but despite his wife's pleading, he would not stop for a break.

Take seventeen was looking good, but a little over halfway through, Mimi began to slowly slide off her horse. She might have had a bad fall had I not reached over to grab her arm.

Bernie called "Cut!" once more and ambled our way with a dangerous expression in his eyes.

"You stupid cow," he said to his wife. "Aren't you ever going to get anything right?"

"That's entirely uncalled for," I said, feeling myself getting red in the face. "Perhaps if you had managed to get a decent script to us on time, if you had worked out your technical problems in advance, then maybe the actors would be able to do a professional job!"

I sometimes get a bit pompous when I'm angry, but Bernie got my point. He looked back and forth from me to Mimi several times.

"What are you doing, Steve?" he asked finally. "Shtupping my wife?"

Bernie turned and walked back toward the camera car. I was so furious that words temporarily failed me. They were beginning to come, however—all kinds of words—when I felt Mimi take hold of my arm.

"Please don't say anything, Steve. It will only make matters worse. If he gets too angry, he'll beat me up tonight."

"That son of a bitch!"

Mimi gave me a weak and endearing smile, poor lady. "It's okay," she said. "I'll cook him a six-egg omelette for dinner, with some fatty bacon on the side."

"Why not just stick a knife in his back?" I muttered. "It would be a hell of a lot faster."

I didn't mean it, of course, and the moment I said it I remembered I had a microphone in my lapel. I looked at the sound man huddled over his little Nagra tape recorder, headphones on his ears, trying to decide if he had overheard this somewhat incautious remark.

The man was small and dark with a bushy mustache. To my surprise he looked my way, grinned, and flashed a $V$ with the fingers of his right hand.

# chapter 14

**B**y the end of the day, after twenty-four tries, Bernie finally got something in the can with which he was satisfied. My own opinion was that after seventeen takes Mimi and I had become as wooden as the horses upon which we sat—two zombies mechanically repeating lines. Maybe that was what Bernie was after. I wasn't about to argue with him when he said it was a wrap.

It was getting on toward twilight, a gray, diffuse light in the sky behind the huge, dark buildings on the Upper East Side. As usual, I declined the offered limousine to return to my hotel. In some parts of Los Angeles walking is a near criminal offense; one of the pleasures of New York is the chance to be a pedestrian and window-shopper again. I exited the park near the zoo and strolled downtown along Fifth Avenue, watching all the hurly-burly motion of New Yorkers on their way to restaurants and theaters and cocktail parties and home.

As is my custom, I began to speak softly into my ever-at-hand pocket-size tape recorder. On an average day I will dictate a dozen or so jokes, a few extended philosophical observations, answers to backlogged letters and memos, and assorted notes related to my activities of the moment. In this case I found myself dictating thoughts about Barnes, Mimi, Trip Johnson, and some of the other characters I had newly come to know.

My ruminations were suddenly interrupted by the sight of a homeless young woman sitting on the cold sidewalk with a small, sad-faced child in her arms. Deliberately avoiding her eyes, I stepped over to the woman and handed her a few dollars, a gesture to which she responded with a soft, impersonal thank-you.

There is no city in America where you feel the legacy of Reaganomics quite so clearly as New York: The rich here have become fabulously rich, the poor, poor beyond comprehension. Between 65th Street and 59th I was hit up for money four times. After the second instance I found myself averting my eyes and walking on. The city has become a new Calcutta; eventually you harden yourself to some of the misery you see around you. Then, too, it's difficult to distinguish between the junkies and winos and the more deserving poor.

At the corner of Fifth and 59th Street next to the Park, a booth was set up where some young people were collecting money to help the homeless. I found a twenty-dollar bill in my wallet and pressed it down into the box. I don't want to present myself as some paragon of charity, but you have to do something. Frankly, I was glad to find something to think about other than *Murder in Manhattan.*

It was at that moment I heard a vaguely familiar voice not far away: "You son of a bitch, you're going to do what I tell you to do or else. . . ."

I didn't hear what followed *or else.* I glanced through the crowd, and to my surprise saw that the vaguely familiar voice belonged to Jack Wolfe, the publicist who had met me at the airport. He was standing about five feet away with his hands rather angrily on Trip Johnson, holding the third assistant by his pinstripe lapel. God, more intrigue. I really didn't wish to hear what they were arguing about. Neither Jack nor Trip had noticed me, and, to avoid their doing so, I stepped a few feet from the curb toward the edge of the park. When I thought it was safe, I glanced around to see the two crossing 59th Street toward The Plaza. Their backs were turned to me, but their hand gestures suggested they were still involved in dispute.

"When people have everything they want, they then create totally imaginary problems for themselves in order to accommodate the deep human need to suffer, do they not?" came a deep rumbling voice from somewhere behind me, sounding like the voice of God in an Old Testament film. I turned around but saw only an old bum sitting on a bench alongside the park wall.

It had been a long day. I turned back toward the intersection when the same voice came again: "You do well to give to the homeless, Mr. Allen. Now, if you were clever, you would leave all this greed and stupidity and return to your sunny California."

I felt a shiver on the back of my neck. The light was green across 59th Street to the safety of my hotel, and I was momentarily tempted to run. This was irrational; I forced myself to turn around. The bum on the bench was looking at me. On closer examination I saw this was not just any derelict but Clancy Donahue, the ravaged rose himself. I hesitated, but something drew me forward. I walked over and sat down next to him on the bench.

"Well, Mr. Allen, was it guilt that inspired you to give to the needy of this dark city?"

"Not guilt, Mr. Donahue. Compassion."

Clancy shrugged and offered me a pint bottle from his coat pocket. I declined. He shrugged again, took a hit himself, then returned the bottle to his pocket.

"Guilt. Compassion. Love. Fame. Death and dishonor. It's all the same to me," said the alcoholic philosopher somewhat obscurely. "So how do you enjoy being a hack?"

"I beg your pardon?"

"I'm referring to Toots Gable, ruined writer and social aspirant, who has sold his inner treasure for the empty glitter of being so briefly in vogue."

"Ah, *that* hack," I said, having mistakenly thought he was referring to the quality of some of my books. "Never mind me. You should get back to serious writing. You're a very talented man, and it's a pity to let talent go to waste."

He grinned at me rather hideously. Up close I could see the veins in his nose and a face that had begun to look like a roadmap of old disasters. With a beard Donahue might have resembled Willie Nelson.

"How do you know I'm talented?" he asked. "Maybe I'm just an old fake."

"I read *The Ravaged Rose*," I told him.

"Did you? I thought people in Hollywood didn't read books."

"Please. Those New York put-downs of the movie business have been clichés since the 1930s. Stop feeling so sorry for yourself. If you got off the booze, you could be a successful writer again."

"Oh, could I now?"

I was trying to be encouraging, so I didn't admit I had managed only the first half of *The Ravaged Rose*. The book was heavy going, with a few sentences that stretched on for a page and a half. I had bogged down about page 350, over an entire chapter subsection devoted to the description of a woman's earlobe. I'm sure it's my own fault for not being more sensitive. I had the impression that if I had managed to force myself onward, the book would have yielded untold treasures of philosophical insight.

"Talent is a blessing of the gods," Clancy was telling me. "You must prove yourself worthy, my friend, or the gods go away."

"Forget the gods," I advised. "Find yourself a good typewriter."

Clancy suddenly took hold of my right wrist and squeezed surprisingly hard. "Look over there," he ordered.

A long black limousine had just pulled up to the 59th Street entrance of the hotel across the street. Out of the limo stepped the unforgettable Victoria La Volpa, followed by the bloated figure of Bernard Barnes. Donahue became so excited he stood up on the park bench to get a better look. He weaved slightly on his perch.

"What is she doing with that sleaze merchant?" he cried. "Oh, Victoria, you're breaking my bleeding heart. Not him. Anyone but *him.*"

"Clancy, come down off there before you do a Humpty Dumpty!" I advised.

Clancy watched La Volpa and Bernie disappear inside the hotel and then, with a sigh, accepted a hand down to the pavement.

"Victoria is the only pure one among us," he mourned. "She is a light in the wilderness."

"Isn't she, well, a bit young for you?"

"Of course. She is youth itself," Clancy agreed. "She is the first blessed day of spring captured in female form."

"She certainly is pretty," I agreed.

"Pretty! What a dull word. Don't you understand? Victoria isn't *pretty!* My God, man, she's a whore, an astonishingly beautiful slut, everything a man wants but can never have."

"Clancy," I said. "What do you mean by the word *have?* If you're talking about a one-night fling, you've got a point. We are all creatures of the flesh, after all, and the most moral man on earth cannot possibly be blind to such a combination of eyes, lips, legs, and all that. That's why many such women end up in pictures. They are recognized by directors and producers as marketable products. There are many actresses in films, but only rarely does one have that mysterious animal quality—it has nothing to do with talent—that quality that attracts a certain kind of attention by sheer physicality. Marilyn Monroe, Sophia Loren, Dolly Parton—every man finds the image of such women attractive. But it's purely sexual. Surely you can't seriously be talking about wanting to settle down with someone like Victoria, wanting to marry her, for God's sake."

To my surprise, Clancy suddenly fixed me with a strangely sober, almost calculating look. "I've read some of your work," he said. "I know you're a rationalist of sorts. You want everything to be reasonable. You want discourse to be civilized, as it was on that program you and your wife did for public television. My God, man, don't you know that sex, by definition, is *not* rational? Don't you know that love isn't rational? I assure you, the beauty of this little Italian darling has not blinded me to the reality behind that beauty. I'm perfectly aware that she's a greedy, grasping selfish little bitch who will destroy any man foolish enough to love her, yet—don't you see the magic and curse of it all?—we will love her anyway, for she is our very life-force, the essential primitive woman, and what she exudes is untrammeled by civilization!"

He turned to me, almost pathetically eager to have me agree upon the object of his love.

"Clancy," I said. "There happens to be a very nice young

lady who seems to be truly concerned about you. Suzanne Tracy—"

"Suzanne Tracy? My God, man, she's a copy of a copy! A third-rate epigone! Have you ever listened to her environmental nonsense? To people like her—men or women—that sort of thing is somehow a distraction from the reality of their lives. They throw themselves into causes because they are emotionally restless. They have no creative gift that consumes them and they—"

"You know what your problem is, Donahue? I think you're not too happy with almost the entire human race. Suzanne happens to be a relatively normal young woman. You might even say average, but doesn't it matter to you at all how deeply she admires you, respects you?"

"No, it doesn't," he said. "If she happens to be fond of me, it can't be because of anything I've done to encourage her. Perhaps she had a problem with her father, so she gravitates toward men older than herself. Only Victoria is real. My God, man, a totally authentic person in all her greedy graspiness! She is the very rose, I tell you, that is not yet ravaged—and if that slime Barnes harms a single petal, I am personally going to strangle that son of a bitch until he is dead!"

# chapter 15

Jayne flew into JFK the following evening. She stepped off the plane amid a clutter of hat-boxes and overnight bags—last-minute objects that wouldn't quite fit in the luggage she checked through—and I can't remember ever being so glad to see anyone in my life.

"You look ravishing," I told her. "And I've brought you a rose."

"Darling, how sweet!"

I had for her a single, long-stemmed, dark red flower, which I exchanged for various boxes and bags.

"Well, how's life in Manhattan?" she asked as we carried our respective burdens down a long corridor.

"Murderous."

"Aren't you having fun?"

"*Fun*," I repeated, trying out the word in an experimental manner.

"It can't be that bad."

"It's worse. Picture a group of pathologically over-stimulated eccentrics in heat, and you might begin to imagine our cast and crew."

Jayne gave me a long look. "By the way, speaking of heat, you never did explain what that actress wanted when she came to your room."

"Oh, that was nothing," I assured her. "She's simply in love with somebody who's in love with somebody else. She wanted a shoulder to cry on."

"Well, a shoulder's all right, I suppose, as long as that was the only part of your body involved."

"Jayne, all kidding aside, it's been terrible—I may be the

only normal, happily married guy in the lot.''

We were waiting for the baggage carousel to deliver up Jayne's three overstuffed T. Anthony suitcases. She gave me another of her long looks.

"Darling, if *you're* the most normal person in the company, I'd say they're in trouble. But of course, there's always Jasper."

My silence regarding Jasper North spoke louder than words.

"Jasper isn't part of the . . ."

"No, no," I lied.

Jayne was silent while a porter with cart followed us out to our limousine. The chauffeur and porter eventually managed to find space for everything, and then the limo lurched forward into the free-for-all frenzy New Yorkers call traffic. I saw Jayne's eyes grow a little wide as we passed a truck on our left by using the shoulder.

"So," she said, "besides the romantic intrigue, how do you like working with Mr. Barnes?"

"Well, Fellini he ain't. He treats his cast with all the sensitivity of Godzilla tearing up Tokyo. I hope the director they find to replace him has a somewhat lighter touch."

The skyline of Manhattan came suddenly into our sight, like some magnificent city of Oz lit up against the night across the East River. Jayne was silent a few moments, watching the view and rethinking my words.

"What do you mean, the director they find to replace him? You think Barnes is going to quit?"

"Permanently," I said. "The way he's going, I think he'll get himself murdered."

"Steve! That's a terrible thing to say!"

"Well, he deserves it—if anyone does. I've heard almost everyone in the cast suggest they'd like to put him away in one diabolical way or another. Yesterday I even found myself suggesting to his wife that she stab him in the back."

"That's not funny."

"I didn't mean it to be. I was furious with the bastard. Honestly, I wouldn't be at all surprised if someone tried to give Barnes the big cancellation before this picture is in the bag."

Jayne regarded me suspiciously. "Steve, you're not getting detective fever again, are you?"

"Detective fever?" I asked innocently.

"You know what I mean. Personally, I think you were lucky not to end up dead or in jail on that last little caper."

Jayne was referring, of course, to a double murder I'd happened to solve last year in Los Angeles, an adventure I recounted in *Murder on the Glitter Box.*

Some people like solving crossword puzzles; I happen to find it mentally stimulating to solve crimes. My interest in such exotica goes back to childhood and a peculiar interest of my aunt Margaret's—called Mag—my mother's sister.

Let me digress for a moment and tell you about Mag, a sweet, semi-saintly soul who never married and was the most sensible member of her family. My mother and all the others were heavy drinkers, and managed to raise hell in other ways too, but Mag was, as I say, always a bedrock of strength and sanity, except for the fact that she couldn't read enough detective stories. I don't mean of the Raymond Chandler or Dashiell Hammett sort. What Mag was interested in was found in magazines such as *True Detective,* in which the stories were always accompanied by grisly photographs of dismembered corpses, decapitated heads, bodies burned in fires, and other evidence of human savagery. Habitually reading literature of this sort is commonly assumed to corrupt, to somehow harden the heart. If this is so, then Aunt Mag was an exception to the rule, since to the day of her death she was sweetness personified. But she could not get enough news of gory violence to satisfy her. I can still see her sitting in a rocking chair, at the end of her hardworking day, eyeglasses held about four inches from her one good eye, clucking and saying, "My God, isn't that terrible," as she read about various atrocities and crimes.

When she had finished with the magazines, I was welcome to them, so from the age of about ten to seventeen I read a great deal of this sort of thing. The grisly details were not of passionate interest to me, but I took a sort of intellectual delight in seeing how various policemen, sheriffs, detectives, and private investigators around the country had developed their solutions to the thousand and one murders described. I don't know why Jayne makes such a fuss about it.

"Steve, you're being awfully melodramatic," she said. "But now that I'm here, I'm going to make certain you eat right, get enough exercise, and *don't* have any murders to solve."

"Tell that to the suspects," I suggested.

"Suspects! Aren't you getting a little ahead of yourself?"

"I doubt it. Honestly, if I were holding Barnes's life insurance policy, I'd raise the premium."

I noticed the chauffeur's eyes looking at me through the rearview mirror and realized I was providing a slightly bizarre conversation to overhear. I raised the glass partition.

"I think you have this all wrong," Jayne was saying. "Jasper North is one of the most gentle men I've ever met, and I'm sure that nice young man who plays in *Bermuda P.D.* would never think of murdering anyone either."

"Zachary Holden? He does seem nice," I said, half putting her on. "But that might be only a clever ruse to avoid suspicion."

A few minutes later, as we went through the Midtown Tunnel into Manhattan. I mused aloud, "I wonder what Zachary's motive could be?"

Jayne took my hand. "Do you hear yourself, darling? Don't you think you're being premature?"

I had to laugh. She was right, of course, and I told her so. Wasn't it absurd trying to identify a murderer who hadn't even struck?

# chapter 16

**L**ife changed with Jayne's arrival in New York. A week went by with no young blond actresses knocking on my door for a morning tête-à-tête, no new confessions of twenty-five-year-old secrets of the heart, and definitely no more corned beef hash on the breakfast tray. The world treats you differently when you're a married man. Even Bernie Barnes was relatively amiable.

I decided that *Murder in Manhattan* was only a brief interlude in my life that would soon be over. With Jayne's arrival, the main part of the day seemed to begin after work, at favorite restaurants, seeing a few plays and concerts, and visiting old friends. We dined with my long-time friend, TV producer Bill Harbach, and his wife, Barbara, went to the theater with producer/writer Jim Lipton and his beautiful lady, Kedikai, laughed our way through an evening with two of my comedy friends, Herb Sargent and radio personality Mark Simone, and, on the street, ran into super-agent Irving Lazar, a dear fellow. Through it all we gave scarcely a thought to Barnes and company.

I wish it could have stayed so simple. There were omens— small things really: a box of flowers arriving at my dressing room with a note that said: "Thanks for being so wonderful! XXX, Mimi;" an overheard conversation in which young Trip Johnson actually seemed to be selling Bernie a gram of cocaine. But, these and other small signs of trouble I chose to ignore.

On the Wednesday after Jayne came to New York I was sitting in my trailer waiting to be called to the set when I gave into an inscrutable urge to peek at the unfinished manuscript Suzanne Tracy had forced upon me—Chapter One and assorted fragments of Clancy's new novel, *Busted in Babylon*. We were filming that day in an elegant old Greenwich Village brownstone just off Washington Square, with our equipment trucks and trailers strung out along West 4th Street for nearly a block, and I had brought the manila envelope along to return to Suzanne. I'm really not certain why I decided to give it a quick glance, but as soon as I read the first page, I couldn't put it down.

*Busted in Babylon* began at the funeral of a fictitious and thoroughly despicable film director, Mort Sugarman, who has just been murdered by his wife, Clara, who, as coincidence will have it, happens to be an aging actress, once famous but now hitting the bottle a little too hard.

It was one of those stories that begins at the end and works its way forward in flashbacks. We meet various colleagues, lovers, and rivals at the funeral, and then go to the beginning and tell the entire story of the rise and fall of Mort Sugarman, and how he happened to end up murdered by his wife. From the notes I could tell Clancy saw the murderous wife as the heroine of the story—after all, she rids the world of a corrupt menace and fulfills the secret wishes of every character in the book, including the author. Clancy's prose, I was surprised to see, was wonderfully concise, and he brought his characters to life in quite a remarkable way. Suzanne was right: The man obviously had talent. I only wished he had written about a subject not so close to home.

The manuscript was nearly forty pages long, but thanks to Bernie Barnes, who was proceeding that day at a snail's pace, I had time to read the entire thing and sit with the pages on my lap staring out my trailer window onto 4th Street, pondering on their message. Clancy might be a part-time drunk, but he was no fool. I had nearly convinced myself that my fears about someone ending up murdered on this production were groundless, but this manuscript awakened the concern again.

There was a knock on my trailer door, and I assumed it was one of the assistant directors saying they were ready for me on the set. I was wrong. It was Mimi Day.

She smelled heavily of perfume, albeit a particularly delicious one, and was wearing a lavender and pink garment that I think women call a housecoat, which had buttons from the neck to the ankle.

As she climbed up into the trailer I could not help noticing that the top three buttons were undone, and since her breasts were still remarkably youthful, despite her age, there was no way they could have escaped my attention. It made me uneasy.

She plopped herself down upon the window-wall sofa and gracefully crossed her once-famous legs. I seated myself opposite and gave voice to a quite meaningless, "Well, here we are."

"I hope you don't mind the interruption," she said.

"Oh, no." Having just read Clancy's manuscript, it was hard not to think of Mimi as Clara, the murderous wife. Perhaps I was staring at her a little oddly.

"Is anything wrong?" she said.

"Not at all," I said. "How are things going on the set?"

My brain definitely was getting mixed signals. On the one hand I was fond of Mimi. Her inner sweetness, warmth, and womanliness would make that inevitable, but something about the perfume and the open buttons on the housecoat was making me uneasy, a reaction that was intensified when, at that moment, she recrossed her legs, an act that permitted a view of a good part of the upper leg.

"Did you get my flowers?" she asked.

"Yes," I said. "How nice of you. Jayne and I love roses."

Finding it difficult to remain seated in front of her, trying not to be too obvious about keeping my eyes on her face, I thought that part of the problem might be alleviated if I sat next to her so that I would not have to look at her at all as we continued our conversation.

To my surprise, however, she seemed to interpret this change of position as indicating an interest in greater intimacy and patted my thigh, not suggestively, but in an open, friendly way.

"I had to find some way," she said, "to thank you for helping me through that ghastly scene on the carousel. Something about it made me feel, at the time, as if—I know it will sound silly—but as if you were my only friend in the world. Am I sounding foolish?"

She turned her face to me at that moment, again looking into my eyes, and she seemed somehow so naive, so sincere that it took me a few seconds to realize that our mouths were now only inches apart and that unless I was very much mistaken, she would not have minded in the least if I had taken advantage of the situation. I must confess I wanted to. Mimi Day was still an attractive woman, and her vulnerability made her even more appealing. As a compromise between what my simple animal, physical self very much wanted to do at that moment and what I knew the rules of the game dictated, I took her hand, kissed it with straightforward tenderness, and tried to light-touch my way out of what was not only a titillating but an embarrassing situation.

"Jayne thought it would be fun if all of us had dinner together some night soon," I said.

"How nice. And where is Jayne at the moment?"

I glanced at my watch. "She's at The Four Seasons having lunch with her sister, Audrey, I believe."

"May I confess something?" Mimi said, and I knew she was going to regardless of my answer.

"I don't sleep around," she said.

"I never would have thought you did."

"But at the moment I find myself very attracted to you."

"Well, thank you, Mimi. To tell the truth, I'm attracted to you, too, but I'm trying to summon up what little common sense I seem to have left at the moment because I don't really think we ought to do anything that we'll both be sorry about later."

"I wouldn't be sorry at all," she said softly.

"I have no doubt," I said, "that during the, well, the experience, neither of us would be sorry at all, but eventually I'm sure we'd regret it."

At that, an incredibly sad look came over Mimi's face. There was a strange half smile to it, but she also looked as if she was going to cry. She took my face in both hands and kissed me, tenderly rather than passionately, on the mouth. For a moment my resolve weakened—whose wouldn't?—and I had not the slightest doubt what I wanted to do. To make quite sure that she would not feel she was being personally rejected, I returned the kiss, with fervor, but then forced myself to stand.

"Mimi dear, at the moment I find you irresistible, but I—"

She put her hand, in a flat open position, on my stomach, and then leaned her head next to it. I patted her head half affectionately and half clumsily, and at that moment there came a knock at the trailer door.

"Yes!" I called out loudly.

"Steve, we're not going to get to you today, babe," came the voice of Trip Johnson. "Bernie says I can send you home."

"You see how fate smiles on us," whispered Mimi. "Now we have all the time in the world!"

I managed a matador-like maneuver, slipping past her to the door.

"Trip!" I called. "Wait a minute. When does Bernie want me on the set tomorrow?"

"It depends how far he gets today, dude. I'll put a call sheet in your hotel box."

"I'll walk with you back to the set just to get an idea," I insisted.

"Hey, you don't have to do that—"

Trip had assumed I was alone, but he stopped in midsentence when he glimpsed Mimi behind me in the trailer. That miserable third assistant looked from Mimi to me and back to Mimi—and then, with a smirk on his face, he turned to me, and, unseen by Mimi, winked!

# chapter 17

I was walking uptown from Washington Square along Fifth Avenue, thinking I'd flag down a taxi after a few blocks, when I heard a shout and, turning, saw a Catholic priest running after me.

"Mr. Allen! Would you wait up a minute?"

The priest had a beard, wore dark glasses and a hat, and cut an odd figure, though I couldn't quite put my finger on what was wrong with him. He was separated from me by 18th Street, and as I watched, he sprinted through the traffic like an athlete, dodging a van that nearly ran him down.

"You should watch the jaywalking, Father," I said as he jogged up to my side.

"Don't you recognize me?"

"I'm sorry, Father, but I—"

"It's *me,*" whispered the priest, looking around cautiously. To my surprise he raised his dark glasses and tugged at a false beard that was attached by a little piece of elastic to his hat.

"It's me—Zach Holden," he whispered.

"Zach, what the hell—"

"This is my disguise. I have to go around like this if I'm going to go out in public without being mobbed."

"Ah, the price of fame."

Zach let the glasses and beard fall back into place. "In Los Angeles last year I was nearly torn apart by a gang of teenage girls who wanted a piece of my clothing for a souvenir," he said. "After that I started being careful. The priest outfit works great—no one dares look you in the eye. I hope you don't think I'm being irrelevant—er, irreverent."

"No, not at all."

"You know, I don't have much of an education—that's why I'm coming to you. What I was hoping, well . . . tell me if this is asking too big a favor, okay?"

I was struck by the difference between Holden's dashing good looks and his shy, apologetic manner. I told him, quite sincerely, that I'd be glad to help him if I could.

"Well, it's women," he said. "Or one woman, anyway. I was hoping you could give me some advice on how to score with an intelligent chick."

I tried to keep a straight face. This was TV's hottest detective, just voted the sexiest man in America, at least by the readers of *People* magazine, asking *me* for advice!

"I never imagined you'd have trouble in that department, Zach."

"With Suzanne Tracy I have trouble," he mourned. "I'm sick of all the beach bunnies and bimbos. I want someone I can talk to about—oh, world events, the environment, life, important things like that. I want someone who appreciates me for my mind."

"Look, Zach, perhaps Suzanne isn't interested in you because she's in love with someone else. That sort of thing can't be helped. You could get a Ph.D. in astrophysics, and she still might not know you're alive."

"Yeah, she's in love with that drunken writer." Zach stared at the ground, scuffing the concrete with the black toe of a lizard-skin boot that peeked out from his priestly trousers. "She thinks she's going to save him. How can a smart woman like that be so dumb?"

"I.Q. refers to the brain, not the heart."

We fell into step together walking up Fifth Avenue.

"Do you think it would help if maybe I read some books on pollution and stuff like that?"

"Environmentalism?"

"Yeah, that's the word. Suzanne is really into that stuff. She's such a terrifically sensitive person, Mr. Allen. Why, last Christmas she stood outside Saks Fifth Avenue in a snowstorm and yelled at women in fur coats."

"That's real dedication all right. But, Zach, you'd do best

just to be yourself. You have a lot to offer."

"Nothing·Suzanne seems to want. That's why I thought if you could recommend some good books . . ."

"Have you tried *The Ravaged Rose?*" I suggested.

"By the booze hound?"

"Right. Maybe if you showed an interest in Clancy's work and tried to befriend him, Suzanne would see what a decent person *you* are—in fact, a lot more decent than Clancy in comparison."

"Great idea! Thanks, Mr. Allen. I'll stop off at a bookstore and start reading the damned thing tonight, even if it is Wednesday and it'll mean missing *Jake and the Fatman.*"

"That's the spirit, Zach. But remember, just be yourself."

"Son of a bitch!" said Zach loudly, startling two old women who didn't seem to think this was appropriate language for a man of the cloth. "With your help I'm going to murder the competition!"

"*Beat* the competition," I tempered.

"Isn't that what I said?"

"No, Zach. The word you used was *murder.*"

# chapter 18

We filmed the grand finale costume ball on a clear Wednesday evening aboard the 150-foot yacht, *Easy Money,* moored in the East River. The craft had belonged to a thirty-seven-year-old whiz kid from Wall Street who had been earning three hundred million dollars a year—for at least a year—before retiring to one of our local penitentiaries. *Easy Money* was a seductive ship all right—white and sleek and modern with a helicopter pad, Jacuzzi, hot tub, and just about every convenience a modern, unethical young billionaire might require.

"Oh, I *do* love a sea cruise!" Jayne said as our limousine made its way slowly eastward through the thronged rush-hour streets.

"The boat's not even leaving the dock," I explained. "And besides, there seems to be some confusion about whether we're really filming tonight."

The problem had to do with an argument between Bernie Barnes and our producer, Nashville Stuart. I had gotten the lowdown on the situation from Annie Locks as she was doing the final alterations on my Superman outfit the previous afternoon: Bernie wanted to delay the filming of the costume ball for another three weeks, since he was behind schedule, and shooting the climactic scene now would be out of sequence. In film making, of course, scenes are often shot out of sequence, but this was not Bernie's way. In this instance, however, Nash had apparently prevailed; the good ship *Easy Money* had been reserved for three nights starting today and any delay would be an intolerable expense to an already plundered budget.

The yacht, docked at the end of East 37th Street, looked like

a graceful white sea bird sitting on the gray sludge of the East
River. Crew members were milling about the dock, loading camera and lighting gear up the gangplank. Trip Johnson came
ambling toward our limousine. He was dressed in pleated white
flannel trousers, a white V-neck sweater, and white deck shoes
*sans* socks. Except for the missing socks, he was your compleat
British yachtsman, circa 1927. I should mention that there *was*
a first assistant director, and a second assistant director, too, on
the film, but they kept a low profile. For all practical purposes,
the third A.D. had apparently taken over.

"Steverino! Ready for the big adventure? Jayne, it's great
that you came to see your husband off," Trip said in greeting.

"Off?" I repeated with some irritation. I don't stand on a
great deal of ceremony, but there was something annoying
about this nineteen-year-old treating us like bosom buddies.
"What do you mean, see me off?"

"On the great sea voyage, of course," Trip said.

"But we're not going anywhere. We're filming at the dock
. . . aren't we?"

"That was *yesterday's* plan. Today Bernie woke up with one
of his famous flashes and declared we'd sail a quarter mile out
from lower Manhattan to have the New York skyline in the
background."

"Well, I don't like it," I grumped. "It seems a little dangerous heading out to sea with a maniac like Barnes in control.
Someone knows how to steer this thing, I assume?"

Trip laughed good-naturedly, yachtsman to landlubber.
*"Easy Money* comes with a captain and five-man crew, so no
sweat."

Jayne was squeezing my hand in a reassuring way. "Well, I
think it sounds lovely," she said. "It's always exciting to see New
York from the water, particularly at night."

"As long as we're not *under*water," I said skeptically. "I'm
not getting near that boat unless I see life jackets for all hands
and passengers."

Trip was looking back and forth from me to Jayne. "Oh,
dear, this is a little embarrassing," he said.

"What are we talking about now?"

"You were expecting Jayne to come on board? Didn't they tell you?"

"Tell me *what?*"

"It's a closed set—no one's allowed who's not actually involved in the specific scenes tonight. There just isn't room. I'm awfully sorry, Mrs. Allen, but you can see if we make an exception for you . . ."

"Either Jayne goes or I stay behind," I announced. "So you'd better lead me to Barnes, pops."

"Bernie and Nash are in a last-minute powwow at the moment. I don't think it's a good idea to disturb them, not even for you, Steve."

I folded my arms and prepared to be difficult.

"Darling, maybe I *should* stay behind," Jayne said.

"If it makes you feel any better, even *I* couldn't bring a friend," Trip said. "There was this terrific girl I met last night I was *dying* to impress, but no deal."

Jayne squeezed my hand somewhat harder than before. "Steve, I think I will stay behind. I could use a nice long soak in a hot tub and I can understand not wanting extra people. It *is* reasonable."

"I don't care if it's reasonable or not. I'm tired of all the confusion on this film."

"Darling, it'll soon be over. Then maybe you and I will take our own cruise somewhere."

"Promise?"

Jayne sweet-talked me into accepting the inevitable. With dire misgivings I watched the limousine take her westward, back to The Plaza, wondering briefly about the negative feeling in the pit of my stomach.

The last light of day was fading from the sky as I walked up the gangplank to the deck of the ship. Against the twilight the numberless windows of the great monolithic buildings of midtown Manhattan were already lit with the power of a billion candles. As always in New York, there were sirens in the distance that sounded like the very voice of doom.

I walked up toward the bow, where I could get out of the way of the various cast and crew coming aboard. After a few minutes Trip drifted my way with a black leather attaché case in one hand.

"Hey, Steve, I didn't want to say anything in front of the old lady, but if you need a little potion to ward off the seasickness, I've got a few things in my bag that might really knock your socks off. . . ."

"I intend to keep my socks on, thank you, and to tell the truth, I think drugs are for idiots and losers."

"Hey, man, I only thought . . ."

"Stop thinking," I snapped.

"Whatever you say, Mr. Allen. See you around." With an insolent look Trip went quickly on his way.

I sighed and looked out across the water. The moon was rising over the smokestacks of Long Island City as I felt a shudder deep down in the bowels of the ship. The engines had started; the lines were undone. I saw Bernie and Nash hurry up the gangplank from a parked limousine and then, too quickly, we were heading out to sea.

# chapter 19

**W**e made our merry way down the East River. *Easy Money* seemed to have been designed as a party boat, and I'm not talking about fishing expeditions. The main deck consisted of a huge unbroken salon, possibly eighty feet long by thirty feet wide, with a polished hardwood dance floor in the middle, a bar at one end, and all the conveniences necessary to entertain a small horde of fun-loving tycoons and their women.

It certainly was a beautiful craft. All the furnishings were white with gleaming chrome around the edges—white leather sofas, white tables, lamps, armchairs, and plush white carpeting thick enough to lose your pet chihuahua in. At the moment two burly technicians with tattoos on their arms were setting lights and laying cables while the rest of us milled about, now wearing our costume finery. It was quite a sight to see the cast as well as approximately forty extras dressed up as gods and Valkyries, gladiators, rock stars, and various famous people from history, including Napoleon, Marie Antoinette, and Jim and Tammy Bakker, both of whom wore heavy eye makeup. To manage all this, Annie Locks had taken over the master stateroom, and a small army of her assistants were making last-minute alterations. Every few minutes *Easy Money* rolled through the wake of a tugboat or barge, and we would all sway back and forth just enough to remind me that this particular party was not on dry land.

I was, of course, wearing my Clark Kent outfit, an extremely square, single-breasted gray suit straight from the fifties, my own dark-rimmed glasses, and an old-fashioned gray fedora, precisely the sort I used to wear when I did the Big Bill Allen sports reporter sketches and the old letters-to-the-editor bit, where I would read actual angry letters, usually from the New York *Daily News* or the *Post,* in the emotional tone in which they had been written. Wearing the comedy wardrobe should have been fun now, but it wasn't. I was nagged by the uncomfortable realization that on this boat, separated from land, we were all at the mercy of Madman Barnes. Outside the windows, the night skyline of Manhattan was passing by from an unfamiliar POV— the water. Before long we reached the tip of lower Manhattan and then began moving through the dark night farther offshore. A shiver prickled the back of my neck.

I noticed Jasper North in a corner, having an intense conversation with Clancy Donahue. I went over to say hello and immediately had the awkward feeling of intruding. Jasper and I exchanged a bit of small talk while Clancy stared rudely out the window. When I moved away, they both seemed relieved.

"All right, places everyone!" shouted Trip Johnson.

The first shot was a crowd scene in which I had to stand next to Mimi Day and pretend to have a conversation. Mimi was stuffed into a tiny fairy costume—a little silver bodice, tights, and sparkling wings. She was Titania, the fairy queen. The heavy cooking Mimi was doing for her husband seemed to be getting to her as well, a fact that was painfully apparent in this revealing attire.

"Do I look okay?" she whispered.

"Magnificent," I lied.

"I told Bernie I was too old to be dressed like this, but he insisted," she confided.

"Your outfit was Bernie's idea?"

"He wouldn't hear of me wearing anything else. Do I look all right, Steve, *really?*"

That bastard! Barnes was deliberately embarrassing his wife by putting her in a skimpy outfit. I was so angry I took her hand.

"Mimi," I said, "Zaftig is in. You look very sexy."

"Truly?" She was blushing with pleasure. "You look just super yourself!"

I smiled and kissed her hand reassuringly.

La Volpa drifted by, flashing Mimi a catty smile. "Are you being unfaithful to your husband, darling?"

"Every chance I get," Mimi lied.

La Volpa gave a wicked little laugh and kept going. She was dressed as Aphrodite, goddess of love, in a shimmering silk tunic that clung to her firm young body.

"I'm not jealous of her," Mimi said as we watched La Volpa drift through the crowd, leaving every male eye lingering after her. "Not anymore." I felt Mimi clutch my arm more tightly. "I'm not jealous because now I have you."

"You want me," I said, keeping up the game, "just because you think that under this mild-mannered exterior I'm really Superman."

"Cut!" called Bernie. The spontaneous crowd scene was a keeper. Mimi took advantage of the break to make her way to the powder room, flashing me a last long-lidded glance before she left.

If she was even semi-serious, this was turning into a problem. After all, I had only been trying to be nice to the lady.

The ship was now dead still in the water, some distance from land. There was a spectacular view of lower Manhattan just off the port bow. Not far away, an enormous ocean liner, lights gleaming, passed on its way out to sea. I found myself wondering how deep the water was at this point. It was certainly well over our heads.

My mind flashed back to first one and then another instance in which, on live television, I had actually been in danger of drowning. The first had happened at the old St. George Hotel in Brooklyn, in 1952, one afternoon when we were doing our daily CBS show there. A few people over the years who saw that particular telecast have told me that its opening provided a surprise they've never been able to forget. We had brought along a wooden frame across which was stretched a silver and blue spangled curtain like the one that usually backdropped my opening monologue. Consequently, when the show started, the at-home audience naturally assumed I was in our theater, whereas I was really standing on a diving board out over one end of the hotel's enormous swimming pool, though fully clothed.

After a few minutes of standard jokes, I said, "Well, it's time to get over to home base," and started the usual walk to the stage-right area. The camera pulled back into a wide shot just as I suddenly dropped into the frigid water at the deep end of the pool. So far so good, except that I'm quite a poor swimmer and, being fully clothed and wearing heavy shoes, I came to the surface far too slowly for my taste, got water into my mouth, nose, and eyes, and floundered about momentarily, unable to head for the side of the pool. Luckily our guest that day was former Olympic swimming champion Buster Crabbe of Flash Gordon fame. He promptly came to my rescue.

In the other instance, a few years later, we were doing the *Tonight* show from Florida and had staged a mock military invasion as our opening.

This involved my being on an actual GI landing craft and assaulting the beach with a boatload of marines. About five minutes before air time, 11:30 P.M., I was told to wade out into the water in full military uniform, including a rifle strapped over my back, and clamber aboard. But by now the tide had shifted and the water was deeper than we had anticipated. Again I couldn't seem to keep my head above the surface as I splashed and thrashed out toward the landing craft. Just in time, a couple of marines lent a helping hand and dragged me aboard, a task further complicated by the fact that the entire scene was played out in pitch darkness.

Now, reminded of those frightening experiences, my sense of uneasiness began to grow. Glancing around, I felt a sense of intrigue in the air: a glimpse of Suzanne Tracy whispering something into Jack Wolfe's ear, then both of them looking my way; La Volpa taking Zachary Holden by the hand and leading him off on deck while Bernie watched them with his cold, reptilian eyes; Nash Stuart deep in conversation with the ubiquitous Trip Johnson. Were they buying and selling drugs? Passing secrets? Making strange assignations? Catching sight of these vignettes made me feel paranoid. For some strange reason I was suddenly relieved that Jayne had not come along. All I wanted was for the ship to return to the dock.

According to the script, I was to emerge, at the stroke of

midnight, from the colorless cocoon of Clark Kent into my alter ego, Superman. In order to do this, I had to visit Annie Locks in wardrobe to don my blue tights, red cape, and boots. We had been filming more than three hours by now, and I was glad to get away from the crowd into the quieter depths of the ship. Descending the stairs, I followed a long corridor toward the bow. Since I was the only one in double costume, there was no one around to tell me the way, but I finally found a cardboard sign taped to one of the doors: MEN'S WARDROBE. I knocked, but there was no answer. The door was unlocked, however, so I went in.

"Annie? Anyone here?"

Apparently Annie, too, was on the upper deck. Seeing my costume folded neatly on the bed, I decided I was quite capable of dressing myself. With no telephone booth in sight, I took the entire outfit into the bathroom, removed my suit and fedora, and stepped into the tights and snug-fitting sweatshirt with the big $S$ on the chest.

They say clothes make the man. I had never appreciated the truth of that until, in television and a few films, I had occasion to wear various costumes and uniforms. Although it may sound odd, you do tend to feel strangely like the characters you play. Dressed as a policeman, for example, you carry yourself like one and actually *feel* somewhat more masculine and dominating. Attired as a priest, you become more compassionate. Anyway, it was indeed odd how I felt as I finished clasping the long red cape around my neck. I found myself standing straighter, breathing deeper, thrusting out my chest, pulling in the old waistline. When I was ready, I stepped back into the stateroom and stood in front of the floor-length mirror, posing with my knuckles on my waist, really Supermanning it up.

Nothing worried me any longer. Boy, was I tough! Reluctantly, I removed my glasses, making my world a little blurry but essential for the final transformation from mild-mannered reporter to Man of Steel. I was flexing my muscles when I heard a knock on the stateroom door.

"Come in," I roared in a voice loud enough to derail a

speeding train. There was no answer. "The door's open," I called.

When there was still no answer, I went to the door. As soon as I turned the knob, the door pushed in on me. I stumbled backward into the stateroom. A great bulky figure swayed in the doorway, then toppled forward. The enormous hulk of a man fell limply into my arms. We did a kind of crazy waltz for a moment and then crashed backward on the bed, face-to-face, with him on top. Even without my glasses I recognized Bernie Barnes. His eyes stared hideously into mine, and a small trickle of blood oozed from his mouth and landed on my chin. "Holy Christ!" I shouted, and slid out from under him as fast as I could, leaving him facedown upon the snowy white eiderdown, arms outstretched, an enormous carving knife protruding from his back.

Before I could react, a roaring explosion rocked the boat beneath my feet. *Easy Money* yawed wildly to the starboard, sending me sprawling backward onto a chaise longue. I was momentarily stunned, but knew I'd better get up and moving. As my feet hit the floor, I felt something wet. At first I had the horrible idea it was Bernie's blood, but I reached down a tentative hand and discovered something even worse: water!

I brought a small sample to my lips, fearing the taste. My suspicions were confirmed. It was saltwater, not a plumbing leak.

I'm not much of a sailor, but I knew this was not a good sign. A half inch of the saline liquid now swirled about my feet. Strangely, I still felt idiotically capable of leaping tall buildings in a single bound, but I also knew damned well that I had better get the hell to a higher level. The simple instinct of self-preservation led me to the immediate conclusion that the good ship *Easy Money* was going down off the rocky shores of Wall Street. And there were no Buster Crabbes or marines in sight.

It would be an exaggeration to suggest that my whole life flashed before my eyes, but I did think, quite sadly, of Jayne, my four sons, and my nine grandchildren. I knew that if I let myself get trapped down here, God knows how many feet beneath the surface of the river, I might never see any of them again.

# chapter 20

I tried not to panic. Because the hallway was listing to one side at a crazy angle, getting myself back up to the deck of the ship was like passing through a slanted fun house at a carnival. Though I could hear shouting, I didn't see another soul until I climbed the stairs and reached the grand salon. Where the orderly film cast and crew had been, now there was pandemonium. People were arguing and trying to climb out the main door and windows onto the deck. The floor beneath our feet was now a slippery hill upon which women in high heels lost their balance and went tumbling down among the chairs and tables. The colorful costumes gave the scene a surreal air, like some Hieronymous Bosch vision of hell.

"What happened?" I heard someone ask.

"The captain said the bilge pump blew," someone answered.

I don't know a bilge pump from a head gasket, but the explanation didn't sound right. What I had heard sounded more like a bomb. I was looking around for someone familiar when I spotted Trip Johnson standing by the stairs from where I had just come.

"Trip, Bernie's down there," I shouted. "He's dead."

"Bernie?" said the young man, giving me a strange look. His white yachting outfit was still immaculate, but there was a cut on his forehead where he had bashed into something.

"He's dead," I said again. "There's a big carving knife sticking between his shoulders."

"I can't believe that," said Trip, and I was surprised to see a very small smile work at the corners of his mouth. "Guess I'd better go have a look."

"Don't bother. This boat's going down fast."

"Hey, I'm third A.D.," he said with noble purpose. "This is my job. Besides, there might be someone else trapped down there."

Johnson was the last person from whom I would have expected heroics, but, then, emergencies bring out the unexpected all around.

"I'll be okay. I'll do it fast," he told me, bounding down the stairs.

"Trip!" I called, but he was gone. I shook my head. Bernie was dead, and I actually didn't think anyone else was down there. As far as I could see, Johnson was risking his life for nothing.

Then there was a scream, and the lights went out as the ship's power suddenly failed. I knew it was time to get out of there. There was a milky light in the night sky outside, the reflection of nearby Manhattan, which guided me toward the door, my hands held in front of me to ward off dimly seen objects. With a horrible groan the ship settled farther on its side. I managed to grab hold of a chrome railing and felt a strong hand take hold of my arm and pull me outside onto the deck. It was Zachary Holden.

"Gotcha, Mr. Allen! You okay?"

"I'm fine, but Trip just went below to see if there're any others down there."

"I'll find him," said Zach. "You'd better get into a life raft."

The starboard side of the yacht was now level with the water, and it looked as if the ship could sink any moment. A few people, wearing orange life vests, were already in the water. Two life rafts were bobbing on the surface not far away, desperately overloaded with people. I saw Jack Wolfe kneeling in the nearest raft, using a paddle to beat off the director of photography, who was in the water and trying to come aboard.

"We can't *take* anyone else!" screamed the publicist in a high, unnatural voice. "Can't you see? We'll sink, goddammit!"

"Are there any more life jackets?" I asked Zach.

"We couldn't find any, and the captain and most of the crew got off in the first raft."

"Lovely!"

"You'd better get moving, Mr. Allen. There's only one more raft, and it's filling up fast."

"What about you?"

"I used to be an Olympic swimmer. I'll stay and help the stragglers."

Zach had a humble and heroic way about him—very unusual to Hollywood he-men, some of whom are not particularly macho in real life. I could see the last life raft being lowered into the water and was about to take Zach's advice when a new explosion shook the boat. I found myself tumbling through the air, landing into the shock of cold, dark water. I came up sputtering. The nearest life raft was at least twenty feet away and seemed to be sinking under the weight of well over a dozen hysterical people. A wave hit me in the face, and I went down beneath the surface. When I came up again, I found myself staring at a truly terrifying sight: *Easy Money* was standing nearly straight up on end, bow in the sea, stern in the air. I could see the twin propellers and the rudder hanging free of the water in an improbable way. The cold was beginning to get to me. I had a vague notion that when a ship went down, it created a suction that would be good to avoid, so I began swimming energetically in the general direction of Manhattan. But as I've mentioned, I'm only a fair swimmer, and the cold and dark and feeling of panic crowding the edges of my consciousness debilitated my strength. It also did not help to be weighed down by a long red cape. I stopped, treading water, and tried to undo the clasp around my neck, but my fingers were too numb to control.

I floated for a moment, trying to catch my breath. When I looked up, *Easy Money* was a good distance across the water but still hovering in its impossible position, pointing regally toward the sky. Then, as I watched, something seemed to give. The ship arched gracefully forward and into the deep. I saw the smokestack disappear, the main cabin, and then with a loud *whoosh,* the entire craft slid from view toward the harbor floor. After a moment great bubbles came up from the depths. It was the eeriest spectacle I had ever seen. And probably the last spectacle, I reminded myself grimly.

With the yacht gone, there was a dead quiet upon the water. Because of the darkness, I couldn't see any of the life rafts or any other people in the water, though I could hear distant voices. The solitude was devastating.

"Hello?" I called. "Hel-lo! Anybody out there?"

I went down and came up coughing saltwater, saying a prayer of thanks that Jayne was safe at The Plaza.

*This was really it,* I began to realize. *This was the final curtain for Stephen Valentine Allen.*

I sank once more into the clammy depths, too weak to fight anymore. Obviously, I had never thought I would drown off the island of Manhattan. Perhaps from a heart attack at receiving the bill for dinner for four at Spago's, but never this.

I was going down for the third time, asking myself: What's it all about, Alfie? Life, death, the bitter war with calories, the struggle to get a good table at the best restaurants. . . . I was face-to-face with the big questions and feeling the answers nearby, like a curtain about to part. Then I heard a roar in my ears, and a mighty wind came upon the water. From the heavens a great light pierced the gloom and shone down upon me.

I heard a thunderous voice: *"Grab the line!"*

A rope dangled from the sky and something dropped into the water beside me. *God was about to haul me off to heaven!* I had always imagined a more metaphysical ascent to the afterlife, but I didn't wish to be rude.

*"Put the harness around your waist!"* came the Great Voice in the Sky.

I took hold of the rope. At the end was a little seat that reminded me strangely of a device called a Johnny Jump-up, in which very young children can dangle and hop before they're old enough to walk. This, too, seemed part of the Wizard of Oz's mysterious plan.

*"Yank the rope two times when you're ready,"* said the voice.

I managed to strap myself into the Johnny Jump-up, swallowing more oily seawater as I did so.

Of course, I had no idea what to expect. It really was rather glorious. There was a mighty roar, and I was yanked up out of the watery grave and into the beautiful sky. I found myself dangling a hundred feet above the water, being carried swiftly toward the city, my red cape flying behind me like a flag.

Risking a glance upward, I saw the underbelly of a helicopter with its green and red running lights flashing. It took hardly more than a minute to reach land.

Below me I could see a wharf crowded with people and various emergency vehicles with revolving lights. Everyone was staring up at me and pointing. I couldn't imagine what was so special about seeing someone descend from the sky until I remembered I was still wearing my Superman outfit.

Okay, I'll admit it—I posed a little, hammed it up, flexing my biceps and making sure my cape was free of the rope so it could wave in an impressive way. After all, this was the opportunity of a lifetime.

*Is it a bird?* I could almost hear the crowd asking. *Is it a plane?*

No, by God, it's Steve Allen, Super-Comic, returning from the very jaws of death!

# chapter 21

I was soaking in the bathtub back at The Plaza, a big, old-fashioned marble-topped tub with lots of room to stretch out in. I lay back, only my head above the water, and savored the hot steam that rose toward the high ceiling.

Jayne strolled into the bathroom.

"There's a Lieutenant Carlino and a Sergeant Dimitriev of the NYPD here to see you," she said. "Why don't I tell them to come back tomorrow? It's not every day one gets shipwrecked and plucked from the sea."

"No, I'd better talk to them now," I said wearily. "Offer them a drink or something. Policemen generally drink scotch. Just make sure they don't smoke."

I was the one who had contacted the police, making the call not long after I had returned to the hotel. Now, lying in the tub, I had been meditating upon the motives different people might have had to murder Bernie Barnes and, more important, who had had the opportunity. In retrospect, I wished I had had the presence of mind to look out into the hallway after Bernie made his final plunge into my stateroom. It seemed he must have been stabbed only seconds before he knocked on my door—thus the murderer could not have been more than a few feet away.

I dried myself and stepped into a thick terry-cloth robe. The two policemen—police*persons* I suppose I should call them— were being entertained in the sitting room by Jayne, who was plying them with peppermint tea, not scotch, and telling stories about her childhood in China.

The officers rose when I came into the room. I found myself

shaking hands with a good-looking man in his late thirties who had dark hair and dark eyes.

"Good evening, Mr. Allen. I'm Lieutenant Carlino and this is my partner, Sergeant Natasha Dimitriev. I understand you have a murder to report."

"I'm afraid so," I said. "Would you like something a little stronger than tea?"

The lieutenant flashed a wan smile. "Thank you, but no."

We all sat down in a circle around the coffee table. Lieutenant Carlino was dressed in a well-cut dark suit and didn't look like anybody's idea of a cop. He had pale skin, a sensitive, ironic mouth, and long, almost girlish eyelashes. He was the sort who could be the leading man in an old black-and-white French film. Quite debonair.

Sergeant Dimitriev, on the other hand, was chewing gum and looking about as tough as you might expect a New York cop to be. She was a rather pretty young woman, but her dark auburn hair was pulled back in a bun and she wore no makeup. Additionally, she was dressed in a no-nonsense black pants suit that did its best to conceal the curves beneath it, and I got the impression that she was trying hard to be one of the boys. I couldn't help notice, however, that her aquamarine eyes—beautiful eyes, actually—seemed to rest upon her partner more often than they did on Jayne and me.

"The murder, Mr. Allen?" prompted Lieutenant Carlino.

"From the beginning?"

"Please."

"Well, I was sitting in our home back in Encino when my agent called . . ."

"Not *that* far back."

So I told them about the night, about the filming of the party on the yacht, and how eventually I went below to change into my Superman outfit.

Jayne was sitting on the edge of the sofa as I recounted how Bernie Barnes had fallen into the stateroom with a knife in his back. I told how his great weight pinned me to the bed, how I rolled out from under him, about the explosion—and finally how I barely escaped with my life. All the time, Lieutenant

Carlino watched me with good-natured skepticism and Sergeant Dimitriev scowled as if she were trying to think of some offense she might charge me with. I noticed that neither of them took notes.

"Tell them about Bernie's eyes," encouraged Jayne. "How they were all glassy and bulging out."

"It was pretty horrible," I said. "He looked like a big dead fish."

"Let's go back over this, if you don't mind," the lieutenant suggested. "Now, right before you heard the knock on the stateroom door, what exactly were you doing, sir?"

"I was looking at myself in the floor-length mirror, imagining myself as Superman."

"Imagining?"

"Well, I was a bit of a blur, to tell the truth."

"In other words, without your glasses you couldn't see too well?" asked the lady sergeant.

"Yes," I admitted. "Superman, as you may be aware, does not need glasses—only Clark Kent."

"But Steve Allen needs glasses, right?" Sergeant Carlino put in with mild reproach. "They've been your trademark over the years, haven't they?"

"Yes, but I don't see . . . uh—"

"That's exactly the point I'm trying to make—*you don't see* too well. So if you had your glasses removed, and by your own admission all you could discern of your reflection in the mirror was a blur, how can you be certain the man stumbling into the stateroom was Bernie Barnes?"

*He didn't believe my story!* I glanced over at Sergeant Dimitriev for support, but she looked even less believing. As I watched, she took a wad of orange chewing gum from her mouth and put it into the ashtray on the coffee table.

"Sergeant," rebuked the lieutenant, frowning at the gum.

The sergeant's aquamarine eyes flashed angrily at her partner, then at me.

Jayne stepped in to smooth things over. "Don't worry about the gum," she said graciously. "It's much better than cigarettes."

"That's the reason I'm chewing the stuff," admitted Sergeant Dimitriev. "I went cold turkey from two packs a day. Down to zilch. I've gone six days now without a smoke."

"Isn't that wonderful!" Jayne said.

"Yeah, but she's driving me nuts," the lieutenant complained to Jayne, though good-naturedly. He gave me a man-to-man look. "How'd *you* like to be partners with a woman who's trying to stop smoking? And this isn't the first time she's tried to quit either."

He turned to his partner, teasing. "How many days did you manage *last* time, Natasha?"

"Three," Natasha mumbled sullenly. "But that's only because you were bugging me the whole damn time."

"I think it's splendid what you're doing, Natasha," Jayne said supportively. "Quitting cigarettes is one of the most difficult things in the world."

Now, I don't want to complain about this twist of conversation. After all, I'm in favor of everybody quitting cigarettes—but somehow all hands seemed to be forgetting about a little thing called murder. Fascinating as it was to watch two of New York's finest squabbling, I felt it was time to get back to the point.

"Look," I explained, "Bernie Barnes rolled right on top of me. His face was about an inch from mine—*that* far I can see. And I can assure you, the poor man was dead."

"And you're certain it was Barnes?" asked Lieutenant Carlino.

"Absolutely."

"And then you noticed he had been shot in the back?" The lieutenant was sly.

"*Stabbed* in the back," I corrected him.

The lieutenant smiled at me, the sort of superior smile a professional reserves for an amateur, then flashed my wife a genuine one. "Mrs. Allen, do you suppose I could have a little more tea?"

"Of course, Lieutenant." When the tea was poured, Carlino once again turned my way.

"And then you felt an explosion?"

"That's right. Later, on deck, I heard someone say the bilge pump blew, but it sounded like a bomb to me."

"Have you ever heard a bomb explode before?"

"Not actually," I admitted. "Only in the movies, of course. And grenades in infantry basic training."

"Ah, the movies." Lieutenant Carlino smiled an ironic smile. "Well, Mr. Allen, you'll have to admit, this all sounds a little fantastic, doesn't it?"

"Look, if you don't believe me . . ."

"I didn't say that, sir. I'm simply trying to approach this in a levelheaded way. Did you mention this—er, death to anyone?"

"Only the third assistant director, a kid by the name of Trip Johnson."

"The *third* assistant?" questioned the lady sergeant. "Wouldn't you report a murder to someone in a more important position?"

"You do know that the boat was sinking, right? There was pandemonium everywhere—Johnson was simply the first person I saw."

"And did you take him to the corpse?" asked the lieutenant.

"Of course not. The last time I saw the kid he was heading below deck to check for himself. I hope the little bastard's all right."

I felt the lieutenant studying me. "Well, we'll look into that, naturally. But tell me, why would anyone want to murder Mr. Barnes?"

"Ha!" I cried. "Bernie was a man who could inspire homicidal fury in a saint. Everybody wanted to murder him!"

"If we interpret the word *everybody* literally, it would logically follow that you wanted to kill Mr. Barnes."

"All I intended to convey," I said, forcing myself to control my anger, "was that the man had apparently no friends but a very long list of enemies."

"I see," said Lieutenant Carlino dryly. "And do you have any theories as to who the murderer could be?"

"I've been thinking about this for a couple of days," I told him, leaning forward.

"A couple of days?"

"Sure. Anyone could tell it was just a matter of time before someone bumped him off. This may be a little premature, Lieutenant, but I'd look very closely at Zachary Holden. Nice as he appears to be, he's the only one who doesn't have an obvious motive."

"I'm afraid I don't see . . ."

"Well, neither do I right now. But the one thing I'm sure of, you have to discount the obvious. And Zachary's about the most *un*obvious suspect in the group, which makes him my prime choice."

"That's very clever, darling," said Jayne enthusiastically. At least I had one fan. Lieutenant Carlino continued to regard me with what might have been good-natured skepticism. He smiled and stood up, joined immediately by the tough but pretty sergeant.

"I think we'll let you get some rest now, Mr. Allen. You've been through quite an experience tonight, escaping a sinking ship and all."

He said it in a way which implied that my judgment might be impaired.

And then to my wife he said, "So nice meeting you, Mrs. Allen."

For a moment I thought he was going to kiss her hand, but he merely gave it a friendly squeeze.

"Yeah, nice meeting ya," Natasha said, giving Jayne's hand a firm shake. She didn't say anything to me at all.

"What a cute couple," Jayne said when they were gone.

"They're not a couple," I grouched. "They're police officers . . . and they don't seem to believe a damned word I said."

"Well, *I* believe you, darling," said my wife. "*I* think it's a wonderful story."

"Thank you."

"Incidentally," Jayne said, "you don't really think Zach Holden has anything to do with the killing, do you?"

"Of course not. I was just putting the lieutenant on."

"Well," Jayne said. "If you don't mind my saying so, you could get poor Zach in trouble with that sort of a put-on."

"Hey," I said, "I don't know for a fact that Holden didn't stick that knife in Barnes's back, but I have a strong feeling that

he's innocent, has an alibi supported by the testimony of wit-
nesses, and won't be in any real danger from what I just said to
Carlino."

"You sound a little edgy," Jayne said.

"Well, my God, it isn't every day I have a dead man fall on
me and almost end up dead myself. A day like this could make
a grouch of Mother Teresa."

Jayne smiled sweetly. "Why don't you get back in that nice
tub full of hot water?"

"All right," I said. "And why don't you join me?"

She paused, then smiled noncommittally.

# chapter 22

The next day Jayne and I had lunch in the Edwardian Room downstairs in the hotel. The restaurant is a nostalgic reminder of old New York, renowned for its dark oak-paneled walls, high ceilings, and waiters, some of whom act as if they're doing a tremendous favor by serving you.

Jayne and I were devouring some succulent salmon, sitting by a large window overlooking 59th Street and the park, when I noticed Jack Wolfe step into the dining room. He glanced over the heads of the other luncheoners, found us by the window, and headed our way. I suppressed an urge to hide under the table.

"Steve-er! What a goddamn *coup!*" he shouted. "You see the goddamn *Post?*"

"Won't you sit down, Mr. Wolfe?" Jayne murmured. Most people who are speaking too loudly will automatically lower their voices if you respond in a softer than normal tone. Jayne was obviously trying this tactic with Jack, but the man was either an exception to the rule or too excited to notice. He was grinning from ear to ear. His tie was loose, and I thought for a moment I saw a tiny drop of saliva dribble down his chin. He threw the "goddamn *Post*" down next to my bread plate.

"Son of a bitch! You're beautiful, baby—bee-*you*-tiful! Take a look at the front page!"

I glanced at the paper and saw the reason for Jack's glee: Nearly the entire page was taken up by a photo of me, in my Superman outfit, being lowered out of the sky and onto a wharf in lower Manhattan. Above the picture, in huge letters, was the headline: MOVIE SHIP SINKS IN MYSTERY EXPLOSION. Beneath the photo was a caption: SUPERMAN STEVE ALLEN RES-

CUED LAST NIGHT FROM SINKING YACHT DURING FILMING OF THE NEW BERNARD L. BARNES COMEDY *Murder in Manhattan.* SEE PAGE 3.

"They even got the name of the goddamn picture right there on the fucking front page!" Jack gloated, his voice still too loud.

Jayne was regarding him with the curiosity of an anthropology student meeting her first real savage.

"Won't you join us for lunch, Mr. Wolfe?" she asked demurely.

"I wouldn't want to intrude . . . but, to tell the truth, I haven't had a goddamn thing to eat since last night."

A waiter appeared. Jack didn't want any of the better things on the menu—which didn't surprise me—but inquired if "the cook" could rustle up a hamburger with plenty of onions, extra pickle, and a side of fries. The waiter reacted as if he found it distasteful even to write down such a request.

Meanwhile, opening the newspaper to the story inside, I saw a photograph of Zachary Holden helping sex goddess Victoria La Volpa from a life raft. La Volpa managed to look as ravishing as ever, despite the disarray of her hair.

Another picture showed Jasper North and Suzanne Tracy wrapped in blankets and looking cold and uncomfortable on the wharf. I read what I already knew—miraculously there had been no fatalities or serious injuries, with the exception of Bernard L. Barnes, whose body was still missing. An extensive coast guard search of the waters off lower Manhattan had failed to reveal the fate of the renowned director, although it was assumed he had joined the yacht in its watery grave.

I sighed and found myself with little appetite. I had been no admirer of Barnes's, but it was painful to think of him lying dead in polluted waters. To my great surprise, there was nothing in the paper to indicate he might have been a victim of foul play. Either the police were keeping this information to themselves, for clever reasons of their trade, or Lieutenant Carlino and Sergeant Dimitriev simply hadn't believed me.

Jack was enthusiastically telling Jayne how this was the best thing that could have happened to *Murder in Manhattan.* Publicity like this could not be bought for love or money—the entire "goddamn country" would now hear of the film.

"Yes," I said, "but you're forgetting we don't *have* a film anymore. Not without Bernie."

"Oh, he'll turn up. B.B.'s too nasty to drown."

"He didn't drown—he was murdered."

Jack's feral eyes narrowed. He lowered his voice to a whisper. "Murdered?"

"That's the story, Jack." I didn't see any reason not to tell him what I knew. His hamburger came, and he ate it with ravenous speed, nodding and grinning while I recounted the gory details of Bernie's demise.

"Murdered!" he said, smiling hideously. "Hot damn, this is better than I thought! I mean, if B.B. had just drowned, the story would be news for a few days and then forgotten, but *murder!* Holy hell, they're going to be talking about this for years!"

"Swell," I said sourly.

"Can't you see it? Say they catch the killer and put him on death row—ten years from now the son of a bitch will be screaming for a stay of execution, and the newspapers will still have to mention that the crime occurred during the filming of *Murder in Manhattan.* What we got here, my friend, is name recognition!"

"Forget it, Jack. As soon as the police let us leave New York, Jayne and I are going to fly back to L.A. and try to never think of this film again."

"You think the police are going to be . . . difficult?" Jack frowned for the first time.

"You're not getting the picture. Someone on that boat last night is a murderer, and until the police find out who it is, we're all suspects."

Jack bit off half a dill pickle and chewed thoughtfully. "I see what you mean," he said.

"Just to give you the idea," I said casually, "where were you, say, the last five minutes before the explosion?"

"*Me?*"

"You understand, I'm sure, that documenting each of our movements right before the explosion is going to take on some importance."

"Well, I'm in the clear," Jack assured me. "I was having a conversation with Suzanne, trying to convince her to pose semi-nude for *Playboy*. You see, I got this idea: "The Girls of *Murder in Manhattan.*" I thought it would be a dynamite publicity angle—Suzanne and La Volpa—for a spread. But that Suzanne, what a prude! You know what that chick called me? A toad!"

"And where were you having this conversation?"

"Right in the main cabin, in sight of everyone." He glared at me defensively. "I saw *you* go downstairs, though."

"That's right," I admitted. "I had to change my costume. What about Bernie? When's the last time you saw him?"

Jack shook his head. "I don't really remember. When they were doing the last shot, I guess. Maybe twenty minutes before the explosion."

"Did you notice anyone go downstairs after me?"

"Nooo . . . hey, wait a goddamn minute! There *was* somebody after you! Mimi Day. I remember now. Mimi went downstairs just a few minutes after you. I thought—" Jack stopped in midsentence and peered over at Jayne.

"What did you think?" she said.

"Well, maybe she was going to the bathroom . . . or something." Jack managed to give me a conspiratorial smile that I didn't particularly like. "Hey, maybe Mimi did it," he added brightly. "Kill her husband, I mean. It would be hard to blame her. Jeez, this is going to make a sensational trial—enough glamour and infidelity to keep the tabloids going for years!"

At that moment, over Jayne's shoulder, I saw Lieutenant Carlino and his svelte sidekick, Sergeant Dimitriev, enter the room.

"Jack," I said. "You'll be able to tell your story to appreciative ears. Here comes the law."

Jack sputtered, wiped the catsup from his mouth, stood up from the table, and said he really had to run.

I watched him circle the room, going out of his way to avoid the police officers. Lieutenant Carlino, I noticed, wore a light gray double-breasted charcoal suit, pink shirt, and tasteful burgundy tie. Sergeant Dimitriev had on the same shapeless dark pants suit we had seen her in the night before.

"You know, Steve, beneath those dowdy clothes lurks a beautiful young woman," remarked Jayne thoughtfully, watching Natasha walk our way. "Someone should take her aside and show her how to dress."

There was something in her tone that worried me. "Jayne," I said gently, "a New York cop does not necessarily need to look like a fashion model."

"True, but if Natasha wants to catch Carlino, she'd better start using a few feminine wiles."

"Darling, I'm sure Sergeant Dimitriev only wants to catch murderers and muggers and nasty people like that—*not* Lieutenant Carlino."

"A lot you know," said my wife.

The officers had now arrived at our table.

"Mr. Allen," said the lieutenant, shaking my hand. "Mrs. Allen," he said more softly. "How lovely you look today."

"Oh, brother!" said Sergeant Dimitriev, rolling her eyes. Jayne obviously was wrong about there being any possible romantic interest between these two.

"Your partner's quite the sophisticate," I said quietly to the sergeant as the lieutenant and Jayne chatted.

"Ain't he though? Carlino's the only cop in New York who eats tempura for lunch instead of a corned beef sandwich."

"Speaking of lunch, can we order you something?"

"No, thank you." The lieutenant answered for her. "We'd prefer to talk to the two of you downtown . . . if that wouldn't be too great an inconvenience."

"You want to talk to Jayne as well? What for? She wasn't even there."

The lieutenant glanced at nearby diners and smiled charmingly. "Why don't we discuss this at my office? It'll be more comfortable . . . and discreet."

The lieutenant was as polite and formal as a fencing master about to make a lunge for your heart. I signaled for the check and the waiter brought it quickly, seeming not at all surprised that we were leaving the table abruptly in the company of the NYPD.

# chapter 23

**L**ieutenant Carlino's office at One Police Plaza was hardly more than a cubbyhole, but it had a certain *je ne sais quoi*. There was a framed photograph of Charlie Parker on the wall behind the desk, a small Chinese vase full of flowers, and some unexpected reading material on the bookshelf: works on Zen Buddhism, a fakebook of jazz standards, a slim volume of Shakespeare's sonnets, and a gourmet guide to Basque cooking. This was clearly a new breed of cop.

Some things, however, never change. Jayne and I had been separated—Sergeant Dimitriev had taken her to another office—and I had seen enough crime movies to know this was not a good sign.

"I heard you play on Marian McPartland's radio show a few weeks ago, Mr. Allen," said the lieutenant. "I was impressed."

I raised an eyebrow. "Really?" He was referring to a show called "Piano Jazz," which airs over public radio stations around the country. Marian McPartland, who is a fine jazz pianist in her own right, each week interviews and plays duets with some of the better keyboard players in the business. I had been honored to be included.

"Are you interested in music, Lieutenant?"

"Well, I play a bit of jazz piano and write songs—just as a hobby, of course. I don't have the time to be really serious about it. But maybe I'll have a chance to play you some of my material sometime?"

I smiled but knew music was not the reason I was visiting One Police Plaza.

"Have you found Barnes's body yet?" I inquired.

The lieutenant shrugged. "Not yet. The currents can be a bit tricky off lower Manhattan, but I expect we'll find him eventually. That is, if everything you told me is true."

I flushed with anger. "Why would I lie?"

"I really don't know." He smiled, his eyes probing mine. "Now, let's go over this again. You say the last time you saw Mr. Barnes he was sprawled across the bed in the master stateroom, a knife in his back. Is that right?"

"That's right. The master stateroom was being used for wardrobe."

"You didn't move the body?"

"No . . . maybe an inch or two. I ended up pinned under him on the bed and had to push him aside to get up."

"Mr. Barnes was a very large man, Mr. Allen. That couldn't have been easy."

"It was very easy," I assured him. "You find yourself possessing unsuspected strength when a corpse's big bulging eyes are staring in your face."

"Your adrenaline was flowing?"

"I guess you could say that."

"Did your adrenaline flow so much, by any chance, that you found yourself removing the body from the room?"

"Why the hell would I do that? I left the body on the bed."

"What about the knife? What did you do with that?"

"What do you mean, what did I do with the knife? I didn't do *anything* with it."

"You simply left it sticking in his back? That seems a little heartless, if you don't mind my saying so."

"The man was dead, for God's sake—it wasn't hurting him anymore. Besides, I didn't want to disturb the evidence."

"But the yacht sank. That certainly disturbed the evidence."

"Lieutenant," I said with a deliberately calm voice, "*I* didn't know the yacht was about to sink, did I?"

The officer leaned slightly forward across his desk. "That's a good question. Did you?"

"*No!* Good God, why don't you have your divers try to find that yacht instead of wasting your time with me? You'll find Barnes in the stateroom, just as I said."

"Well, you see, that's the problem. We *have* found the yacht. It's sitting in sixty-five feet of water, and our divers have managed a fairly thorough search. Mr. Barnes is not there. So now how do you explain that?"

"I don't have to explain anything, Lieutenant. I'm only telling you what I saw. Perhaps the currents carried him away. How do I know? You said yourself the water was tricky off lower Manhattan."

"Relax," he said gently. "I'm sure you understand why it's necessary for us to be absolutely certain everyone is telling the truth."

"Well, I am."

"I'm sure you are," he said in a mollifying tone. "And I have only a few more questions." Carlino put on a pair of reading glasses and consulted his notebook. With the glasses on he looked less like Marcello Mastroianni and more like a professor of romantic poetry at a girls' finishing school.

He found what he was looking for in his notes. Off came the glasses, which he now held by the frame in his lap. In this pose he became the picture of an attentive psychotherapist, listening with great concern to some new eruption of the subconscious.

"Mr. Allen," he said in a kindly voice, "how long have you been having an affair with Mimi Day?"

*"What?"*

"You can be frank. Naturally, I won't tell your wife."

"That's because there's nothing to tell!"

"Oh, come now. The relationship between you and Ms. Day is rather common knowledge among the cast and crew."

I felt I had just passed from the ordinary world into the Twilight Zone.

"Lieutenant Carlino," I managed to say. "I want to assure you there's absolutely nothing between Mimi Day and myself."

"But you *have* had several rather intimate conversations with Ms. Day on the set, have you not? *And* in your trailer?" he added suggestively.

"No, not *intimate* talks. I was only trying to be friendly. The poor woman was having a tough time."

"Did she happen to send a box of flowers to your dressing room?"

I had to think back. "Yes, I have a vague memory of something like that," I admitted.

"Do you have a vague memory of the note that accompanied these flowers?"

"No, I don't."

"Allow me to refresh your memory, then," said the lieutenant. He put his glasses back on his nose, consulted his notebook, and read aloud: 'Thanks for being so wonderful. XXX, Mimi.' Was that the message you received, sir?"

"It could have been something like that, I really don't remember. How the hell did you get that note?"

"The third assistant director happened to glance at the message while he was delivering the flowers. He was curious."

"Trip! That little bastard."

"All I'm trying to arrive at here is the truth. Now, to get back to the note, it is signed 'XXX, Mimi.' What do you suppose those three Xs signify?"

"You know perfectly well they represent kisses."

"Kisses."

"Look, I was kind to the woman, that's all. I didn't like the way her husband was bullying her."

"And she was very grateful." He stated it as a fact.

"How the hell do I know? Maybe she was grateful. Maybe she even started imagining something between us. But that certainly isn't what *I* had in mind."

"But you do admit you were . . . shall we say, *friendly* with the victim's wife?"

"I'm friendly with everybody! That doesn't mean Mimi and I are having an affair. Or that I'd commit murder for her. . . . But I'm glad to see that you now at least believe that Barnes was killed."

Lieutenant Carlino shrugged in a fatalistic way. "Well, whatever happened, it's doubtful he could have survived in the water this long. We take matters of this kind very seriously, Mr. Allen—particularly since our divers found traces of a pipe bomb in the forward hold of the ship."

"A pipe bomb! I *knew* that wasn't any bilge pump blowing!"

"Do you know much about explosives, sir?"

"Good God, no!"

Carlino changed the subject. "Do you remember last week you were filming at the carousel in Central Park?"

"Of course."

"You did a scene with Mimi . . . perhaps you forgot you were wired for sound and that the sound man could hear your conversation between takes? As a matter of fact, he accidentally recorded the entire exchange."

I sank lower in my chair. I remembered that conversation, and suddenly the situation wasn't looking good. Carlino took a small cassette player from his desk and held it in his lap.

"Perhaps you can tell me if this is part of the conversation between you and Ms. Day," he said, switching on the recorder.

To my surprise, out of the tiny speaker came not dialogue but a piano chord, followed by a somewhat husky, unprofessional-sounding voice singing a song I wasn't familiar with.

> *Am I crazy,*
> *Or did I just dream we kissed last night?*
> *Am I crazy,*
> *Or was it real?*

"Oh, gosh, I'm sorry," Carlino said.

"About what?"

"That's a song of mine. I forgot it was on this tape."

"No problem. Let me hear it."

"No, I wouldn't want to impose. I mean, it wouldn't be taking care of business."

I confess that the crass-enough thought crossed my mind that it wouldn't hurt to get on Carlino's good side.

"It would be taking care of music business," I said.

"Okay. If you really don't mind . . ."

> *Did it happen?*
> *Did I really see a wish come true?*

*Did you let me know how you feel?*
*Can't believe it—*

After that there was nothing but silence.

"Where's the rest of it?" I asked.

"That's as far as I've gotten," he said. "Give me your honest opinion."

"Do you really mean that?"

"Sure. I mean, you're a pro—I'd really appreciate knowing what you think."

"Well," I said, "I hate to have to say it, given the nature of our present relationship, but both the melody and lyric are quite good."

He nodded without saying thank you.

"Pardon the interruption. I guess we'd better get back to business."

I listened now to Mimi's voice coming—loud and clear—from the tiny speaker: "Help me through this, darling, and I'll love you forever." And then there was my voice replying: "It's going to be oodles of fun, sweetheart, give or take an oodle or two," followed by the definite sound of a kiss.

The lieutenant stopped the tape. "So tell me, Mr. Allen, what was that all about?" he asked.

"Lieutenant, cops have their own private lingo, right?"

"Yes," he said.

"Well," I said, "so do show business people. It may sound dumb, but we are constantly using words like *darling* and *sweetheart* to the point where they've almost lost their meaning, and I'm as great an offender on that score as anybody. In my case it's partly because I sometimes have trouble remembering people's names, so if I see a woman walking toward me, and I know her but can't recall the name, I naturally say, 'Sweetheart, how are you?' "

"You're not suggesting that you forgot Mimi Day's name, are you?"

"Of course not. I'm just telling you that all that lovey-dovey language doesn't mean the same thing as it does to other people. And you must have noticed that little show-biz kiss on the cheek. Men and women kiss each other that way. Women kiss each other that way. I even know some guys in the business—chiefly my Jewish or Italian friends, come to think—well, listen, you're Italian, right?"

"Yes."

"Then you know what I mean. If you meet an old friend, you might give him a kiss on the cheek. It's no big deal."

"Okay," Carlino said. "So how about *this* part of the conversation?" The lieutenant started the tape again, and I had a bad feeling about what we would hear next. I was right. Our tiny voices filled the room:

MIMI: It's okay. I'll cook him a six-egg omelette for dinner, with some fatty bacon on the side.

ME: Why not just stick a knife in his back? It would be a hell of a lot faster!

"A knife in his back," repeated Lieutenant Carlino with great interest. "Who were you referring to, Mr. Allen?"

"Barnes obviously."

"Isn't that curious? A knife in the back. And that was to be Barnes's very fate."

I didn't know what to say. Carlino might look like a *GQ* model, but he was one savvy cop. I was beginning to wonder what the accommodations were going to be like at Sing-Sing.

"Cheer up, Mr. Allen. You can go now if you like. But perhaps you'll be so good as to remain in New York? Maybe I can play you a few more of my tunes."

"I can go?" I blinked at the sudden dismissal. I had been expecting the metallic clink of handcuffs.

"Enjoy yourself," said the lieutenant cheerfully. "While you can!"

# chapter 24

I found my wife in a windowless waiting room with Sergeant Dimitriev. They were laughing at some private joke. Clearly Jayne had fared better than I with her interrogation.

Jayne saw me coming—her grumpy, somewhat disheveled husband moving down the grim corridors of One Police Plaza. She smiled brightly, as if we were meeting in a lovely flower garden.

"Aren't men splendid creatures?" Jayne chuckled.

"Yeah," said the sergeant as if she were talking about insects. "Most of the time I don't know why we bother."

With that cheerful thought, Jayne and I departed.

"Guess what?" she asked as we walked down the corridor toward freedom. "Natasha and I are going shopping tomorrow. We're going to spend tons of money."

"Whose?"

"Don't be such a grouch. When you see how I make over that sweet girl, you'll agree it was worth it."

"Jayne, she's a cop," I reminded her. "And New York cops, whatever else they are, are not sweet. We don't pay them to be sweet."

It compounds guilt to be in a bad mood and find yourself in the company of someone in a very good mood. Jayne took my arm and smiled at two uniformed policemen who were leading in a bedraggled-looking fellow in handcuffs. The prisoner winked at me—as if he recognized a future jailbird who might soon be sharing his cell.

"Isn't this fun?" asked Jayne. "We'd never be having such

fascinating experiences with the police if we'd stayed home in boring old Los Angeles."

"Boredom," I said, "is looking better all the time."

Once outside and trying to flag down a taxi, my mood did not improve. Yellow cabs sped by with off-duty signs or stopped for more aggressive souls who hurled their bodies into the path of the oncoming traffic, to either get a cab or die. I was about to give up and go for the subway when Jayne called out sweetly, "Oh, yoo-hoo!" and to my astonishment a cab screeched to a bone-jarring halt at our side.

"You see," Jayne said. "All you have to do is smile."

"Next time you'll probably do Claudette Colbert in *It Happened One Night*," I groused.

As we climbed into the cab I voiced the question in my mind. "Well, what did you and Sergeant Dimitriev talk about besides shopping sprees?"

"She wanted to know all about our love life."

"Swell. Don't you see what they're trying to do? They have this stupid idea—if you can believe it—that I was having an affair with Bernie's wife. They're trying to pin the murder on *me!*"

Jayne began to laugh, then scowled instead. "Oh, dear," she said.

"Oh, dear, *what?*"

"I suppose that's why Natasha asked if you'd ever been unfaithful."

"And of course you were kind enough to give me a clean slate on that?"

Jayne looked out the window and didn't answer.

"Jayne!"

"Well, darling. I didn't want to make you sound too tame."

"Oh, great. Should I tell the driver to just take us directly to the New York offices of the *Enquirer* so we can provide them with all the details?"

"Well, I never . . ."

"Oh, I bet you have once or twice," I said, giving her a line from one of our old Senator Phillip Buster sketches.

"Don't be mad, darling," Jayne said.

Just then we hit one of New York's ten million potholes at

fifty miles an hour, and Jayne and I bounced toward the roof. It was that kind of day.

"Anyway, Steve, poor Natasha wasn't paying much attention to *our* old story. You know how it is when people ask about your love life—what they *really* want to do is talk about their own."

"You're kidding. You ended up talking about *her?*"

"Naturally. Natasha's a very attractive young woman and love is very much on her mind. The lieutenant certainly isn't making it easy for her. They've been working together more than a year now. Even went out on a date once and, according to Natasha, had an absolutely marvelous time, but nothing more came of it. He won't even admit he loves her, though it's obvious he does."

"Why is it obvious? He seemed to ignore her pretty well when I've seen them together."

"Steve! Use your eyes! Sure, he ignores her. But he ignores her in a way only someone in love who's afraid to show it can ignore a person—if you see what I mean."

"Oh," said I. There was no answering such logic. I shook my head glumly. Out of the entire New York police force I wondered how I had drawn such an odd pair as Carlino and Dimitriev. Cops in love, for God's sake.

"It's a good thing I have a plan," said my wife. "After I finish with Natasha, that girl is going to look so devastating, Bobby won't even know what hit him."

"She doesn't look too bad already," I mentioned. "Especially if you could get her out of those drab clothes."

"Don't get *too* carried away, darling."

"Oh, you know what I meant."

"I hope so, because you're the second part of my plan. I think it's time to make Bobby Carlino suffer the pangs of jealousy so he'll begin to take more notice of her. Perhaps we can make it look as if you and Natasha are having a little flirtation."

I didn't scream, but I did take a small blood-pressure pill out of my vest pocket and swallow it.

I turned my body to the right and faced Jayne directly. "Earth to Jayne Meadows," I said. "Do you read me?"

"Oh, stop," she said.

"I'd love to. In fact, that's exactly the end I'm trying to achieve here. We must stop this crazy scheme of yours before it develops legs, as they say in film marketing. Lieutenant Carlino already entertains the bizarre notion that I've been having an affair with Mimi Day. If you haven't lost track of our cast of characters, you'll recall that she's playing the role of the victim's wife. This means that Carlino thinks I'm actually capable of stabbing the voluminous Mr. Barnes in the back with a carving knife. Or maybe he thinks I carved him in the back with a stabbing knife, and I—"

"Can't you ever be serious?" Jayne said.

"I'm deadly serious right now," I said. "Don't let the jokes fool you. If the lieutenant thinks I'm also having an affair with his girlfriend, he could—well, who knows what he could do? He could go berserk and kill me."

"You think so?" Jayne said thoughtfully with a reading that would have done credit to Gracie Allen.

Perhaps I should explain that Jayne—being an actual flesh-and-blood human being—is far more complex than the kinds of characters you ordinarily run into in mystery novels. If she were just someone I made up, for example, we could describe her as cute and ditsy—like, say, Goldie Hawn or Lucy Ricardo—or else intuitively brilliant, incredibly quick-minded, and gifted with near-total recall. Actually, she's all of the above. Our dear friend Groucho Marx once explained to her why he had so admired her performance in the old Kaufman and Hart classic, *Once in a Lifetime.*

"Jayne," he said, "you are, without a doubt, the most bewildered woman I know."

But behind all the bewilderment, as I say, is one of the sharpest minds you'll ever encounter.

"Well," Jayne said, "if he did try to do you harm, at least Natasha would know he cares."

You see what I put up with? I slumped in the back of the taxi as Jayne squeezed my hand in a way that was meant to be reassuring. Things were not looking good. I had a wife who was a cross between Spring Byington and Joan of Arc, and I had somehow managed to make myself a prime suspect in this season's most sensational murder case. It would be nice if Lieutenant Carlino and Sergeant Dimitriev found the real killer and got me off the hook, but with a romantically distracted pair like that, I didn't have much cause for optimism.

No, as far as I could see, there was only one way out for me. As our taxi pulled up in front of the awning of The Plaza, I decided I would simply have to solve this murder mystery myself.

# chapter 25

There was a note slipped under the door of our suite. Jayne was the one who found it, since I'd bounded over the threshold on my way to the baby grand that I had not had much chance to play. I was loosening up with a little little rendition of "Makin' Whoopee," when Jayne dangled the folded sheet of paper before my eyes.

"This was on the floor by the door, darling," she said.

"What does it say?"

" 'Dear Steve,' " she read. " 'I must talk with you, if that's all right. Sincerely, Zach Holden.' My, what a polite young man."

I went over to the couch and dialed Holden's room.

"Hello, Zach. Steve Allen. What can I do for you?"

"That you, Mr. Allen?" For some reason Zach was whispering. "This is me, Zach."

"I think we've already covered that pretty well. I'm me, and you're you. But what can I do for you?"

"I'd like to talk to you," he said.

"By remarkable coincidence," I said, "that's exactly what we're doing right now."

"No," he said. "I mean, you know, face-to-face."

"You'd have the advantage there," I joked. "Your face is much nicer than mine."

"Please," he said. "It's important."

"Okay," I said. "Come on up."

"If your wife is there, I'd rather not. If it wouldn't be too great an inconvenience, could we meet by the sea lions in fifteen minutes?"

"You're talking about the sea lions in the park, right?" In

a city like New York you have to check such details. For all I knew The Sea Lions could have been the name of a new Danish restaurant. I agreed to meet Holden and hung up the phone.

"Well?" Jayne said, as wives always do at such moments.

"I have to go to the zoo to meet Zach, and if you say, 'Why, how could they put a nice young man like that in a cage?' I don't know what I'll do."

"I usually don't know what you're doing anyway," Jayne said. "Will you be long?"

"I don't think so."

"What does he want to talk about?"

"I don't know. It must be something serious, though. He sounded sort of—I don't know—scared, now that I think back."

I went into the bedroom closet to pick up my Burberry scarf. When I returned to the sitting room, Jayne was studying *Vogue,* probably looking for clues to the right look for Sergeant Dimitriev.

Outside, the sky had turned gray and a light drizzle made me turn up the collar of my trench coat. Spring was temporarily in retreat. On gloomier days such as this, Central Park tends to be empty of secretaries, white-collar office types, lovers, old women out for constitutional exercise, and tourists wondering if they can afford a ride in a hansom cab. Fifty-ninth Street always has its own busy traffic, of course, but once I was in the park I encountered chiefly unsavory teenagers who probably should have been in school, old men sitting on benches deep in thought, pigeons, and the usual assortment of homeless, the poor lost souls who now wander aimlessly through all large American cities.

I made my way briskly to the zoo and found seals—not sea lions—swimming happily in their tank. Probably there are worse things to be in life besides a seal—they always seem so wonderfully playful, at least when there are no sharks around. Zachary, however, was nowhere to be seen. There wasn't even a Catholic priest. I was trying to decide whether to feel miffed or mystified when I was approached by a jogger in a maroon sweatsuit. He was wearing dark glasses and had the hood of his sweatshirt tied snugly around his head so that there was little of his face to be recognized. It took a moment to realize it was Holden.

"It's me, Mr. Allen. What do you think of this disguise?"

"Get tired of life as a priest?"

"I like to change around, just so no one can get a fix on me. You know, in case the *Enquirer* or the *Star* have any photographers staked out. Those are the guys you really gotta watch out for. You're out in public, you scratch your nose thinking no one sees you, and the next thing you know you got your picture by the checkout counter in every supermarket in America. It's not easy being famous. Especially when the woman you love is the one woman who doesn't want you."

Speaking of priests, I guess I wouldn't have made a very good one, although I was raised as a Catholic, because I'm always made uncomfortable when people share intimate confidences with me, particularly if there's anything confessional in the disclosure. I feel appropriately sympathetic, but the various responses that leap to mind almost invariably strike me as dumb. I mean, saying things like "Oh, that's too bad" really doesn't do your companion of the moment much good after he's just told you that he and his wife are getting a divorce, that his only child is in the hospital, or that his TV series has just been canceled.

"Listen, Zach," I said. "I could probably give lectures, maybe write a book about sympathy, but all by itself it doesn't accomplish a hell of a lot. And then, too, all the wise psychological advice in the world really can't change the reality. A woman either loves you or she doesn't. If it'll make you feel any better, we've all been through that. Anyway, was that what you wanted to talk to me about?"

"No, not really."

Then why the hell had he brought it up?

"I hope you won't think I'm being rude or nosy," he said, "but I wanted to check with you about something Jack Wolfe happened to mention today."

"Happened?"

"He said that the cops came and dragged you out of the Edwardian Room. Is that true?"

"There is, tucked into your version of whatever it was that Wolfe said to you, a small increment of truth, but not much. I certainly wasn't dragged. A Lieutenant Carlino asked Jayne and me to accompany him to police headquarters and, uh, we did."

Zach and I had, during the preceding few minutes, moved from the seal pools to the monkey house, and at this moment we stopped in front of a rather melancholy baboon who scratched his head and gazed at us through the bars.

"Then it's true," said the handsome TV star in maroon jogging suit.

"What's true?"

"That Bernie's been murdered."

I nodded grimly. "Looks that way."

"Can I ask you something?"

"Why not?"

"God, this is embarrassing. I hope I don't sound like a real idiot, but . . . do the cops think I did it?"

Swell. I suddenly felt terribly uncomfortable. If Holden was indeed under suspicion, it was almost certainly because of my casual theorizing in Carlino's presence. What we're touching on here, of course, is a problem that has perplexed both philosophers and administrators since the earliest days of human life on planet earth. It's relatively easy to think abstract thoughts, to imagine philosophical solutions to practical human problems. The tough part comes when you suddenly realize that as a result of your alleged solution, some actual flesh-and-blood standing in front of you is either going to be fired, arrested, forced to move to Fargo, North Dakota, or otherwise profoundly affected by whatever you've proposed. So now, just because earlier I had expressed aloud an insight derived from having enjoyed the work of Agatha Christie, Dashiell Hammett, Raymond Chandler, Conan Doyle, and other practitioners of the art of detective fiction—that a story character who at first seems both likable and innocent often turns out to be the guilty party—because of my big mouth it was now probably quite true that poor Zachary Holden was indeed under suspicion.

"Well," I said. "If you are a suspect, welcome to the club, not to coin a phrase. They've got their eye on me too."

"You? That's ridiculous."

"Tell me about it. Zach, if you really didn't do it, and if

you've got no possible motive for wanting Barnes out of the way, it seems to me that you don't have much to worry about."

"But that's just it. There is a motive." Zach seemed to deflate. His tall, athletic body sank a few inches in despair. "They asked questions about me, I guess?"

"They wanted to know where you were on the boat those last ten minutes before the explosion. Stuff like that. I told them how you helped me onto the deck."

"What did they say to that?"

"Well, you know how cops are, they have to be cynical. They suggested maybe you were playing hero because you had a guilty conscience about stabbing Bernie and sinking the boat."

Zach walked away from me, too upset to talk. I followed him out of the monkey house into the melancholy afternoon.

"Did they . . . did they mention blackmail?" he whispered.

"Blackmail," I repeated thoughtfully. "Actually, they *did* use that word once or twice, but I told them I didn't know anything about it."

Zach moaned. "God, wait till my mother hears about this! I'm so ashamed."

My brain was working overtime. "A lot of people get blackmailed, Zach," I mentioned cautiously.

"Maybe I should have told Bernie no right at the beginning. But I was scared."

"You let Bernie blackmail you, and in return he wouldn't expose your big secret."

"I feel like such a slime."

"How much did you have to pay him to keep quiet?"

"Oh, it wasn't money, it was doing the picture."

"You've lost me."

"I'm talking about *Murder in Manhattan*. You see, I didn't want to do it, but Bernie made me. I had a chance to be the new James Bond. Had to turn it down. I would have done just about *any*thing to be 007!"

"So Bernie was blackmailing you," I said. I tried to imagine what Holden's deep dark secret could be, but couldn't. As far as I could tell, the kid was as open and clean-living as a choirboy. Besides, in today's anything-goes society, it's hard to imagine any scandals that are still blackmail material. Thirty or forty years ago the list was long. Now, at least so far as actors are concerned, shocking news actually seems to increase their popularity.

We started walking haphazardly back along the paths in the general direction of 59th Street.

"What a mess!" said Zach. "Sometimes I wish I'd never become a celebrity. That I was still a water-ski instructor back in good ol' Fort Lauderdale."

"We all wish that sometimes," I consoled him. "But maybe I can help you, Zach."

"Can you, Mr. Allen? Gosh, I don't know where else to turn."

"What you need to do is give the cops someone else to point the finger at. We have to find the real murderer and then they'll forget about you."

"Do you think so? I'm innocent, Mr. Allen. I swear to God."

"Okay, Zach. But you know how the cops are once they get an idea."

"But what can I do? This is like a nightmare."

"What you can do, Zach, is tell me the truth. Let's start with what Bernie had on you, because as far as I know, that's the only real damaging thing the cops might dig up."

"I can't tell you, man. It's too embarrassing. I *can't.*"

"It's hard to help you, pardner, unless I'm armed with the facts. Can't you give me even a clue?"

"It's too horrible."

"Tell me this," I said, actually just joking. "Whatever it was, was it animal, mineral, or vegetable?"

To my great surprise, Holden cast his eyes on the ground and said, "Animal."

I was so puzzled that I was momentarily speechless. But if a joking approach had released Holden's tongue, I thought perhaps I should continue in a light vein.

"I see," I said. "Now, did this animal have four legs, six legs, or perhaps . . . two legs?"

"Two," he admitted, looking down at the ground like a little boy. "Only they were facing the wrong way."

At that point I very much wished that I had kept my mouth shut in Carlino's presence and that I had never agreed to meet Holden at the zoo.

"Was this a two-legged *female* animal?" I said.

"I'm sorry," Holden said. "I can't . . ."

It was obvious that as far as Zach was concerned, the subject was closed for the moment. We walked in silence past an old woman feeding a flock of pigeons crumbs and crusts from a soiled paper bag and back to the hotel.

Once at The Plaza I could think of nothing to say to Holden except, "See you later."

# chapter 26

"**M**aybe he's a closet homosexual?" I suggested to Jayne after I had filled her in on the details of my meeting with Zachary.

"I'll never believe that," she said. *"Not* Zachary Holden."

Jayne was, of course, aware that not all male homosexuals are effeminate. There are football players, cowboys, truck drivers, and other rugged types who betray no public trace of their sexual preference. I'll never forget one night during my three-year service as master of ceremonies for the old *I've Got a Secret* show for CBS when we had for our celebrity guest a famous professional football player who had gone on to a career in action films. At the point of the show where I said, "All right, panel, our guest will now whisper his secret to me while we show it to the folks at home," the burly chap whispered not his actual secret, but what, in more circumspect times was called an indecent proposal.

"But," Jayne was now saying, "there are so many famous actors today who are gay that, so far as public relations are concerned, it just isn't the big deal it used to be."

"Right," I said. "Except as regards that sizable category of ostensibly macho and romantic actors who have not come out of the closet and whose livelihood depends on being perceived, chiefly by women, as the most romantically attractive thing since Clark Gable."

"Still . . . let's see, what else could it be?"

"Drugs?" I wondered.

Jayne shook her head. "Zach seems such an overgrown boy scout."

We spent the next several minutes, I confess, dreaming up

idiotic scenarios that might explain Holden's present fear. He seemed such a straight-arrow type, he might have worked briefly as a page boy in the U.S. Senate and been compromised by a sexually omnivorous representative of the people. He might have succumbed to the wiles of a KGB agent. He might have studied for the priesthood or ministry and been thrown out of the seminary for God knows what reason. He might have worked briefly, early in his career, as a television game-show host and been ashamed of the fact ever since.

We tossed the question back and forth for some time. It was clearly important to discover by what means Barnes had been blackmailing the handsome actor. I have to admit it gave me a kick to be a step ahead of Lieutenant Carlino in the matter—that clotheshorse of a cop probably hadn't even considered the blackmail angle.

"I have scotch, vodka, gin, tequila, and Irish whiskey," said Jayne with seemingly total irrelevance to the entire record of western history. I should perhaps explain that Jayne almost never provides a context for her out-of-the-blue pronouncements. She invariably assumes—usually incorrectly—that you know exactly what she's talking about and therefore does not gladly suffer those of us foolish enough to be without a clue at such moments. I sometimes work my way to the context by way of humor.

"You also have high heels, red lipstick, a lot of talent, a high I.Q., and a small, loose thread hanging from the back of your skirt, but why are we both taking inventory?"

"Steve, you know perfectly well that Clancy will be here at nine o'clock."

"I do indeed, but I had absolutely no way of knowing that that was the connection in which you were itemizing the booze."

"Well, why else would I be doing it? You do remember, I hope, that we had planned to deliberately ply Clancy with liquor to free his tongue."

"What I clearly recall," I said, "was that you came up with that crazy idea and talked me into going along with it."

When she had earlier proposed the scheme, I had started to protest. One hardly encourages alcoholics to continue to kill themselves. But I realized that it was highly probable that our visitor would arrive already moderately intoxicated. Somehow this made us feel semi-justified in encouraging, at least for a portion of the evening, his ingrained self-destructiveness.

Clancy came late. I was in the bedroom on the phone to my son Bill in California when he arrived. Hearing a crashing chord on the piano in the next room, followed by another, I became aware that I was listening to an alcoholic interpretation of the Rachmaninoff Prelude in C Sharp Minor. I told Bill I'd better go.

Stepping back into the sitting room, I found Clancy in a disheveled tuxedo and ruffled shirt, thunderously pounding on the baby grand. His bow tie was loose, unraveling on his collar. In the middle of a passionate arpeggio, he reached for the Irish whiskey and took a long slug directly from the bottle.

"I love Russian music, don't you, Steve?" asked Jayne politely.

"Particularly when it's played by an Irishman. . . . Would you like a glass with your whiskey, Clancy?"

The author's eyes briefly glanced my way, but he continued in wild abandon to the final chord, at which point he sat with his fingers still on the ivories and his head bowed, the sound slowly fading away. For a moment I was afraid he had fallen asleep.

"Bravo!" cried Jayne, clapping. "Wasn't that splendid, darling?"

"Splendid," I said, clapping along. "Good old Maninoff. I never knew him well enough to call him Rock. They don't write 'em like that anymore."

Donahue managed to turn his body around on the piano stool until he was facing our way. His hair was wild, his eyes owlish and red.

"Do you know what happened to him?" he challenged.

"Sergei Rachmaninoff?"

"Himself. What's the worst thing that can befall an artist, I ask you?"

"I don't know."

"Dear me," Jayne said. "Did he die in some awful garret, starving and forgotten?"

"Worse. He went to Hollywood." Clancy gave a small hiss. "Yes, that's right, my dear, the great Russian composer turned out to be a great whore."

"Maybe he simply liked the California sunshine," I murmured.

"He was a whore!" Clancy insisted. "Like all artists . . . everywhere."

"Let me freshen your drink. Why don't you make yourself comfortable on the sofa?" fussed Jayne. Few men can resist my wife when she's in her mother-to-lost-boy mode. "Poor thing, you look exhausted. And I'll bet you haven't eaten a proper dinner. Wouldn't you like me to order a nice omelette from room service?"

"No, thank you. You have to break eggs to make an omelette," said Clancy gloomily. "And that might make me cry."

"Such sensitivity," cooed Jayne.

Clancy stretched out on the couch with his feet up, balancing his half-empty glass precariously on his chest. I raised an eyebrow at Jayne.

"Clancy," I said gently, "what do you think about Bernie getting killed?"

"Artists . . . they're all a bunch of whores," he muttered.

"Yes, I see what you mean. But do you have any idea who might have wanted to blow up *Easy Money* and skewer Barnes with a carving knife?"

Clancy shrugged, jiggled his glass, then raised his head only far enough to take a big gulp of the whiskey. "It could have been anyone," he said. "Who cares? The irony, you see . . . the wild, delicious irony is that while all artists are whores, it takes a whore to be a true artist. Don't you agree?"

I sighed. Conversing with drunks is not my favorite pastime. Donahue was getting more and more relaxed on our sofa, looked as if he might pass out at any moment. Jayne and I exchanged glances over his head. I knew what she was thinking: inviting the man here tonight was proving to be a waste of time.

I tried to save the day. "Clancy, do you remember the ten minutes or so before the explosion on the boat? I've been trying to put together all our movements—just a little hobby of mine. Do you remember where *you* were?"

"I remember everything," Clancy said. "I remember the smell of rain on the asphalt streets when I was a child. I remember the damp, delicious dew on my first love's lips as we sank down, down, down into chaotic swirls of ecstasy."

"Clancy, we don't have to go back quite that far into your memory vaults. To tell the truth, I'm interested only in the time right before the explosion—particularly if you saw Bernie leave the main salon and go down to the staterooms."

"Oh, we were sailing dark seas that night," he muttered, closing his eyes and drifting. The glass tilted as his hand relaxed, but he jerked it upright in a reflexive motion.

I was getting fed up. "Wait a minute, Steve," said Jayne. "I think he's trying to tell us something. Aren't you, Clancy?"

Clancy opened his eyes and gazed at Jayne with drunken rapture. "You are a good woman, Mrs. Allen. Tell me now, you don't think a man the likes of Bernie Barnes deserved to possess a glorious and pure goddess on earth the likes of Victoria La Volpa, do you?"

"Of course not," Jayne agreed readily.

I was beginning to think she was onto something.

"And yet Victoria and Bernie seemed quite . . . chummy," I suggested mildly, inside feeling like a chef who has just added a box of cayenne pepper to his recipe.

"Chummy!" Clancy roared. He half sat up, his eyes flashing in anger. His drink sloshed slightly but stayed in the glass. "But what choice did she have, I ask you? Do you think a true artist like Victoria would agree to appear in a shabby Bernard L. Barnes comedy if she had a *choice* in the matter?" He slugged down the rest of the whiskey.

Feeling a surge of excitement, I took a long, deductive leap. "So Bernie was blackmailing her to appear in the film?"

Clancy gave me a wary look and lay back down lethargically. "How do you know about that?" he asked.

"Simple. It seems it was one of Barnes's favorite ways to gather talent when normal methods wouldn't do. What dirt did he have on her, Clancy?"

Clancy wouldn't meet my eye. "I think I'll have that other drink now, my dear." He held his glass out to Jayne, his voice hardly more than a whisper.

*Make it a strong one,* I silently mouthed over his head.

Clancy took the drink and guzzled it down, staring at me in silence for a moment or two before he said simply, "When Victoria was sixteen she was—again the word—a whore. In a very expensive house in Milan actually. I don't know how Barnes found out, but he had developed his own library of pornography and apparently he had a picture of this lovely young creature in what might be called a compromising position. I told Victoria there is no disgrace being a whore—the profession is without pretense. The disgrace, you see, is to be an artist. But she wouldn't listen to me. She is naively foolish—a foolish little flower of love. Ah, such innocence! Now that she is more respectable, she wants no one to know about her past. I told her . . . I told her . . ."

"Clancy . . . *Clancy* . . ."

There were a lot of things I still wanted to ask him, particularly if he had seen his foolish little flower of love stick a not-so-foolish carving knife into her blackmailer's back, but after making his startling revelation, Clancy closed his eyes, settled back into the soft white cushions, and at once was sound asleep.

# chapter 27

"How," I said to Jayne, "without resorting to the bizarre, are we going to wake this guy up?"

Had he simply been asleep, the problem would not have been severe. Any loud noise or elbow poke would have done the trick. But our guest had passed out and was therefore in quite a different state of unconsciousness. Nevertheless, since we had ruled out leaving him on the couch all night, we continued our efforts to wake him. I spoke loudly in his ear, shook his right arm vigorously, even gave him a light tap or two on the cheek. Finally we were desperate enough to think that loud music might do the trick. I sat down at the piano and banged out a fortissimo version of "This Could Be the Start of Something Big," even ad-libbing a not especially clever parody of the original lyric:

> You're walking along the street,
> Or you're at The Plaza;
> Or else you're a hopeless drunk, asleep on the couch;
> Then suddenly there you are,
> And you want to stay where you are,
> And I'll punch you so hard that you'll say "ouch."

Jayne laughed, but Clancy didn't give me a tumble.

"This is dreadful, darling," Jayne said. "I don't think I'm going to get a wink of sleep with Mr. Donahue snoring here all night."

"Swell detectives we are!" I complained.

"I think you're *very* clever," Jayne assured me. "Just think, you've discovered Bernie was blackmailing *two* members of his cast."

I gave my wife a sarcastic look. "Jayne," I explained, "what we're attempting to do is *narrow* the field of suspects, not expand it endlessly."

"Oh. Well, I'm still proud of you. But we really are going to have to get rid of Mr. Donahue."

"Remember the other time a famous writer zonked out in our living room?" I asked.

"Are you talking about Jack Kerouac?"

"Yes. Remember, he came for dinner—I think back in 1957 or '58, when we lived on Park?"

"Of course I remember," Jayne said. "The poor man put away two and a half bottles of cognac and began snoring right there in the living room, unfortunately at two o'clock in the morning, as I recall. But apparently Jack could hold his liquor better than Clancy can. He was asleep only a few minutes."

I stared at Donahue, who had now settled onto his right side and was snoring with gusto—great thunderous arpeggios that built expressively to a long crescendo and then faded away with a faint, breathy whistle. It was really the most horrendously irritating noise I could imagine.

"I've got an idea! Let's abandon our suite and move across the street to the Sherry Netherland," I suggested.

"That would be a ridiculous expense," Jayne said, ever the practical one. "Why don't you just call a bellboy or security and have them carry the poor man back to his room?"

"Sure, and then it would probably end up in the *Enquirer*," I said. "What are you doing now?"

"I'm looking for his room key. I've got a brilliant idea."

Jayne managed to find the key in Clancy's right-hand jacket pocket. She held it up to me like a hunting trophy.

"It's Room 910, dear, just down the hall. We can carry him there ourselves."

"The man probably weighs a hundred and eighty pounds."

"I know what! We can stretch him out on the room-service cart and wheel him down the hall. Isn't that clever?"

"*I'll* tell you something more clever. Let's pack our bags

and catch the first flight home," I grouched.

"Yes, dear. But didn't that nice Lieutenant Carlino suggest that you remain in New York? We wouldn't want him to think you're running away."

Just then Clancy let out a real earth-shaking snore. *Something* had to be done. Despite my better judgment, I was soon helping Jayne remove the various items from the room-service cart and wheel it over to the sofa.

"This is crazy," I muttered.

"Think of it as a simple kindness to another human being. I'm sure Mr. Donahue will be much happier in his own bed."

"Okay." I sighed. "Though I doubt that Mr. Donahue will know the damned difference."

I got hold of Clancy's arms, Jayne took his legs, and we managed to more or less flip him over from the sofa unto the cart. I was hoping the unkind motion might wake him, and he would be able to leave on his own power after all, but no such luck. Clancy lay sprawled across the cart, facedown, his arms and legs dangling toward the floor. In his tuxedo he looked like a headwaiter who had died on the job.

We got off to a shaky start, crashing into a coffee table and nearly dumping our load. The cart had obviously not been designed to hold this much weight, but with Jayne pulling and me pushing, we managed to wheel our author to the door.

"I'm *never* going to accept another movie offer in New York," I grumbled.

"Just think of this as a fun adventure," Jayne advised.

"Boy, am I having fun! Let's just make certain there's no one in the damned hallway while we experience this little adventure, shall we? I'd rather not end up in the loony bin."

"Whoops, here comes the elevator."

We had to back up and wait while Victoria La Volpa swept out of the elevator and strode imperiously down the hall toward her room. She was followed by two bellmen, each of whom led a very small dog on a leash. We waited, peering out a narrow crack of our door, until the bellmen had deposited the dogs in La Volpa's room, received their tips, and disappeared around a corner toward the service elevator.

The hotel corridor was as empty of life as it was ever going to be. Clancy nearly slid off the cart as we pushed forward out of the room, but we managed to rebalance him. It wasn't really until we were out in the hall with our own door shut behind us that I realized just how dumb this was going to look if we met anyone.

"Let's not dawdle," I whispered nervously. We began wheeling Clancy at a pretty good clip down the hall when I heard the telltale ding of an elevator car about to stop at our floor. Jayne giggled.

"This is no laughing matter! Quick! Let's try this door!" I opened an unlocked door near the elevator bank. It was a linen closet with stacks of neatly pressed sheets and towels piled high on the shelves. We wheeled Clancy into the closet and shut the door behind us just as I heard the elevator slide open and disgorge its passengers. Jayne and I waited in the dark, listening to two pairs of feet step our way.

"Remind me never to do anything like this again," I whispered. "Just in case I get the urge."

"I think it's rather romantic, dear," said Jayne, snuggling closer in the dark. Jayne's the sort of person who can look on the bright side of any situation, even hiding in a linen closet with a drunken writer passed out on a room-service cart. Her eyes did widen a little, however, when the feet in the hallway stopped directly on the other side of the door.

"Hold on," said a voice. "Let's talk a minute, Mr. North. I need some money."

"Haven't I given you enough?"

"Not nearly. Not after what I've done for you."

Jayne's eyes quizzed me as our friend Jasper tried to appease the man whose voice, although tantalizingly familiar, I couldn't quite place.

"All right, I'll give you another five thousand, but that's it, do you understand? You and I are even."

"Make it ten thousand, and we have a deal, Mr. North."

"Hell I will!"

"Of course, I could always send an anonymous little note

to the police: 'Dear Cops, Are you aware that Jasper North, the famous British actor, is—' "

"Shut up! All right! You'll get the bloody ten grand. But I warn you, if you ever try to hit me up for money again . . . I have a pistol, my friend—and I know how to use it."

There was a moan in the dark. Jayne and I each uttered a small cry of terror until we realized it was only our drunken companion, probably dreaming of sugar plum fairies. I put my hand over his mouth and prayed he wouldn't let out a snore next.

"What was that?" Jasper asked nervously on the other side of the door.

"I don't know, but we'd better get out of here," said the man whose voice I still couldn't quite recognize.

To my great relief, I heard the voices move away. A door opened down the hall. Closed. Jayne and I waited a few more moments in the dark, hardly daring to breathe.

"How horrible!" whispered Jayne. "Do you think poor Jasper is being blackmailed too?"

"I don't know what to think. It sounded more like they were in cahoots together about something."

"Probably Jasper has a perfectly innocent explanation."

I had lost faith in the innocence of anyone on this crew except myself and Jayne. I cracked open the closet door and peered down the hall in both directions.

"All clear," I said. "Hurry. Let's get this over with and get back to our room. Lurking in dark closets isn't exactly my idea of a good time."

We wheeled our literary burden once again into the hall. I pushed and Jayne pulled and we made our way down the long corridor toward Room 910. I had Clancy's key in his lock when I heard the ding of the elevator once again arriving at our floor.

"Hurry up!" Jayne commanded.

"I'm going as fast as I can!"

I got the door open and then stepped around to help Jayne push the cart into the room. We might have made it, too, but the wheels stuck on the small metal runner holding down the carpet beneath the door. The elevator opened, and the worst two people who might appear at a time like this stepped out.

It was Lieutenant Carlino and Sergeant Dimitriev, and they did not look happy to see Jayne and me playing room service with an unconscious body in the hall.

"My, my," said the dapper lieutenant. "Is this à la carte or simply the plat du jour?"

# chapter 28

We were still in the hallway. Lieutenant Carlino was checking the pulse in Clancy's neck to make sure he was alive when a middle-aged couple in evening clothes walked past on their way to the elevator, not giving our little tableau a glance. Probably it takes considerable social skill to completely ignore a body sprawled face-first on a room-service cart in a hotel corridor, but that's New York, a city that demands selective vision.

"I know this looks bad," I said to the officers. "But there is an explanation."

"We got Clancy drunk only to make him talk," said Jayne cheerfully.

"Talk?" asked the lieutenant. "Talk about what?"

"Oh, this and that," I put in. "Irish literature, Russian music, the usual sort of chitchat."

"Including murder and blackmail," said Jayne breathlessly. I felt like giving her a small, decisive kick but gallantly restrained myself.

"I think we'd better get this gentleman to bed," said the lieutenant. "Mr. Allen, will you give me a hand?"

The women waited in the hall, heads together in conversation, as Carlino and I pushed the cart into an extremely messy bedroom. It looked as if it had not received maid service in days. Beer cans and full ashtrays littered every surface. Books, loose papers, half-finished plates of food, socks, and underwear spilled over the bed onto the floor. Clancy had managed to turn his swank room at The Plaza into an East Village pad.

"A good thing he's a bachelor," I said, clearing off the bed to make room for the body.

"You must make allowance for genius," said the lieutenant as we tossed the author onto the bed and pulled off his shoes.

"This is your idea of genius?"

*"The Ravaged Rose* is one of the great pre-postmodern masterpieces," said the cop.

*"Pre*-postmodern—doesn't that sort of cancel itself out?"

"It's a *subtle* concept," Carlino said. He gave me one of his superior smiles, as though a mere TV celebrity might not grasp such a thing. "We're talking about a small body of literature that is post-Jack Kerouac and pre-Stephen King. I'm taking a course in the subject at CUNY."

"Ah," I said vaguely. I thought it wise not to mention that a little learning is a dangerous thing. We left Donahue, genius or hack, snoring loudly on his bed and rejoined the ladies in the hall.

"So you see," Jayne was saying to the sultry sergeant, "Steve found out that Bernie Barnes was blackmailing Zach Holden *and* Victoria La Volpa. Isn't that the most amazing thing you've ever heard?"

"Honey, some of the stuff I've seen come down in this city makes blackmail look like kindergarten stuff," the sergeant assured her.

Hoping to keep our newly gained information to myself for the time being, I took Jayne's arm and gave her a warning squeeze. I was surprised when neither Dimitriev nor Carlino appeared particularly interested in the blackmail revelation.

"Let's have a little talk in your suite, shall we?" the lieutenant suggested.

The two followed us down the hall to our room and seated themselves on the sofa upon which Clancy Donahue had so recently reclined.

"Oh, I had a conversation this afternoon with Sergeant Walker of the Burbank police," said Lieutenant Carlino. "He sends his regards."

"Good old W.B.! How is he?"

"He says police routine is dull without you, Mr. Allen. I understand you like to dabble in detective work."

I grinned happily. "Only as an amateur. Of course, W.B.

and I *did* solve a rather intriguing murder last year—I described the case in my book *Murder on the Glitter Box.*"

"Steve was a suspect in that case too," said Jayne proudly. I looked at her in amazement.

"Jayne, *suspect* is much too strong a word, even if I did accidentally poison that poor guy on television. . . ."

The lieutenant held up a hand. "Please," he said. "Sergeant Walker filled me in on all the details. I was only trying to get a background on your personal life, Mr. Allen. Curious, isn't it, how murder seems to follow some people around?"

"I wouldn't say it *follows* me," I protested. "Most of my life has been spent in quite normal endeavors, like doing TV comedy, playing piano, being a husband and father."

"A husband and father who just happens to dabble in murder?"

"Only as a hobby," I said. "You study pre-postmodernism at CUNY, and I enjoy the mental stimulation of solving a good old-fashioned whodunit. What could be more simple?"

"Just your average Joe, huh?" Carlino gave me a long, hard look.

I smiled from ear to ear and concentrated on looking average. I noticed Sergeant Dimitriev studying me intently, apparently unimpressed.

"What do you know about Nashville Stuart?" she asked suddenly. The question caught me by surprise.

"Nash? Very little, really. He seems quite a gentleman. I understand he was the CEO of some corporation that took over a film company. He got into show biz by mergers."

"That's right," added the lieutenant. "He's connected with Henderson Oil in Oklahoma and Texas, and also, interestingly enough, International Chemicals of Atlanta, Georgia."

"Why is that interesting?" I asked.

"Because International Chemicals manufactures dynamite," said Sergeant Dimitriev impatiently, as if any fool would know such a thing.

"The very kind of dynamite used in the pipe bomb which sank *Easy Money,*" added the lieutenant.

"Are you sure you don't know anything about this?" Dimitriev eyed me suspiciously.

"If you're holding back any information, it could look pretty bad for you," said Carlino.

"Why the hell should I know anything about dynamite?" Jayne patted my hand.

"Now, Mr. Allen, what kind of relationship have you observed between Nash Stuart and Bernie Barnes?" asked Lieutenant Carlino.

"Well, I haven't had a chance to know either of them very well. But they seemed to be like oil and water."

"You mean, Nash liked to make money and Bernie liked to spend it?" asked the sergeant.

"There was that, of course. But even beyond the money conflict, they struck me as an odd couple. Nash is rather aristocratic in his own way, genteel, whereas Bernie was just the opposite. A real vulgarian."

"They weren't the sort of men you'd expect to have a partnership?" asked the lieutenant.

"Hardly! Though sometimes opposites do attract."

"And they fought on the set?" asked the sergeant.

"Almost every time I saw them together."

"As an amateur detective, would you think it's possible that Mr. Stuart might want to . . . cut his losses, shall we say?" The lieutenant almost seemed genuinely interested in my opinion.

"By murdering Barnes? I don't know, Lieutenant, that doesn't sound very likely to me."

"But *Murder in Manhattan* was millions of dollars over budget, and there's still a month and a half of shooting left to do. For a businessman like Mr. Stuart, I'd imagine a free-spender like Barnes would be a real liability."

"Why didn't Nash simply fire him, then?" I asked.

"Ah-ha!" said the lieutenant. "That's the question I've been asking myself: Why didn't Nashville Stuart fire Bernie Barnes?"

"I bet Bernie was blackmailing him along with all the others!" Jayne said.

The lieutenant turned to her and smiled. "You'd almost

think Mr. Barnes was asking to get killed, wouldn't you? Anyway," he said, turning back to me, "it's interesting that Mr. Stuart is going to finish directing the film himself."

"Nash is going to direct? That's crazy!" I couldn't believe it. "He doesn't know a thing about directing."

Lieutenant Carlino shrugged. "Well, his son's going to help with the technical aspects, I understand."

"His son?"

The lieutenant flashed me one of his now-familiar superior smiles. "Don't you know about his illegitimate son, Mr. Allen? It was supposed to be very hush-hush, of course—Stuart has a very proper wife and family who know nothing about this—but a great *amateur* detective like yourself . . . well, I would have imagined you'd have guessed."

"His son?" I repeated in astonishment.

"His secret, illegitimate son," the lieutenant insisted, as if this were of prime importance. "A son he was trying to help, perhaps from a guilty conscience."

The name came to me before Carlino supplied it. I suppose I should have suspected something like this earlier.

"My God, of course, the third assistant! Trip Johnson!"

# chapter 29

**O**ur encounter with Lieutenant Carlino and his sidekick was on a Tuesday night. Bright and early Thursday morning, the filming of *Murder in Manhattan* resumed—with Nash Stuart in the director's chair.

The location was a vast, old-fashioned apartment on the Upper West Side, just off Riverside Drive. Nash gave a little speech to the cast and crew before we began:

"I know we're all going to miss Bernie," he lied boldly with just a trace of a southern accent. "We'll miss his great humor, his compassion, and his dedication to the art of film making. Some of you may think this is rather sudden to be resuming work after so great a tragedy"—there was an indiscreet snickering from the back of the room—"but I believe Bernie himself would be the first to say, 'On with the show.' So let us bow our heads in a moment of silence and then put aside our grief and go out and make this a great one . . . for Bernie!"

I had underestimated Nashville Stuart. This was hypocrisy with a vengeance. We all knew it, but we all bowed our heads and stood in the living room of the West Side apartment and had our separate thoughts of our former leader. I thought of him washing out on the tide somewhere, carried off to sea, for at this point in the search the police and coast guard were saying the body might never be found. It was strange to think of Barnes floating in the cold currents, perhaps prey to sharks. Poor bastard. I tried to work up some sorrow, but the emotion wouldn't come. Any way you looked at it, dead or alive, Bernie Barnes had been a real son of a bitch.

"All right! Onward to the Academy Awards!" cried Nash, and the death of Bernard L. Barnes was put behind us. I was amazed how easily ex-businessman Stuart took to playing film director. Gone was the conservative pinstripe suit and quiet demeanor of the boardroom. Nash dressed for his new occupation in jeans, tennis shoes, and V-neck sweater. He wore a viewing lens on a silver chain around his neck and a pair of dark glasses perched jauntily on the top of his head. I was beginning to wonder if being a director had been his secret ambition all along.

I thought of the story, famous among film people, that starts with the death of Mother Teresa. After having lived such a saintly, selfless life, she is, of course, rushed immediately into St. Peter's presence, and he gives her the warmest possible welcome.

"We've been admiring you up here for quite a long time," he says. "And now, to reward you for your long years of heroic sacrifice, I'm pleased to tell you that whatever you wish to do up here shall be granted to you."

But not entirely to St. Peter's surprise, the good nun says, "In life I never wanted anything for myself, and I shall be content, here in heaven, to be guided by the same principle. I am happy and honored to be here with all of you, but I require no special favors."

At that point St. Peter smiles, gives the newly arrived woman his special blessing, and starts to walk away.

"Oh, come to think of it," Mother Teresa adds, "if it wouldn't be too much trouble, I *have* always wanted to direct."

"What a difference a murder makes!" Jasper said cheerfully, coming up to my side, interrupting my musings. "Would you believe this is the same crew?"

I shook my head in amazement. With Bernie gone, it was as if a great weight had been lifted—everyone was cheerful as could be. Electricians were whistling as they trimmed their lights. The first setup was ready in record time, and Nash was beaming goodwill upon one and all.

"Look over there," Jasper continued.

"Now, that I don't believe!" I muttered. Across the room, Suzanne and Victoria were laughing at some shared joke, looking like the very best of friends. It was hard to believe that the first time I had seen them they were nearly scratching each other's eyes out.

"Makes you wish old Bernie had had the sense to get himself knocked off months ago!" observed Jasper.

"That's not very funny," I objected. "Nobody misses him, but the chances are someone in this room is a murderer. And you realize, of course, we all could have bought the farm in that little boating mishap."

"Steve, don't be shocked, but that little boating mishap, as you call it, was the most fun I've had in years! God, for a little while there, life was full of drama—wasn't it? Danger and adventure. I swear, I felt twenty years old!"

Jasper indeed looked great. There was color in his cheeks and a new vibrancy in his speech.

"Weren't you worried about the ticker?" I asked, remembering our conversation in Trader Vic's.

"Not a bit, old man! And now Bernie's death has made me feel almost immortal."

I hadn't seen as much of Jasper in New York as you might expect of old friends on the same production. Jayne and I had had dinner with him once since she'd arrived from California, but we had somehow avoided each other afterward—the old friendship just wasn't the same.

"I left a message for you yesterday," I mentioned. "You didn't call back."

"Ah, sorry, old man, Annie and I took off for a day in the pastoral pleasures of Connecticut. There's a nice little inn we've been going to for years." Then he added, "You looked shocked."

"Jasper," I said. "I haven't been Mr. Perfect as a husband myself, but reactions to this sort of situation do come automatically."

"I know," he said with a note of sadness in his voice. "Whenever I hear that one of my friends is doing this kind of thing, I'm always, well, disappointed."

"It isn't just that Jayne and I are fond of Emily," I said. "I'm concerned about you too. Your health, your age."

But like everyone else on the crew, Jasper looked as if he might at any moment kick up his heels in glee. I found it all depressing. We had seated ourselves in folding chairs behind the camera and had to stop speaking while Suzanne and La Volpa did a short scene. I noticed Trip standing importantly by his father's side, shouting "Silence on the set!" before every take. Now that I knew they were related, I could see a certain resemblance in the nose and structure of the cheekbones. Probably Bernie, who never missed a dirty trick, had been keeping Nash in line with the threat of exposing this relationship.

"The crazy thing is, almost everybody seems to have a motive," I said, thinking aloud, once we were able to talk again.

"I beg your pardon?"

"A motive for murder. It makes finding the killer rather difficult."

"Why bother?" asked Jasper. "Unless perhaps you want to give him a medal."

"Or *her*," I said.

"You think the killer is a woman?"

"I'm keeping an open mind. It could be anyone, cast or crew. It could even be you, Jasper."

He laughed with Shakespearean gusto. "Good God, you're serious about this, aren't you?"

I flashed him my hard-boiled film noir detective look. "Jasper," I asked. "What were you doing in the hallway of the ninth floor the night before last?"

"Which hallway, old man?"

"You know. The one in which you were agreeing to pay ten thousand dollars and threatening to use your pistol if you were ever asked for more."

Jasper's blue eyes lost some of their dazzle. His mouth went a little slack.

"Good Lord, where were you, Steve? Lurking in the shadows?"

"I was in the linen closet," I said with as much dignity as this admission would afford.

Jasper seemed to find this funny. "The linen closet? Whatever were you doing there?"

"The point is, I heard your conversation, Jasper, every word. And so did Jayne."

"Er, Jayne was in the linen closet as well?"

Trip Johnson called for silence as the scene between Suzanne and La Volpa was filmed once more, from a new angle. I kept an eye on Jasper. He wasn't looking as jaunty as before.

"Well, I suppose you have me," he admitted when the shot was finished. He moved his chair closer so that no one could eavesdrop. "You realize who I was talking with, don't you?"

"Of course," I bluffed, though for the life of me I still couldn't connect that second half-familiar voice with a face.

"Damn!" he said softly. "I really wish you hadn't become involved in this."

"Jasper, I'd like to help you, but I have to know exactly what this is about, from beginning to end."

Jasper had gone a little pale. He sat upright in his chair, looking as if he had been hit by a bolt of electricity. He put a hand over his heart.

"Steve, I don't want to frighten you, but I've just experienced a rather nasty feeling in my chest."

"Good Lord, let me call for a doctor!"

The hand that was not over his heart reached out and grasped hold of my arm with amazing strength. "No, no . . . I'll be all right. Let me just sit here a moment."

"Jasper, please, if there's any question of a heart attack, we should get you to a hospital right away."

"Steve, it's nothing, really. I have these pains all the time. Now, let me just sit and rest a few seconds and not have to answer a lot of silly questions."

"Certainly," I said. "Just relax."

He smiled in a fragile way and waved me away. What a trooper the man was. When Trip called him before the cameras a few minutes later, he gave the performance of his life—not for an instant letting it show that his heart might stop beating at any moment.

# chapter 30

In the film Jasper plays a character by the name of Richard Fallsworthy, a fake British aristocrat actually from Newark, New Jersey, who is trying to make it to the stratosphere of New York society by sheer guile and charm. The funny part was the way Jasper masterfully let little bits of New Jersey occasionally show through the very upper-crusty British manner he so naturally conveyed. As soon as the camera was rolling, every person on the set stood transfixed, trying not to laugh or applaud until after the director cried "Cut!"

I was watching Jasper at work, enraptured along with everyone else, when I noticed Annie standing off to one side, shyly following the progress of the scene. I knew by now she must be in her late forties to have had a relationship with Jasper for twenty-five years, but there were moments when she looked hardly older than a teenager. Though she was "the other woman," she had a waiflike innocence to her.

I edged my way over. "Hello, Annie," I said.

She jumped and turned around. "God, you scared me, Steve."

"I'm sorry. Do you think we could step off somewhere and have a chat?"

The big, childlike eyes regarded me solemnly. The way she had jumped, one might imagine she had a guilty conscience. Without a word she led the way off the set. I followed her out of the big old-fashioned West Side apartment into the hall.

"Where are we going?"

"Let's go up to the roof," she suggested. "We can get a breath of fresh air."

We took an elevator up to the seventeenth floor and then walked a flight of stairs to the metal door that opened out upon a flat tar and graveled rooftop. This was a poor man's terrace, with various pipes and chimneys sticking up here and there, but the sky overhead was a pale blue, and we could see Riverside Park below us, the West Side Highway, and the broad expanse of the Hudson River clear to the Palisades of New Jersey.

"This is where real New Yorkers go to get away from it all," said Annie, gazing out. "Up on the roof."

"Annie, I was remembering my first night in New York. You said I might come to you if I were having any problems with Barnes. Well, I'm having one."

"With a dead man?" Annie asked, reaching into her bag and pulling out a cigarette. I was a little shocked that she smoked. She hardly looked old enough.

"I want to know more about him," I prodded. "To know what made Bernie tick."

"Maybe it's best to just leave it alone. After all, does it really matter now?"

"Of course it matters. Among other things, it could help us find his killer."

Annie seemed amused. "Jasper told me you're something of an amateur detective. Aren't you ever worried that you might stumble across something . . . dangerous?"

I smiled an unworried smile.

"Steve, do you carry a gun?"

"What for? Now tell me about Bernie."

"Bernie? Well, now, *he* was a little crazy."

"That I know."

"No, I mean *really* crazy. He was once diagnosed as being a borderline schizophrenic. Most of the time he could function fairly well, but he went through drastic mood swings. Not too many people know this, but three months before this movie began he tried to commit suicide with an overdose of sleeping pills."

"Good God! Why?"

"He was having trouble getting financing for *Murder in Manhattan.* Nash Stuart's company wasn't his first choice, you know.

He'd been turned down by Fox, Paramount, Warners. . . ."

"But I always heard that Bernard L. Barnes films made tons of money!"

Annie stamped out her cigarette on the gravel of the roof.

"Sure, the films made bundles, but they also *cost* bundles. And unfortunately Bernie was getting more extravagant just as the films were becoming less popular. The last one barely broke even. The big studios began to think Bernie no longer presented a very good risk. They couldn't reason with him, so they turned him down. Bernie got depressed, thought the world was against him—thus the pills."

I shook my head sadly at the idea of anyone taking an overdose of sleeping pills. Though I had never been a fan of Barnes's, it put him in new light to see him as weak.

"You see what I'm driving at, don't you?" asked Annie, watching me carefully.

"No, I'm afraid not."

"I don't think Bernie was murdered at all."

*"You're saying he committed suicide?"*

"Why not? His mood swings were irrational, and it would be just like Bernie to check out in a way that would make life uncomfortable for other people—maybe even have someone falsely accused of his murder."

This was an astonishing thought, but it didn't add up. "Look, Annie, clever as Barnes might have been, you can't commit suicide by stabbing yourself in the back."

"Are you sure about that?" mused Annie. "You have to remember Bernie was a film maker, a master of illusion. He was used to faking all kinds of things. So maybe—I don't know—he could attach the knife to the wall somehow with the point sticking out, and then fall back on it?"

"You think that's possible?" It was a wild theory, but Annie gave it some plausibility.

"With Bernie, *anything* was possible."

I was feeling a bit stunned. In a funny way, I could almost imagine Bernie getting his last joke on the world by having his suicide blamed on some innocent soul, like me! It would be the ultimate revenge of the paranoid schizophrenic.

"Was Bernie depressed recently?"

"I told you, he had these irrational mood swings. Sometimes he was on top of the world, other times at the bottom—and it generally didn't have much foundation in reality. Just the other day I ran into him on the set after everyone had left, and I could tell he'd been crying."

"Crying? What about?"

"When I asked him, he wouldn't say. Just laughed and said the tears were an allergic reaction."

"Well, thanks for the information," I said. "And, Annie, to change the subject, where were you the other night on the boat when I went down to change into the Superman costume? I thought you were supposed to meet me in the stateroom to give me a hand."

Annie flashed me an unreadable look with those innocent china-blue eyes. "Steve, you don't think *I* helped Bernie stick that knife in his back!"

"Lord, no. I'm just wondering if you saw anything, that's all."

"No, I'm sorry. I was in the main salon playing cards with Jasper and Mimi. I guess I lost track of time. I didn't even realize you'd gone below to change, or I would have come to help you. Just my luck, I was two hundred dollars ahead at five-card draw when the explosion happened."

"I see. Well, speaking of Jasper, I'd keep an eye on him if I were you and try to persuade him to take it easy. He's pushing himself pretty hard for a guy with a heart condition."

Annie gazed at me blankly. "Heart condition? I don't understand."

"You know, the heart attack he had in North Africa last year. Surely he must have told you."

"Steve, Jasper's *never* had a heart attack—certainly not in North Africa last year. Why, I was with him nearly that entire time."

Suddenly I was angry. "Excuse me, dear, I've got to get back to the set."

I left Annie on the roof—she said she wanted to smoke another cigarette before returning below—and I huffed off down the stairs and the elevator to the apartment where we were filming.

Jasper had just finished the scene and was stepping off the set toward his dressing room.

"Jasper," I said. "I think it's a pretty lousy trick you've played on me."

"What are you talking about?"

"I'm talking about the heart attack in North Africa you never had. I was fool enough to believe you and be worried. Now maybe we should get back to some of those questions you've been trying so hard not to answer, like what you were doing in the hotel hallway offering someone ten thousand dollars to keep quiet!"

Jasper, that miserable faker, put his hand over his heart and started looking pale again. "Oh, dear. I'm afraid I'm feeling those pains . . ." His voice even wobbled.

"You're as healthy as a horse," I scoffed. "If you were able to survive a sinking ship, I'm confident you can deal with a few simple questions about murder and blackmail."

Jasper staggered two paces forward, struggling for breath. This was award-winning stuff from Britain's greatest actor.

"Jasper, you can't get away with not answering my questions as easily as this!"

"Steve . . . if only . . ."

He never finished the sentence. He made a horrible gurgling sound deep in his throat and fell forward onto the floor to the accompaniment of a few screams from people standing nearby.

# chapter 31

The nearest hospital was a few blocks uptown near Columbia University, and that's where Jasper was taken. I followed the ambulance in a taxi and sat wretchedly in a bright, depressing waiting area off the emergency room. I watched two policemen lead in a bloody teenager in handcuffs, and a few minutes later came medics with a stretcher on which lay a moaning pedestrian who had evidently mistakenly believed New York taxis would not run down a jaywalker. There's a lot of pain passing through a big-city emergency room, and I was feeling pretty badly myself—causing an old friend to have a heart attack and then being so insensitive as to accuse him of faking.

"How is he?" Jayne asked, sweeping into the waiting room, responding to my frantic telephone call like an angel of mercy.

"I don't know," I admitted. "You have to be a relative or the doctors won't tell you a thing. I'm just sitting here out of guilt."

"Let me try."

"The nurses are too busy to—"

Jayne didn't wait for me to finish. She approached a nurse who had a hard face, and in a moment my wife had the woman smiling and making a phone call, jabbering about Jayne's years as a panelist on *I've Got a Secret* as they waited for the phone to be answered. Finally Jayne came back across the waiting room to me.

"Well, Jasper's in stable condition, but they're taking him upstairs to intensive care to keep an eye on him."

"But he *did* have a heart attack?"

"They don't know for certain—they think so, of course, but

for the moment he seems fine. Actually the doctors are puzzled."

My suspicions were beginning to return. "That son of a bitch just wanted to get out of answering my questions!"

"Steve, that's a terrible accusation."

"Is it? I'd just confronted him with that conversation we overheard from the linen closet—a pretty damned convenient time to have a heart attack, I'd say."

Jayne told me *Murder in Manhattan* was turning me into a real cynic. She was right, of course. I could hardly wait to get back to California and reclaim my usual sunny disposition, but for the time being I was ready to see falsehood and murderous passions behind every smiling face.

The intensive care unit was on the third floor, and Jayne and I found ourselves in a smaller waiting room, surrounded by a large Iranian family—sisters, grandparents, aunts, and uncles—who were wailing into handkerchiefs and trying to keep the smaller children from running down elderly patients in the halls.

We hadn't been there more than five minutes when Jack Wolfe appeared out of the elevator with a two-day growth of beard and an unlit cigarette dangling out of his mouth. He pushed aside the Iranians to make his way to the reception desk.

"How's Mr. North?"

"I beg your pardon? Are you related to the patient?"

"Lady, I'm more than relation, I'm his publicist."

"I'm sorry, we give out information only to immediate family," said the nurse, a serious young woman. "And would you please remove the cigarette from your mouth? There's no smoking in the hospital."

Wolfe saw us in the waiting room and hurried over.

"What a break," he gloated. "Another headline story, just when the editors were beginning to cool on *Murder in Manhattan.* You guys know the details?"

"Not a thing, Jack," I said.

"Well, I guess I'll have to make it up, then. Won't be the first time, huh? Look, kids, I gotta run if I'm going to get this heart attack in the afternoon papers. See if you can pump the broad behind the desk, okay? *Ciao.*"

Jack, moving fast, crashed into Lieutenant Carlino coming out of the elevator. "Goddammit, watch where you're going," he snarled to the officer, and then was gone.

"What a repulsive little man," Jayne commented.

Carlino was by himself this afternoon. He gave us a wry smile. "I'd appreciate it if you two would stick around a few moments," he said. "I'll just check with the doctors and be right back."

"Natasha took part of the afternoon off to have her hair done," Jayne whispered when the lieutenant was gone. "He's not going to be able to resist her."

"Jayne," I said. "We're too busy to take on the love life of the police!"

"Steve," she answered just as calmly, "don't be an old grouch. What's more important than love?"

Lieutenant Carlino disappeared inside the ICU and returned about ten minutes later with little more information than Jayne had gathered from the nurse downstairs.

"He's going to be fine," he told us. "The doctors aren't even certain he had a coronary event, as they call it. He might simply have fainted. They're going to keep him overnight for observation."

"Steve thinks Jasper was faking, don't you, darling?" Jayne said, not realizing that in the detective business information like this was not given away without getting something in return. We sleuths are a cagey lot.

"Mr. Allen? Why should Mr. North fake a heart attack?"

"Because Steve had him cornered, didn't you, darling? You absolutely pinned him down with questions until the poor man had no recourse but to tell the truth or be rushed to the hospital."

"Jayne, I—"

But she was off and running, telling the whole story of what we had overheard in the linen closet. Listening to her account, I found myself wondering again what it all could mean. It had occurred to me, of course, that Jasper was being blackmailed about his twenty-five-year-old relationship with Annie Locks, but I had trouble visualizing his so casually putting up ten thousand dollars to keep that sort of thing quiet. Perhaps he'd even been looking for a way to break the sad news to Emily himself. That could have been the case if, for example, he was so in love with Annie that he wanted to ask for a divorce. Or sometimes, in situations of this sort, men feel such guilt that they unconsciously want to be caught and exposed, by way of letting external circumstances force them out of the predicament they have stumbled into.

"Well, well," said the lieutenant, turning my way. "Why didn't you tell me about this conversation Tuesday night?"

"I didn't think it was important," I murmured, giving Jayne a murderous look.

"Actually Steve's trying to solve the murder himself," said Jayne with a smug smile.

It isn't easy being married to a totally honest person. Lieutenant Carlino gave me a condescending look. "Ah, that's right—the famous amateur detective," he smirked. "Well, Mr. Allen? What do you think the conversation was all about?"

"More blackmail?"

"In other words, Barnes was not the only blackmailer in the group?"

"Apparently not."

"And neither of you recognized the voice?"

"Sorry," I said coolly. "You know, I've been thinking, the killer could have been anyone on that boat. The way Bernie made enemies, one of the extras—maybe even one of the ship's crew—could have stabbed him in the back, then planted the bomb to get rid of any traces of the crime."

"We're looking into that, of course," said the officer. "You may be interested to know there were exactly sixty-three people on board *Easy Money* that night, and right now our computers and investigators are checking out each and every one, particularly to see which of them had any past association with Mr. Barnes."

"If you discover anything interesting . . ."

"Of course, I'll tell you right away, Mr. Allen. We'll be

partners in this, shall we? That is, assuming you begin to be more forthcoming with me."

"Absolutely. Besides, how can I keep a secret?" I said, nodding toward Jayne.

"Then there'll be no more hiding in closets?"

We were grinning at each other in an earnest new spirit of detente when I overheard a half-familiar voice address the nurse at the reception desk.

"Look, I got to speak with him. Won't you at least tell Jasper I'm here and let him decide if he's well enough to see me? I promise not to wear him out."

The grin froze on my face. This was, in fact, not just any half-familiar voice. It was the half-familiar voice from outside the linen closet. I very carefully did not look toward the reception desk to give myself away. Jayne, fortunately, was regaling the lieutenant with hints about the shopping trip she and Natasha had planned—an excursion with exotic black lace underwear at the top of the list.

If Carlino had only been a bit less condescending, I think I would have told him about the mystery voice being right here among us. As it was, I pretended interest in Jayne's story while my mind raced overtime on murder and intrigue. It was only when the nurse convinced the visitor it was impossible to visit Mr. North that I risked a quick glance—at Trip Johnson, shaking his head and moving away from the desk toward the elevator.

# chapter 32

"I'm going to find the men's room," I murmured, excusing myself. I had the feeling that Jayne and Lieutenant Carlino barely heard me; their conversation had moved on from ladies' underwear to men's suits, and the vain lieutenant was soliciting Jayne's expert opinion.

"I do feel," she was saying, "that the traditional lines are much more attractive than those ridiculous bulky jackets that some young men wear these days. It always makes them look like little boys trying on one of their daddy's suits."

I hurried out of the waiting room after Trip, just in time to see the elevator door closing on him. He was apparently too preoccupied to notice me. There was a frown on his face and his hair—long in front, short on the sides—fell limply over his eyes.

I pressed the down button and waited impatiently. The elevator that eventually came was definitely no express—it stopped endlessly on the second floor to admit an elderly woman in a wheelchair—and by the time I reached the lobby Trip was nowhere in sight. Sometimes we detectives are simply out of luck.

I decided I might as well walk outside the building and glance up and down the street, but I didn't have much hope. Certainly if Johnson had known he was being followed, he could have easily gotten away.

Fortunately I spotted him almost immediately. He was shuffling along, hardly looking where he was going, wearing his allegedly stylish clownlike pants—pegged legs and balloon thighs—loafers without socks, and a baggy sweater because there was an unseasonable nip in the air. He had his hands stuck down in voluminous pockets and occasionally cleared his vision by tossing back his hair with his right hand. Without being sure of my own intentions, I followed him.

The young man walked westward to Broadway, where he headed uptown, sometimes stopping to look in the windows of the bookstores, sushi bars, and Chinese restaurants on the southern edge of Columbia University. I have to admit to a growing interest in Johnson—I couldn't figure him out: yuppie drug pusher, illegitimate son of Nash Stuart, young man seemingly without a shred of idealism. He had appeared brash on the set, but now that I had a chance to observe him on his own, he looked only sad and lost.

It was at that moment that my mind went back to the question as to why I hadn't recognized his voice that night in the hallway at The Plaza. The explanation, it struck me, was that the Trip Johnson Jayne and I had heard speaking in somewhat low, threatening tones was quite different from the usual false-front, superficial, hey-dude con man I'd originally met. The public Trip Johnson, then, was glib, spoke rather loudly, and fended off real intimacy by pretending to a quick friendliness that was without authentic content. The voice in the hallway had been that of the real Trip Johnson.

He led me a few blocks onto the main quad of the university itself. Columbia is not a particularly attractive campus, dominated by the ponderous neoclassic structure of Low Library and surrounded by drab red brick buildings that make you think you could be on the edge of Moscow rather than New York City. My quarry sat down dejectedly on a stone bench with the vast steps of Low Library rising up behind him. Hundreds of grim-faced students marched by on their way to success without glancing in his direction. Trip rested his chin on his hands and seemed to sigh.

I came up behind him.

"Why is Jasper North willing to give you ten thousand dollars?" I said close to his ear. The young man bolted to his feet and looked around wildly. "What the hell do you have on him?" I continued.

Trip looked at me, and I was sure he was about to run. I put a hand on his arm and said firmly, "Sit . . . down!" He had youth and energy and certainly could have gotten away, but I had the sound of God Almighty in my voice. Trip sat.

"Hey, what are you doing up here?" he said, as usual trying to sound casual and in control.

"I'm here to get an education, kid, and I'm majoring in you. What's going on between you and Jasper? And I want the truth."

"You must have been at the hospital. What's the story?"

"You're the one in the hot seat at the moment. What's the answer to my question?"

"Look, there's nothing between me and Jasper. I don't know what you're talking about. I went to the hospital to see how he was making out, you know. I wanted to find out when he'd be well enough to work again, that's all."

"Did your father send you?"

Trip's brown eyes grew larger, then wary. "My father?"

"That's right—Nash Stuart."

He looked away from my steady gaze. "Hey, I don't know where you get your information, but just because some dude knocked up my mother doesn't mean he's my father. I mean, what the hell's he ever done for me?"

"He gave you a job."

"Oh, yeah—big deal. Third assistant director. And the only reason he did that was because he was afraid—"

"Afraid?"

But Johnson had caught himself and was now looking at me suspiciously.

"What's it to you, anyway?"

"It's called a murder investigation. The cops are putting the heat on me—and I'm passing it on."

Trip sneered. I liked him better when he looked sad and lost. "You know, you'd better be nice to me," he said. "If you bug me too much, maybe I'll tell your wife about you and Mimi Day."

"Ah! Blackmail and intimidation. I had a feeling we'd get to that."

"I don't care what you think. I've learned to take care of

myself, because sure as hell no one else will."

"Your father—"

"My *father!* That son of a bitch bent over backward to pretend I didn't exist for about eighteen years. I never would have
known about him at all if my mother hadn't finally told me. She
was his secretary, for chrissake. Twenty years ago in Dallas. Why
*she* kept quiet all these years I'll never know. As soon as I found
out, I went to the old man and told him he'd better start helping
me pronto, or I'd blow his cozy little scene with the wife and kids
on the East Side. So what does he do? He gives me some dumb
job as third assistant on some crummy film!"

"He's giving you more than that, Trip. He's giving you an
opportunity to learn an interesting profession."

The young man laughed nastily. "I don't want an interesting profession. I want money."

It was discouraging talking to Johnson. All the good quali-
ties of youth seemed to have passed him by. While I had him,
however, there was a big question I had wanted to ask ever since
the night *Easy Money* sank beneath the waves.

"Listen, kid, right before the boat went down I saw you in
the main salon and told you Bernie was dead. Remember?"

"Yeah . . . so?"

"You went below to check it out. What did you see down
there?"

"What do you mean, what did I see? An empty corridor. A
bunch of doors."

"You didn't see anyone else?"

"Not anyone alive—only Bernie, and he was as dead as they
come. There was water rushing in around my feet, so I got the
hell out of there."

"And you left Barnes in the wardrobe room on the bed?"

"What the hell was I supposed to do? Take him home? Of
course I left him. What kind of stupid question is that?"

"His body still hasn't been found."

Trip shrugged. "Who cares?"

"You're all heart. Anyway, let's get back to why you're
blackmailing Jasper."

"I don't know why I have to be talking to you at all," he muttered.

"I'll tell you why. Either tell me the truth, or I'm going to go to the cops and let them know you've been pushing drugs on the set. I'm sure they'll find that quite interesting."

"You can't prove a thing," he taunted.

"I can point them your way, and I'm sure once they start looking . . ."

"Okay, okay. I'll tell you about Jasper. The old jerk's cheating on his wife—just like you, man. He gives me money to keep quiet."

"First of all, Trip, I am *not* cheating on my wife, not that I care if you believe me. Secondly, I know all about Jasper and Annie, and I don't believe he's giving you ten thousand dollars to keep it quiet. It's simply not important enough."

Trip grinned at me. "Hey, you're right, man. You're pretty sharp."

"Then what is it?"

"Why? You want to cash in and squeeze me out?"

I stood up. "I'm wasting my time. I think I'll just go to the police and let them sweat the truth out of you."

"Hey, wait a minute. I was just kidding."

"Then tell me now. The truth."

"Okay, okay. Chill out. For starters, how about this: He had to lie to get into the country to do the film. If the immigration department knew what I know, he'd be deported."

"That's ridiculous!"

"Is it? Maybe I found out something about his medical history that would ruin his acting career—like instantaneously. What do you think of that?"

"I don't believe you. Besides, he already told me how he bribed a doctor in England to keep quiet about his heart condition."

"Heart condition? Jesus, is that what he told you? You don't get it, do you? Jasper doesn't have any damned heart condition, he's got AIDS."

"AIDS?"

"You got it."

I let this information sink in for a moment. "This is absurd," I said finally. "How could *you* find out something like that?"

He grinned in a cagey, crazy way and tapped the side of his head with his index finger. "When you're a schmuck like me, you gotta work hard to stay ahead of the game."

"I think you're making this up."

"You don't believe me? Well, it so happens the doctor old man North bribed in England was not your most, uh, upstanding member of the medical profession. He thought he could get money from both sides, so he flew to New York and sold the info to my father."

"Nash knows about this?"

"Sure. I saw the lab report on his desk—that's how I found out."

"But why . . ."

"Why doesn't dear Daddy spill the beans? Maybe hold a press conference and tell the world? Are you kidding? Having somebody like North around is a big plus for the production. Why blow a good thing?"

"Did Bernie know?" I asked.

Trip shrugged. "Probably. I wouldn't be surprised. Anyway, except for it being so shameful and all, what's the big deal? I mean, AIDS isn't all that contagious, or anything."

"No, I suppose not."

"I mean, the guy is too old for love scenes anyway, right?" I had a feeling that Trip imagined people over the age of forty lost all interest in sex. The statement also gave me another thought.

"In the movie does Jasper have to kiss anyone?"

Trip grinned and stood up. "Haven't you read the script?"

"There *is* no real script."

"Sure there is. Look, I gotta run. Nice talkin' to ya."

"Trip! Who—what woman does Jasper—"

He had taken a few steps, but now turned to face me.

"Mimi," he said. "That's right. Jasper has a hot love scene with Mimi coming up. Bernie wrote the scene himself."

The third assistant turned and left abruptly, jogging down College Walk toward Amsterdam Avenue. I watched him blend into the crowd of young people, their faces set with the determination to survive.

# chapter 33

**J**ayne and Lieutenant Carlino had long finished discussing men's suits and had moved on to women's fashions by the time I returned to the intensive care waiting room. At Jayne's instigation, I'm sure, the lieutenant was elaborating on his favorite colors and dress styles. He broke off in midsentence and gave me a skeptical look as I rejoined them.

"I was getting worried about you," he said, and then added quickly with a smile at Jayne, "not that your wife hasn't been very entertaining."

"Ah, well, I made a phone call, and then I was starving, so I ducked downstairs to the cafeteria."

"There *is* no cafeteria downstairs."

"Yes, that's what I discovered. So I dashed outside for a hot dog from the pushcart on the corner."

Carlino continued to look me over. I'm sure I would have come up with a better excuse for my long absence if my mind hadn't still been reeling with the idea of Jasper having AIDS—our modern black plague that comes complete not only with the horror of death but also the suggestion of sexual deviation and drug abuse. Trip was probably right. If word got out about Jasper, he might still have a number of years to live, but his long and distinguished acting career would be over.

"You wouldn't be lying to me, would you, sir?" asked the lieutenant, smiling as if he were joking.

I laughed and gave him my most innocent look. I wasn't ready to pass on Jasper's secret just yet. "Would I lie to New York's most fashion-conscious detective?"

The lieutenant sighed. "I'd keep an eye on this guy, Mrs. Allen. He's slippery as hell."

"You can keep an eye on me at lunch, dear," I said to Jayne, taking her arm. "I'm sure the lieutenant has all kinds of nasty criminals to catch, and we don't want to starve to death on the Upper West Side."

"But you just ate a hot dog," she objected.

"That was just an appetizer," I assured her.

I got her out of there, with Lieutenant Carlino giving me a dark and ponderous look. Flagging down a taxi outside the hospital, I told the driver to take us to the first large stationery shop he found.

"Darling, I thought we were going to lunch."

"Why? Are you hungry?"

"Steve, you know, you really *are* acting strange lately."

I laughed. "Ha! Here I am surrounded by intrigue and consuming passions, illegitimate children, blackmail, and greed—and you say *I'm* strange! Jayne, I'm getting fed up with this little mystery. I've decided you and I are going to adopt a more scientific method to find out who stabbed Mr. Barnes."

"We're going to do this in a stationery store?"

"It's merely a modest beginning," I assured her. "This case needs organization. It's sprawling all over the place. I need colored paper, notebooks, scissors, glue—and pins."

"Sounds interesting, but why all that?"

"Because we're going to pin this on someone, and I've figured out how. You see, up to now I've been concentrating on motive, and that's led to all this confusion. So I'm going to switch tactics and look into something more basic—*opportunity.*"

"I see. Who actually had a *chance* to kill Bernie Barnes."

"Exactly. Nearly everyone in his right mind had a motive to want the bastard dead, but someone actually had to follow him down below deck and do the dirty deed. We're going to make a diagram of the boat, take a different colored pin for each suspect, and map out each person's movement for the time right before the explosion. Someone on that boat is not going to be able to account for his or her movements—and our pins are going to tell us who that person is. *Voilà,* we'll have the murderer!"

"You make it sound so easy."

"To borrow a cliché, it's elementary, my dear."

Actually, I was trying to pump up my own confidence. The situation reminded me of a classic story from the apparently inexhaustible well of Jewish humor. A man attempting to climb a mountain slips, falls, and is cruelly battered as he rolls to the bottom. Rescuers find him with practically every bone in his body broken. The poor fellow is covered with blood and apparently breathing his last. Nobody knows what to do for him, but suddenly, from among the bystanders, an old man steps forth and says, "Give him an enema."

"This poor fellow is dying," an angry bystander shouts. "At a time like this, what the hell good could an enema do?"

"It couldn't hoit," the old man says with a shrug.

So I was going to give my last-ditch method a shot, as we say in the shot-giving business.

Over the next two days I talked with each of the main suspects, as I had begun to think of my coworkers, and also chatted with several members of the crew. Bit by bit I began to put together a reasonably precise scenario of who was where when.

The script girl told me, for example, that the last shot Barnes completed ended at 10:43 P.M. It was after that that I went below to change costumes. The explosion, according to the police report, happened at 11:09. This left a theoretical window of exactly twenty-six minutes for the crime to take place, and I was able to further narrow down the time with information received from the director of photography: Barnes spent at least ten minutes after the last shot moving the camera and trying to decide the best angle for the new setup. When he finished, at approximately 10:53 P.M., he told the cameraman he was going to go for a cup of coffee. After more careful questioning, the gaffer—that's show biz lingo for head lighting technician—told me he had seen Bernie go below deck at exactly eleven o'clock. He was sure of the time because he had just checked his watch— he was curious about how many hours of overtime he was accruing—and so from 11:00 to 11:09 left exactly nine minutes for the knife to be plunged into poor Bernie's back. The bomb, naturally, could have been planted anytime.

I carefully gathered my information as *Murder in Manhattan* continued to film—without Jasper North, I should mention, who remained in the hospital, reportedly for further observation. Clearly anyone on board the good ship *Easy Money* could be the killer, but for the time being I was ready to discount the more casual members of the crew. For this reason, however, I relied primarily on the crew to check out various matters of time and movement among my principal suspects, feeling the workers had less reason not to tell me the truth. I spoke to makeup women and stand-ins, lens pullers and boom operators and carpenters—then finally went to the principal cast. Since I'm perceived primarily as a comedian, no one took my detective playing very seriously, and I was glad to keep it all on a casual, what-the-hey level. Still, I kept notes on a Plaza telephone pad, and when I got back to the hotel Jayne and I were able to place color-coded pins on our diagram of the ship until we had every one of our main suspects accounted for.

It was Sunday afternoon when we finally had all the pieces of the puzzle in place. According to our method, each of our principal suspect's movements had to be corroborated by at least two people. This is what we got:

Victoria La Volpa was out on deck with Zachary Holden.

Jasper North was with Annie Locks and Mimi Day, sitting together in the main salon, playing cards and waiting for filming to resume.

Trip Johnson was with his secret father, Nash Stuart, the two talking together outside near the bow of the ship.

Clancy Donahue was sleeping on a sofa in full view of several people.

Jack Wolfe was with the captain and first mate, talking on the ship-to-shore radio with gossip columnist Liz Smith in Manhattan, apparently planting a story—not a bomb.

And, finally, Suzanne Tracy was sitting by herself in the main salon, also in full view of several people, reading a Russian novel.

And so my oh-so-scientific inquiry had resulted in one disconcerting discovery: *Everyone had a perfect alibi!*

"Therefore it's logical," I said to Jayne with a sigh, "that no one could have committed the damned murder. Thus Bernie is still alive. Only I happened to see him dead with a knife in his back!"

"Of course, it could have been one of the crew," said Jayne. "It could be the caterer, the captain, the clapperboy—"

"Or the prop man, production manager, or principal photographer," I added dismally. "Or Bernie might even have committed suicide, as Annie suggested. It'll take the police to track down this many leads. I'm afraid Detective Allen has met with failure. But damn, I thought it had to be one of the inner circle."

Jayne studied the diagram intensely, her brow puckering in thought, her fingers drumming the table. Suddenly she brightened.

"Steve, there *is* one suspect who doesn't have an alibi."

"No, no, dear. Look at the pins. Everyone's accounted for!"

"Not everyone." Jayne looked at once proud of her powers of deduction and bothered by the conclusion to which they pointed. "There's no pin for . . . you, darling."

# chapter 34

suggested to Jayne that we take a walk to clear the cobwebs out of our minds. Downstairs in the lobby I saw Jack Wolfe lurking behind a potted palm, deep in conversation with Suzanne Tracy—probably still trying to convince her to take off her clothes for his *Playboy* fantasy. Unfortunately, Jack saw us and began heading our way—but I was faster. I took Jayne by the arm, and we broke into an undignified jog, escaping out the side entrance onto 58th Street. We came out into the bright sunshine laughing like kids playing hooky from school. It was a small rebellion, but neither of us could stand the idea of being trapped by Wolfe just then.

"Jayne, will you visit me in prison?" I asked passionately.

"I'll bring you a cake with a small hacksaw in the middle," she promised.

We chuckled and held hands. It was a glorious spring day; sometimes it takes a crisis like finding yourself the only logical suspect in a murder case to make you appreciate the simple joy of being alive. I was about to head up Fifth Avenue toward the park, but Jayne sensed opportunity in the wind and reversed my movements to point us downtown—toward some of the city's most expensive stores.

My mind was still on the case. "It's crazy," I pondered. "Everyone had a motive to kill Bernie, but no one had an opportunity."

"Except you."

"Right, but with me it was just the opposite—I had plenty of opportunity but no motive."

"That's not what Natasha thinks," said Jayne.

"Oh?"

"She thinks you're in love with Bernie's wife."

*"That* nonsense again? I swear, just because I was nice to poor Mimi . . ."

"Steve, *I* understand. Honestly. I told Natasha you're the twentieth century's last chivalrous male."

"And what did the sergeant say to that?"

"She said there *are* no chivalrous males, just guys."

"Nice," I said.

"Ooooh, look, darling! There's Tiffany's. You know what would be terribly chivalrous?"

Well, I was feeling sentimental. If they hauled me off to prison, I probably wouldn't be doing much shopping for a while, so I grabbed the moment—and my wallet—and marched across the street to pick out a pair of diamond earrings for my wife. Jayne was really quite considerate, all in all. The mood I was in, she probably could have gotten me to spring for a necklace.


A few minutes later, back on the street, I said, "The earrings do a lot for you."

"No," she said tenderly. "You do a lot for me."

"No, I mean it," I said. "The adjective that comes to mind is *ravishing.*"

"Really?" she said coquettishly.

"Oh, yes," I said. "By the way, would you mind if I ravished you?"

"Certainly not here."

"It's Sardi's story time," I said, and we both laughed because she remembered one of my favorite story-jokes. A man in his early sixties goes to his doctor and says, "Doc, I'm really worried. My wife and I haven't had any interest in sex for an awfully long time."

"Don't worry," the doctor says. "At your age this sort of thing is common. It even sometimes happens with much younger people. But I've learned, over the years, what is usually involved is a series of missed opportunities. Maybe you're in the mood and at that moment your wife is not. Or she's available, but you're distracted. I wouldn't worry about this at all if I were you. Just relax. But do remember one thing—an opportunity will definitely come along. This time don't miss it. It can be quite casual. Perhaps your wife will drop a spoon on the kitchen floor, she'll bend over to pick it up and at that moment something about the curve of her body, something about her vulnerability will—"

"I get the idea," the man says.

About two months later the fellow is walking along the street and bumps into the doctor. "Ah, doc," he says, "I'm glad to see you. I've been wanting to let you know that your advice was just terrific. It happened just as you said it might. My wife and I were having dinner and, by golly, she did happen to drop a spoon on the floor and when she bent over to pick it up, well, I don't have to go into any further detail, but I'll just say it was one of the great erotic experiences of my life."

"That's wonderful news," the doctor said.

"Of course," the fellow says ruefully. "We'll never be able to go into Sardi's again."

Jayne and I tangoed back across Fifth Avenue toward the Plaza, murder a long way from our thoughts—until we waltzed right into our favorite policepersons, who were staked out near the elevators.

"I'd like to have a word with you, Mr. Allen," said Carlino. He looked exceptionally good, dressed in a white linen suit, a dark blue oxford shirt open sportily at the collar, a thin gold chain around his neck, and wearing soft tan loafers.

But it was Sergeant Dimitriev who held my eye. Blooming-dale's and Jayne Meadows Allen had added their touches, and the results were impressive. Natasha had replaced the shapeless black pants suit with a tailored but very feminine-looking turquoise silk skirt suit that made the aquamarine of her eyes darken and dazzle. For the first time I was able to notice her firm, shapely legs. Her soft, canary-yellow blouse had just the hint of a ruffle at the collar, and there was a touch of muted liner to highlight her eyes. Her hair, freed from the prison of the bun, flowed in full, easy waves around her face and onto her shoulders. Even the color seemed to be a richer auburn. I stared, until the lieutenant's gruff voice brought me rudely back to the reason for their visit.

"Well? Shall we go to your room?"

I sighed deeply. "Lieutenant, although I want to completely cooperate with the police, it's Sunday, and to be perfectly honest, Jayne and I—"

"Mr. Allen, it's either your place or mine." His tone was no-nonsense. Jayne squeezed my hand.

"That's all right, dear," she consoled. "Why don't you two go on up to the room, have your little talk, and I'll take Natasha to tea at the Palm Court."

It seemed to be settled, whether I liked it or not. I watched my wife's expensive earlobes disappear toward the spacious tearoom in the center of the hotel, Sergeant Dimitriev at her side. Then Lieutenant Carlino and I rode the elevator in silence to the ninth floor.

"I don't mind telling you I'm getting a little tired of being hassled," I said as I let us into the suite.

"Just doing my job," said the lieutenant. He glanced around the sitting room, then walked over to the bedroom door, opened it, and looked inside.

"Do you have a search warrant?" I asked sarcastically.

"Do I need one?"

"No . . . go ahead. What do I have to hide?"

Lieutenant Carlino inspected my bathroom and then wandered back into the bedroom, opening the closet doors and moving clothes to look into the darkest corners. Finally he got down on his hands and knees and peered beneath the bed. I knew he must be serious to actually risk putting a wrinkle or two into that white linen suit.

"Do you mind telling me what the hell you're looking for?" I asked.

"We had an anonymous tip that you've hidden a body in your room," he answered casually, standing back up and brushing off his knees.

"Oh, have you? Tell me, Lieutenant, was it a poison-pen letter or a whispered voice on the telephone?"

"A whispered voice." The lieutenant gave me a hard look. "How'd you know that?"

"I was joking!"

But Carlino wasn't laughing. He began pulling open the dresser drawers in the bedroom, riffling through shirts and socks and underwear.

"You think I cut the body into small pieces and hid it with my neckties?"

"Why not?" said the lieutenant tiredly. "In this town we've seen it all."

My mood was not improving. I was supposed to be receiving a reward for chivalry at that moment, not watching the police go through my things.

Whether the explanation was the sublimation of erotica, or something more mysterious, I don't know, but at that very second I got an idea for a melody. Perhaps I should explain that the reference to me in the *Guinness Book of World Records* as the most prolific composer of modern times is legitimate. In many cases—when I'm in a car or walking on the street—the melodies are suddenly just *there,* in my head, as if I were listening to a portable radio. Since I don't have access to a piano at such moments, I often dictate what is, in the music business, called a dummy lyric. Dummy lyrics consist of nonsense so far as thought or coherence are concerned. Their purpose is simply to serve as a memory aid. But when I'm at a piano and have recording equipment with me, no such device is necessary. I simply play the melody while recording it.

Creativity, of any sort, is still largely a mystery, even to psychologists and brain researchers who have given it careful study. In my own case, as regards the composition of music, my situation is somewhat like that of the idiot savant. Such people, as you probably know, are often mentally inferior in some ways but in one way have a remarkable gift. Sometimes it has to do with mathematics; in other cases it might have to do with painting, sculpture, piano playing, or composing music.

In any event, the melodic mood was now upon me. I hurried to the piano and sat down, feeling the slight excitement that always seizes me at such moments, and tenderly touched the keys. To my surprise, the result was absolute silence.

Swell. Here I felt as if I were about to compose what might be one of my better songs, and the instrument had somehow broken down. I ran my fingers over other parts of the keyboard, with the same results, except that on the right hand—or high end—a few notes sounded. The explanation for that sort of problem, of course, is invariably that something is touching the strings of the piano so that they cannot resonate. What idiot, I wondered, could have been careless or malicious enough to store something inside a piano? The top of the instrument was on low-stick, partly raised from the horizontal level. I stood up, stepped around to the right side of the keyboard, and peered in.

"Holy God!" I cried.

"What?" I heard Carlino say from the next room.

"Lieutenant, you'd better come in here."

He came out of the bedroom with one of my sport coats in his left hand. "What's up?"

"What did you say you were looking for?"

"A stiff," he said.

"We've found it."

The lieutenant hurried over, and together we lifted the piano top into the fully opened position. There, lying in an odd position, as if he had been forced into a space too small to accommodate his body, was one very dead third assistant director—Trip Johnson.

# chapter 35

**D**eath attracts some grim characters. Within minutes our suite was invaded by a small army of police, medical examiners, forensic experts, someone from the D.A.'s office, a police photographer who was using a Camcorder to videotape everything in sight—as well as a host of other droll characters whose functions I could barely guess but who stood in the background making cynical comments every now and then like some kind of Greek chorus.

"These yuppie kids don't bleed a hell of a lot," said one. "Not like that guy who got decapitated down on Fourteenth Street last night."

"You're dead either way," said another cheerlessly.

Joining this sample of officialdom was an assistant manager from downstairs who darted hither and thither, rubbing his hands and looking at us all with great sorrowful eyes as if to say, "Oh, what have you done to my lovely hotel?" I had a feeling he wouldn't be renting to another Hollywood movie company in the near future.

"Oh dear, oh dear," I heard him say. "The lobby's full of police and reporters, and the Duke of Donegal is arriving at any moment."

"Screw the Duke of Donegal!" said a member of the Greek chorus.

I was glad to get out of there. After a while Lieutenant Carlino took me down the hall to Zachary Holden's suite, which the police had requisitioned to handle the overflow of business. As the lieutenant and I sat on matching cream-colored sofas, I proceeded to tell him everything I knew—how I had followed Johnson the other day to Columbia University, what he had said about Jasper having AIDS—the works. Finding a corpse in my grand piano had me shaken, I have to admit, and I was ready to be fully cooperative with the police. Carlino listened somberly to my account, occasionally making notes on a small pad.

"Poor kid," I sighed. "I can't say I liked him much, but for a young life to be cut off so abruptly . . ."

"He was asking for it," put in the lieutenant. "Not only was he pushing drugs, but he was also a blackmailer. People like that generally come to a bad end."

"I don't know. I think he was just trying to get even for having a father who didn't want him."

"Mr. Allen, why did you kill Trip Johnson?" The lieutenant's voice was very casual, almost as if he were asking for the correct time.

I stopped in midsentence, my mouth hanging open. And here I had believed we were having a nice, friendly chat.

"Lieutenant Carlino, do you really think I would strangle someone, stuff him in my piano, and then actually be so stupid as to try to play the damned thing during a visit from the police?"

Carlino leaned forward on the couch and gazed at me with a sort of sad resignation. "It's my experience that many killers unconsciously seek some way to confess. Perhaps you were drawn to the piano as a way to—well, express the emotion of guilt? Deep in your soul you were tired of the charade? You wanted the body found so you could be at peace?"

Although I'm not Jewish, nothing could express my reaction of the moment better than a soft rendering of the ancient Yiddish word *oy.*

The lieutenant scowled and rose from his sofa. "Mr. Allen, until further notice, don't leave New York."

"You already said that after the *last* murder."

"Well, it goes double now."

"Lieutenant," I said, "I don't want to sound self-serving here, but I do have some sort of reputation. Doesn't the fact that for the past sixty-seven years I have never been involved with any sort of criminal activity mean anything?"

"I'll tell you something I've learned about at least some

murderers," Carlino said. "When they're finally unmasked, a lot of people who know them, sometimes very well, are surprised as hell. Remember the schmuck, I think it was in Chicago, who killed all those kids and buried their bodies under his house? That son of a bitch actually had a great reputation. He did charity work, helped with kids' organizations, worked—for free—as a clown at little parties and at hospitals, even had his picture taken with the First Lady at some community thing he organized. And how many times have we heard about some guy who has just wiped out his whole family with a rifle that he was a good, churchgoing boy, a model student?"

"Okay, okay," I said. "I've got your point."


Zachary and Suzanne found me a few minutes later, sitting dejectedly on the sofa, my head in my hands.

"Poor Tripper," said Zach. "I told him no good would come of being the company spy."

"What do you mean, company spy?"

Zach seemed reluctant to continue. "Probably I shouldn't be saying this, but I guess I can tell you two. There was some money missing from the budget, and Trip was supposed to keep his eye on things for his father."

I sat up straight. "What? Missing from where? How much?"

"I don't know exactly. Trip and I . . . well, we got a little loaded one night on a few too many beers. He told me some money had been stolen from the payroll account and that his father had asked him to keep his eyes open and report back to him secretly."

"He told you his father was Nash Stuart?"

Zach nodded. "Sure. He said I wasn't supposed to tell anyone—it was a big secret and all. But I could tell Trip was actually pretty proud."

My mind was working overtime. "But he didn't give you any more details about the theft?"

"No, he left it pretty vague. And if he told me, I probably wouldn't remember anyway. As I said, we were both pretty zonked."

"I can't imagine you drunk," said Suzanne, looking at him as if she were seeing him for the first time.

"Well, I was depressed. A certain person I cared about didn't seem to care about me. . . ."

"I didn't realize . . ."

The couple appeared not to remember that I was in the room. I felt as if I were watching an episode of *Time and Tide.*

I definitely felt like a third wheel. Besides, what Zach had told me about missing payroll funds had started my thoughts churning, so I stood up to leave and find Jayne. But Zach took hold of my arm.

"Look, Steve, I really need to tell you something," he said. "Now that both you and Suzanne are here at the same time . . . well, I thought this might be a good time to . . . well, to confess."

"Confess?" I was surprised and not too sure I had the stomach for any new revelations of intrigue or evil. Zach couldn't quite look either of us in the eye as he sat down in exactly the spot recently vacated by Lieutenant Carlino.

"This is pretty hard to talk about . . . but I know I'll feel better if I tell you."

"Don't be afraid," Suzanne said gently as she sat down beside him.

"Well, Steve, remember I told you Bernie had blackmailed me into doing *Murder in Manhattan?* And I wouldn't say what he had on me? Well . . . oh, God, this is so . . . embarrassing."

"Go on," Suzanne said. She smiled encouragingly, her eyes sincere and nonjudgmental. I even thought I saw a faint glimmer of affection in them. She smiled encouragingly.

Zach sat there, staring at the carpet for so long I finally cleared my throat to remind him we were waiting.

As if the sound were a cue, the words finally rushed out. "The truth is, I'm a coward. I was kicked off my high school football team because I couldn't bear to be hurt."

There was another long silence as Suzanne and I waited for the lurid confession to continue. Slowly it dawned on us that there was no more to follow.

"Zach, no sensitive person wants to be hurt," said Suzanne

uncertainly. Probably she had been hoping for something more juicy—like that he was a kleptomaniac or ax murderer.

Zach stared at nothing in particular and talked mostly to himself. "There was one particular Saturday game," he said. "The score was fourteen to ten in the fourth quarter, with Coleville, our arch rival, in the lead. I had injured a couple of ribs in practice earlier that week and probably shouldn't have been playing at all.

"Anyway, Coleville had the ball on our thirty-five-yard line with just minutes to play. It looked like we were out of luck. And then they fumbled! I happened to be the wrong man at the right spot at the right time. The football actually rolled right to my feet. I picked it up, heard the entire school cheer me on, and then . . . and then . . ."

"Yes?" I prodded.

"And then I panicked, bumped into one of my own men, got confused, and ran the wrong way!"

A tiny smile played at the corners of Suzanne's mouth. She patted Zach's hand in sympathy as he continued his confession.

"I saw the entire offensive line of Coleville High moving down the field to squash me, and I—I lost it. I didn't know where I was going! Well, I tell you, my last year of high school was hell with all the damned kidding I got."

"It sounds like you did the perfectly reasonable thing. I would certainly run if a bunch of gorillas were after me," Suzanne said.

Zach signed. "But then, you see, I became a big deal on TV. Here I am, the lead in this detective series, where I'm supposed to be some incredibly macho stud—jumping off buildings, beating up bad guys, crashing cars, rescuing drowning children—you see how bad it would look if word got out I was really chicken?"

"And Bernie got hold of this information?" I asked.

Zach nodded. "He found an old school newspaper with the photo of me running the wrong way, with the entire Coleville team on my heels. It would have ruined me."

I wasn't sure whether to laugh or cry.

"If you're a coward, it's only because you have too much

imagination," decided Suzanne, taking his hand firmly in hers.

"No, I'm just a . . . plain old coward." Zach sighed.

"You weren't the night *Easy Money* went down," I reminded him. "You were helping people into life rafts, you stayed behind until everyone was off that boat. That's not the action of a coward."

"Do you think so?"

"I know so. Listen, Zach, football's just a game, but when the going got rough and people's lives were at stake, you came through like a real hero."

"Only a fool is never afraid," said Suzanne, moving closer to him on the sofa. It was looking as if Zach would replace Clancy in the gallery of flawed human souls requiring her concern.

"Anyway, football is a barbaric and sexist sport. I'm *glad* you're more sensitive than that, Zach."

"You know, I cry at sad movies," he said shyly.

"You're supposed to. So do I!"

I got out of there and let the newfound lovers bare their souls without me.

# chapter 36

**N**ashville Stuart lived in a brand-new skyscraper on the East River, which rose in a dramatic series of terraces and curves like some futuristic Aztec temple. I'm not sure what they call architecture like this anymore, but if you stand on the Upper East Side of New York and look up into the sky, you'll see what I mean—a new generation of construction that defies at least my description. The buildings are enormous and strange; they seem modern yet somehow ancient at the same time.

I took a taxi over to Stuart's futuristic digs on Sunday night, leaving Jayne behind to greet Jasper's wife, Emily, who had just flown in from London. To tell the truth, I was just as glad to leave Jayne behind. The level of danger had risen much too high for comfort.

I had called ahead and Nash hadn't really wanted to see me. When I had mentioned it concerned his son Trip, however, he grudgingly agreed to the visit.

"Steve," said Nash coolly, meeting me at his front door. His penthouse, forty-five floors in the air, had floor-to-ceiling glass and wraparound terraces looking out onto the bejeweled nighttime skyline of Manhattan. In the midst of all this splendor, Nash himself seemed small, fragile, and sad. I briefly met an attractively blond, middle-aged wife, who had a subtle southern accent, and a handsome preppie son in his early twenties. The son had gentle manners and spent a few moments telling me he was down for a few days from Cambridge, where he was attending Harvard Law School. It was hard to look at this polite young man without thinking of Trip, the other son, who had been neither polite nor fortunate.

Nash got me away from his family as fast as he could. We went into his private office, where he sat down behind his desk with a tired sigh. I took a seat on a couch that was so soft, I was afraid I might float out the floor-to-ceiling window into the New York night.

"Well, I still haven't told them," he admitted unhappily.

"About Trip being dead? Or Trip being your son?"

"Neither. You must think I'm an awful coward, Steve, but when you keep a secret as many years as I have . . . well, it's hard to look your wife in the eye one day and say, 'Guess what, dear, there's something I've been meaning to tell you for nineteen years, so you'd better brace yourself.' "

"Would your wife really be that shocked?"

"She's an old-fashioned woman . . . but I suppose there's no way I can avoid telling her now." He pondered for a moment, then added more as an afterthought, "Poor Trip. I guess I've really messed up all around."

I made a vague sound of sympathy. I wasn't there to judge Nash Stuart, but at the same time it was difficult to be supportive.

"When did you learn you had an extra child?" I asked.

"Oh, Sharon—that's Trip's mother—told me when she was pregnant. We'd been having an affair for nearly a year, and when she said she was pregnant, I tried to get her to have an abortion, but she didn't believe in that. Finally I gave her enough money to go to California and have the baby. I never heard from her again."

"She didn't try to contact you?"

Nash shook his head. "I never even found out what became of the pregnancy. I suppose I could have tracked her down in California, but frankly I was relieved when she didn't call. Sharon was an attractive young woman, but I wasn't in love with her. I rather imagined she'd had the abortion after all, or maybe met a man in California who was taking care of her and the child. Actually I didn't think too much about it one way or the other, to tell the truth. Sharon was the kind of woman who wouldn't be without a man for very long, and gradually I put the whole thing out of mind. I nearly succeeded in forgetting I might have a stray child somewhere . . . until about a year ago."

"At which point Trip came to see you?"

"That's right. At first I thought it was some sort of hoax, but he had photographs of himself and his mother." Nash bowed his head. "He even looked like her." He sighed heavily. "I sure haven't been feeling very good about myself lately."

"But you gave Trip a job. You tried to help him," I suggested. He stared at me bleakly.

"What else could I do? Frankly, I would have been happier if—if he'd just gone away."

"What happened to his mother?"

"Killed in an auto accident near San Francisco two years ago. Trip was more or less an orphan."

"I don't mean to be blunt, but was he blackmailing you?"

To my surprise, Nash smiled. "A little," he admitted. "I can't say I blame him much. The kid actually had a lot of spunk. He let me know that either I helped him out or he'd go to my wife and tell his tale."

"Did that worry you?"

"Look, the police were here asking the same question this afternoon. Maybe they think if Trip were blackmailing me I might have had a motive to murder him. But the truth was I rather admired the kid for his fighting spirit. My own family . . . well, they're very genteel, but in some ways our blood has become a little thin."

"Do you have any idea who might have killed your son?"

"My son," he said experimentally. It brought a sad smile to his lips; then he shook his head. "I guess I was so concerned with my grand entrance as film director, I wasn't paying much attention to anything else. It was childish of me, I suppose, but when Bernie died, I found I wanted to make *Murder in Manhattan* myself. Maybe it was a way to get even with Barnes—he'd always treated me like I was just a money machine with no artistic sensibility. So I decided I was going to finish the film and win the Cannes Film Festival—some joke, eh? First Jasper collapses on the set, and now Trip is dead! This has been one disaster after another, and I'm thinking it's about time to turn in my director's chair and get back to what I know."

Nash Stuart looked genuinely humbled by events. Even with his wealth and the luxury of his life-style, I felt sorry for him.

"You know, I've heard an odd story—I heard there was some money missing from the budget."

Nash sat up straighter in his chair and gave me a piercing look. "You know Bernie," he said casually. "If there was a way to waste money, he would find it."

"No, this is a little different," I said. "I heard some money had actually been stolen from the payroll."

"Where did you hear this?" he asked softly.

"Does it matter?"

"It sure as hell does! This is the kind of rumor that can absolutely destroy a company. Before you know it, you have your stockholders up in arms, a police investigation, who knows what else."

"Is it true? About the money?"

Nash deflated. He sat back in his chair looking old and tired. "It's true. On top of everything else, we seem to have a thief in our midst. Wonderful, isn't it? Bernie was the one who spotted it, oh, I guess about a week before the boating mishap. He was going through the production accounts and discovered seventy-five thousand he couldn't account for."

"*Bernie* discovered the loss?" I asked, thinking I must have heard wrong.

"Sure. Are you surprised? He was extravagant, but he was no fool. He liked to know what was being spent where. That seventy-five grand was missing all right. I've been keeping the whole thing quiet, but my auditors can't find a trace of the money. It simply vanished—into someone's pocket, I assume."

"And you asked Trip maybe to do some spying for you?"

"I asked Trip to keep his eyes open. I wouldn't call it spying exactly, but I suggested if he heard anything about the missing money, it would be nice if he passed the information on to me. Hell, I thought it might bring us closer."

"And did he manage to find out anything?"

Nash shook his head. "No. He was friendly with most everybody, cast and crew, but nothing. He was going to continue to ask around, though. . . . You don't think *that* was the reason he was killed, do you?"

I thought of the third assistant director trying to blackmail his way forward in the world and how you can stir up a lot of motives for murder when you live such a life, but I didn't want to say that to even such a reluctant father.

I stood up from the couch and shook Nash's hand.

"You—er—you're going to keep poking around in all this, are you?" he asked.

"Definitely," I told him. "I don't like murder under normal circumstances, and I'm particularly angry that some people think I did it!"

Nash wished me luck and showed me to the door. For all his genteel southern charm, I had the impression he would rather I fall forty-five floors down the elevator shaft than have me look any deeper into his life. Somehow it all left an unpleasant taste in my mouth. I took the elevator to the ground floor and walked out through a brightly lit lobby, past a small squad of uniformed doormen wearing white gloves, and into the cool spring night.

My mind racing, I decided to walk. I found myself on a narrow crosstown street with huge buildings rising up on either side. I put up the collar of my trench coat and began to walk at a more energetic pace. This close to the East River the streets were dark and deserted of pedestrians. Steam came up eerily from the subterranean manholes. I had forgotten how lonely the crosstown streets could be at night. I love to walk, but I realized in this instance it might have been wiser to take a cab.

I began whistling a Jimmy Van Heusen tune to keep my courage up. Looking at the huge, looming buildings pressing overhead gave me an interesting idea: This was a city, after all, where money was everything. Mere human sentiments seemed dwarfed by the great skyscrapers rising into the air.

*"Damn!"* I said aloud to the silent buildings. *"It's not the sexual shenanigans at all, it's the money!"*

Up to this time I had unearthed what I had mistakenly believed to be dozens of motives for murder, but I had a sudden sense that the missing seventy-five thousand was my first real clue. If I could find out who took the money, I was positive I would know who had murdered Bernie *and* Trip.

I was so excited by my discovery, I was only peripherally aware of the dark shape of a long, black Cadillac limousine trailing at my side. I didn't think much about it until I began crossing Second Avenue at 58th Street. I had just stepped off the curb when I heard the roar of the powerful engine and turned, stunned, to see two headlights bearing down on me. I jumped out of the way as the limousine hurled past. I felt a great rush of wind as I fell backward and braced myself for the impact with the pavement, but New York was experiencing one of its famous garbage strikes and I landed harmlessly against a stack of leaking black plastic bags stuffed with something soft—orange rinds and eggshells, I guessed from the smell.

I lay catching my breath and watching the taillights of the receding limousine, wondering who was being so bothered by my questions that they wished me dead.

# chapter 37

I rode the elevator up to The Plaza's ninth floor with a silver-haired woman and a white-haired gentleman in evening clothes who did their best to pretend I wasn't there. To be honest, it was embarrassing to smell like garbage, but there wasn't much I could do about it until I reached my room.

I wasn't sure what I'd find at my suite—presumably the cops and the corpse would be long gone, and Jayne would be back from meeting Emily at the airport. I was surprised to hear piano music coming from the sitting room as I turned the key. Opening the door, I found Lieutenant Carlino sitting by himself playing a pretty little tune on the white baby grand.

"Oh, sorry, Mr. Allen," he said, standing up and looking embarrassed. "Jeez, I lost track of the time. We've been finished for ages, I just couldn't resist trying out the instrument. I have only a small upright at home."

"Go ahead," I told him. "What you were playing sounded interesting."

"Thanks. Little something I wrote. Hey, what's that smell?" The lieutenant sniffed the air and wrinkled his nose.

"What smell?" I countered innocently. "Go ahead and play your song."

Carlino settled back down onto the bench and played a long arpeggio. The melody was quite pretty. I was beginning to think I had been judging him too harshly.

"Bravo." I said when he was done. "Very nice."

"You think so?"

"Absolutely, but let me show you one little thing. . . ."

I sat with the lieutenant at the piano and showed him a

classier way to get from a C chord to an F-major seventh, adding to the C a flat seventh with an augmented fifth, which makes the chord want to slide up to the F in a rather tantalizing way. This is a classic Rodgers and Hart effect; other composers have used the device, but it was new to Carlino.

"Pardon me, sir," he said, "but have you been rolling in the garbage?"

"I had a little accident," I told him. "Actually, a speeding limousine tried to run me over. I had to jump out of the way and fell on top of some garbage bags."

"That doesn't sound like an accident."

"How can you tell in New York?"

"You haven't been asking people a lot of tough questions, have you? If you get too nosy, you know, the murderer might decide to silence you for good."

"I thought you'd decided *I* was the killer!"

To my surprise, the lieutenant smiled in an altogether disarming way.

"I'm sorry if I've given you a hard time, but that goes with my job. I was only trying to put enough pressure on you so you'd be cooperative."

"Then you don't think . . ."

"That you're the murderer? Of course not. What a crazy idea."

I laughed with the sheer relief of finding myself a free man. It hadn't been much fun being a murder suspect, I can tell you. Lieutenant Carlino was suddenly looking like a much more human sort than I had imagined.

"Have you had dinner yet?" I asked. He shook his head, and I told him to order us up something from room service while I took a quick shower and changed clothes. Ten minutes later I felt like my old self again.

Carlino was watching a news channel on television. I returned to the sitting room just as the room-service waiter was wheeling in our cart. The lieutenant had ordered us some sole amandine, rice, Caesar salads, and a bottle of California chardonnay.

"Here's to catching the bad guys," I said, raising my wine-glass in a toast to my new pal.

"May they rot in jail," he agreed. "You sure you're not mad about my giving you a hard time?"

"Not at all. You were just doing your job, right?"

"It isn't easy being a cop sometimes. Hassling people all the time. Always having to be suspicious. No one likes you. You become a kind of breed apart from the rest of humanity. That's why I have this secret desire to be a songwriter—bring joy to the world instead of pain."

Talking about pain reminded me of a subject I'd been meaning to bring up. "Lieutenant," I said, "have you ever considered suicide?"

He looked up quickly from his salad. "Hey, my life isn't *that* bad!"

"No, not you. I'm talking about Barnes."

Carlino blinked, not following my drift.

"This is something Annie Locks brought up. She said Bernie had crazy mood swings, up and down, and that maybe there's a possibility that he committed suicide. According to Annie, he tried an overdose of sleeping pills a few months before *Murder in Manhattan* started shooting."

"As a matter of fact, Natasha—Sergeant Dimitriev—found out about the sleeping pill episode. But come on, Steve, no one commits suicide by stabbing themselves in the back!"

"That's what I said," I told him, and then went on to describe Annie's theory about how Barnes was a master of illusion and that it might be just like him to kill himself in a way that would make life extremely uncomfortable for the unwitting "murder suspects" left behind.

The lieutenant listened carefully, a vaguely astonished expression on his face.

"Well," he said. "That's quite interesting, only there's one big problem with your theory, of course."

"Of course," I agreed, not actually seeing the problem, but not wanting to be left behind in the game of logical deduction. Then it hit me why Bernie's death had to be murder. "If he had

killed himself, the body would have been found in the stateroom, where I last saw it."

"Exactly. It sure as hell didn't go anywhere by itself. We
questioned young Johnson pretty carefully, and his testimony
agreed with yours. He went down below deck after you talked
with him, and he saw Barnes's body in the stateroom just as you
described it. The point is, the boat went down in *one* piece to the
ocean floor. If it had broken up, we might suppose the body had
spilled out of the stateroom and been taken away on the currents. But as it is . . ."

"The murderer had to come back and dispose of the corpse
himself. But why?"

"Ah!" said the dapper lieutenant, sipping his chardonnay.
"Probably because he—or she—forgot something. There could
have been fingerprints on the knife, for example, or some other
clue left behind that needed to be taken care of. But, of course,
the boat was sinking, and there wasn't a lot of time. My theory
is the murderer was already hiding down below somewhere, and
after Trip left, he—or she—simply dumped the body out the
stateroom window and then joined the rest of you on deck."

"You keep saying he or she. Do you really believe a woman
would have been capable of lifting someone as heavy as Barnes
and pushing him out a window?"

The lieutenant shrugged. "You'd be surprised what people
can do when they're desperate."

"But wouldn't the body have turned up by now?"

"Not necessarily. I told you how tricky the currents can be
off lower Manhattan. Remember, you have the Hudson River
spilling out into the ocean, as well as the flow from the East
River. A week from now we might find the body washed up at
the feet of the Statue of Liberty, or it could be swept out to sea
and never found at all . . . this fish is excellent, by the way."

I put my fork down. All this talk about a corpse floating
around the ocean had destroyed my appetite for fish. Carlino
looked at me and laughed.

"You seem a little green. Maybe we should talk about something else. Tell me something, do you understand women?"

"Lieutenant, women remain one serious mystery. That's the reason we write songs about them."

He agreed, pouring us both another glass of wine. "I mean, take Natasha, for example . . . if you don't mind my talking about myself."

"Not at all."

"Do you have any idea what it's like to have a partner who happens to be a very attractive young woman? We're both single, but we're cops, right? So what am I supposed to do? Ignore her?"

"You do a pretty good job of it."

"Well, I *try*. It's bad enough if your partner's a guy, you know? You spend so much time together, after a while you start acting like a married couple. But with a *woman* . . . a gorgeous woman at that . . . I don't mind telling you I'm goin' a little nuts. And she doesn't make it easy to stay professional now that she's started coming to work in all these nice little outfits that really show off her figure. And there's that new hairstyle. I don't understand what's come over her."

I knew, of course, what had come over Sergeant Dimitriev, but I kept my mouth shut. "Natasha seems very nice," I said instead. "Why don't you just ask her out?"

"Date my *partner?* Can you imagine what that would be like? Say we had a fight, and then right in the middle of it we got a Code Three on the radio and had to go arrest somebody? If you were a criminal, would *you* want to be arrested by two cops having a domestic quarrel?"

"Maybe either you or the sergeant should request a transfer. If you weren't partners anymore, you could date each other and fight all you wanted to."

Carlino pondered this for a moment. "That's logical. Only I'd miss seeing her every day, and besides she's a hell of a cop." He poured himself another half-glass of wine and tipped the bottle my way, but I shook my head.

Jayne found us about an hour later—sitting at the baby grand, the lieutenant playing the left hand chords and me improvising on top, both of us singing a ragged duet of "Ain't Misbehavin'."

It was looking like the beginning of a beautiful friendship, but I still wasn't going to let him solve the case all by himself. As it happened, I saw an interesting possibility Carlino had either overlooked or was keeping from me for cagey reasons of his own:

What if Trip Johnson, late third assistant, had been lying through his teeth? What if, on that fateful night *Easy Money* had sunk to the ocean floor, Trip had gone below deck and had found no body in the stateroom as he later claimed? This could mean Trip was in cahoots with the killer, who had already shoved Bernie out the window.

Or another possibility: Trip himself was the killer and used the time below deck to get rid of Bernie's corpse as well as any incriminating evidence that might tie him to the crime.

This was the theory I began to favor, but it left one rather big problem: Who, then, killed Trip Johnson? And why?

# chapter 38

"That man!" Jayne said after Carlino finally left us a little before midnight. "Do you know that, after all the money Natasha's spent on clothes, he's *still* ignoring her?"

"Perhaps he's more interested than he lets on. The poor man *is* trying to solve a double murder, you know."

"Has he been talking about her?" asked Jayne suspiciously.

I smiled innocently. "Would I betray the confidence of a friend? Besides, I think it best to allow the police to work out their own internal affairs. By the way, how is Emily?"

"How should she be? Her husband's dying of an incurable disease, and now he confesses his twenty-five-year affair with a wardrobe woman. Luckily she knew about the affair all the time, of course."

"She did?"

"Steve darling, women only pretend to be stupid. The British simply deal with these matters in a calmer way than we Americans. She knew Jasper would never actually leave her, so it seemed best to just let it blow over."

"But it didn't," I reminded her.

"It has now. A dying man has a way of returning to the comforts of wife and family."

"I wonder if the poor man is going to be able to finish this movie."

"I think so. Even that horrible publicist is keeping quiet, and, according to Emily, Jasper is only in the beginning stages of the disease."

"Then why did he collapse on the set, I wonder."

"The hospital can't seem to find any *medical* reason," Jayne said, staring at me meaningfully. "They're going to hold him one more day for observation, though."

"Maybe I was right all along. Jasper may have simply had a case of evasiveness."

"By the way, I saw Mimi Day downstairs in the lobby," said Jayne, making one of her out-of-nowhere observations. "You really should do something about her."

"Do something? What is there to do?"

"Talk to her, darling. Be nice. She's just lost her husband, and she has a terrible crush on you—anybody can see that."

"Being nice would only encourage her."

"Poor woman, I feel sorry for her," Jayne said.

We sat up in bed and read a few minutes before falling asleep. I soon found myself reading the same sentence over and over without comprehension.

I finally laid the book down and closed my eyes, only to see a long black car rushing at me from a side street. I knew that whoever had killed Trip and stuffed him in my piano, whoever had followed me tonight and tried to run me down—that person had to be someone very close. Someone who knew all my movements.

I awoke in the early morning from a terrible dream in which I was running through empty streets, chased by some nameless fear. Though it was only a dream, I was not reassured.

# chapter 39

*urder in Manhattan* was being produced by Nashville Film Enterprises, a branch of Black Gold Entertainment, Inc., which in turn was a wholly owned subsidiary of the Aardvark Group—which owned everything from oil wells to a fast-food hamburger empire, a chain of department stores, a retirement community in Texas, a commuter airline, and several U.S. congressmen. I find it exhausting even imagining running a business conglomerate of such size, but this is the modern world—the big get bigger, and the small get gobbled up.

On Monday morning I decided to visit the production offices of Nashville Film Enterprises on the thirty-third floor of the Aardvark Building on Seventh Avenue and 54th Street. I was hot on a paper trail. I'm no financial wizard, but I knew that seventy-five thousand dollars could not disappear without a trace, even in such a chaotic production as *Murder in Manhattan.* Someone somewhere had to authorize a fraudulent expenditure, and perhaps if I started digging, it would come to light.

So I showed up unannounced in a muted, well-carpeted reception area and asked a muted, well-carpeted receptionist if I could have a word with a Mr. Donald Tyson, the company accountant.

"I'm sorry, Mr. Allen, but do you have an appointment?"

"I'm a spontaneous fellow," I admitted. The young woman gave me a skeptical look, but after a five-minute wait spontaneity paid off. I was led past a beehive of busy workers in little cubicles toward a narrow office dominated by a tinted window overlooking 54th Street. Donald Tyson was a balding, middle-aged man with chubby hands and a bulging belly. His shirt-sleeves were rolled up for action. I found him sitting behind a computer terminal deep in the land of money. I had a feeling not too many of my fellow performers had ventured this far into the inner workings of film production. Tyson seemed pleased, though a bit flustered by my visit.

"Mr. Allen, how nice to meet you. Are you having any problems with your per diem?"

"My per diem's fine," I assured him, referring to the money for living expenses provided by the company for my stay in New York. "Frankly, I'm hoping you can help me out with a matter that's a bit delicate."

Tyson had a round and pleasant face. He smiled ever so nicely. "You need a cash advance, perhaps? You're having trouble cashing a California check."

"Oh, no. What I'm hoping for, actually, is a little information."

I began by reminding the accountant that two people connected with *Murder in Manhattan* had already died and that there was, therefore, an urgent need to get to the bottom of this before the title of the movie began to seem like a prediction. Tyson listened sympathetically but seemed unsure how he might help.

"It's all quite terrible, Mr. Allen. I hardly know what to say. I'm rather desk bound, far removed from all the excitement. I'd never even met Mr. Barnes or this poor young fellow, Trip Johnson. . . ."

"Be that as it may, Mr. Tyson, the answer to these crimes may be right here in this room."

"Goodness!"

"In your computer." He followed my gaze to the video terminal, which he then stared at as if the screen might momentarily light up and begin printing out dark, bizarre secrets.

"The computer? No, I just had the whole system cleaned and debugged not more than six weeks ago."

"I'm not talking software, sir. I'm talking hard theft—seventy-five grand, as a matter of fact, which has been stolen from the production payroll account."

Donald Tyson sat up straight. "That's a serious accusation!"

"I know this is a touchy matter, but I'm literally begging you to tell me the truth. More lives could be lost if we don't act quickly. You must tell me what you found when you checked out the information Mr. Stuart gave you."

The man's face sagged. He gripped the edge of the desk and deliberately calmed his voice. "Mr. Allen, I swear I don't know what you're talking about. I know there've been problems with this production, but I've never heard so much as a whisper about any missing money. How much did you say? Seventy-five grand?"

"You mean Nash didn't tell you?"

"No."

"Aren't you the production accountant? Wouldn't you be the first one to be told?"

"Yes. But I—you must be making some kind of mistake."

"There's no mistake," I said. "Nash told me himself about the missing money. He was having his son—that is, Trip Johnson—check it out."

"His *son?*" Tyson's voice cracked with wonderment. "But if there was money missing, surely he would have come straight to me."

"You would think so. But you're absolutely sure—"

"I promise you—I've heard nothing of money missing from the payroll account, or any other account used for *Murder in Manhattan.* This is insane! Mr. Stuart should have called me immediately, night or day."

"And yet he didn't," I remarked softly. "Which is very curious . . ."

"I think," Tyson said, "that this really isn't something I should be discussing with an . . . outsider."

"Just tell me one thing, sir: If someone *were* to steal money from the production, how could it be done?"

"Well . . ."

"Please. This could be a matter of life or death."

He wavered, but propriety won out. He offered his hand in a friendly but definite farewell.

"If you find anything, do you think you could give me a call?" I asked in parting.

"If I find anything, I'll give the *police* a call. You can count on that."

I left the Aardvark Building with the unpleasant feeling that Lieutenant Carlino would be the one benefiting from my inspired detective work, but those were the breaks. At least I had a new mystery to consider: If Bernie Barnes had indeed gone to Nash with the news of the theft, why hadn't Nash then gone to his chief accountant, the one person in the company who could most easily check it out?

There were several possible answers to this riddle, and none of them very nice. I meditated on the various possibilities while making my way on foot back to Fifth Avenue.

In an enormous city like New York, you might imagine you'd rarely run into people you knew on the streets, but this is a fallacy, at least as regards the midtown area. I run into people I know all the time in New York, so I was not in the least surprised when, on Fifth Avenue, I saw a familiar young sex goddess wrapped in a fur coat scampering into Saks followed by a uniformed chauffeur. On a sudden impulse I decided to tail the lovely La Volpa. The impulse, I assure you, had less to do with the fascinating way she looked from the rear than with the fact that she had been Bernie's constant companion the last days of his life.

La Volpa led me up four flights of escalators to ladies' lingerie, and here I made my stand.

# chapter 40

**M**s. La Volpa was holding up a black silk semi-transparent negligee, her lips set in their usual pout, apparently trying to decide if the garment was worthy of her. Young and beautiful though she may be, there was something about the way she inspected the piece of clothing that reminded me of an old Italian crone poking at a live chicken in a marketplace.

"Eh, Guido, what you think?"

Guido was the uniformed chauffeur, a handsome young man with a deep suntan. He shook his head. "I should think white would be a better color, *Signora*," he said.

La Volpa carelessly threw the black negligee at the chauffeur for him to return to the rack. This is when she noticed me, smiling from between the bras and the panties in what I hoped was a strictly platonic manner. She gazed at me apparently without immediate recognition.

"Steve Allen," I reminded her.

"Ah! Meester Allen! How nice," she said without much conviction.

Victoria is the kind of young woman who simply does not notice others unless they happen to be young and male and attractive, like Guido, or someone who could help with her film career, like Bernie. Since I fit into neither of these categories, the beautiful young woman had scarcely glanced my way in the more than two weeks we had been working together. It was unnerving to the ego, of course, but one survives such disappointments.

"What you think of this?" she asked, holding up the briefest piece of shimmering flimflam I had ever seen.

"It would be ungentlemanly to say," I replied.

La Volpa giggled, reminding me of the fact that, despite her sophisticated beauty, she was still only nineteen years old.

"Ms. La Volpa," I said in my most fatherly manner, "I've been hoping we could have a little chat. About Bernie," I added, so she wouldn't get the wrong idea.

"Poor Bernardo!" said the young goddess. "He was fat bastard, but he make me laugh so!"

"He made all of us laugh, except when he was being a blackmailing, conniving, miserable son of a bitch."

"Excuse my English, please . . . what is this word *blackmail?*"

"It means threatening to tell the world you were a prostitute in Milan if you didn't consent to appear in his film."

"Ah!" said La Volpa, holding up a pink silk robe with lots of ruffles. "Eet is always good to learn a new word, I think."

She continued rather passionately pulling out garments from the rack, one after another, and now handing them—for some reason—to me.

"Come," she said. "We will try these on. Guido, you keep guard for the paparazzi."

La Volpa imperiously led the way toward the dressing rooms with me following, a bundle of frilly lace in my arms.

Well, actually, there were two of me following. One was a perfectly sensible gentleman in his mid-sixties, married and certainly not foolish enough to have an erotic interest in a former prostitute, however youthful, flirtatious, and dazzlingly beautiful. The other me, however, was a normal human male. It was this Mr. Hyde who at the moment was controlling the movements of my eyes and determining the objects of their interest. But recognizing what a rascally fellow this persona was, my better self quickly shouldered him out of the way. Despite the fact that I stood outside the dressing room door for the next several minutes, handing young Victoria one alluring garment after another, I kept my concentration firmly on what was becoming almost routine detective work.

"Clancy told you this nasty thing about me, I think," she said from inside the dressing room. "About me being . . . how you say? Prostitute in Milano."

"Does it really matter?"

Her face appeared briefly in the doorway as she accepted a salmon-colored robe with a fur collar. "I was young, poor, and very foolish," she said sadly. "There was no one to look after La Volpa but La Volpa."

"My dear, I'm really not judging. I'm interested only in finding out who stabbed Mr. Barnes in his spacious back and stuffed Trip Johnson in my piano."

"Poor Trip," the young girl sighed. "Where will I get my little relaxing pills now, I wonder?"

"Ms. La Volpa, you were seeing Bernie how long before he died?"

Again the face appeared in the dressing room door. "Eet was almost two weeks," she said with a languid look. "I suppose you think this was one of my longest love affairs ever?"

"And he . . ."

"How he make me laugh!"

"Did he ever talk about money?"

"I never charge him. Not once!"

"No, no, I'm talking about money missing out of the production budget. Seventy-five thousand dollars, to be exact."

She narrowed her eyes and disappeared back inside the dressing room with a new assortment of nightwear to try on.

"I tell him, 'Bernie, donna be so damned cheap! Seventy-five thousan' dollar, you canna hardly buy a nice car.' "

"So he did talk about the money?"

You can imagine how difficult detective work can be at such a time. An elderly woman had just gone into the adjoining dressing room, flashing me a dreadfully disapproving look as she went past. I'm sure she thought I was paying for the garments Victoria was trying on, and probably recognized me as well.

"Victoria, about the money," I whispered. "What exactly did Bernie tell you?"

She opened the door wearing a burgundy-colored bra, panties, and matching transparent robe. "You like this?" she inquired.

"Yes! No! Victoria, what I'm interested in right now is the

money. Bernie found there was seventy-five grand missing from the budget, and he went to Nashville Stuart. What did he tell you about it?"

La Volpa's lower lip curled petulantly. "If I tell you, then you will keep my little secret? About Milano?"

"As far as I'm concerned, Milano doesn't exist."

"Then I tell you. Bernie found the money ees gone, and he ees very happy. He tells me, 'Sugar plum, from now on Stuart ees in palm of my hand. We make-a this damned movie any way we like!' "

"I don't understand. Why should Nash be in the palm of his hand?"

The girl shrugged. The subject did not seem to interest her greatly. "All I know ees we laugh and drink-a champagne all night long."

"And you didn't hear anything more about it?"

The goddess shook her head.

My mind was racing. *Could Nash have taken the money himself?*

I tried a couple more questions, but it was obvious the young woman knew nothing further. I mumbled my thanks, and, handing the garter belt, black lace stockings, and fluffy little robes I was still holding to the chauffeur, wandered away.

I was left with the same puzzling question: *If Nash didn't take the money, why the hell hadn't he gone to his accountant to demand an immediate investigation?*

And why did Bernie, by simply knowing about the theft, now have the producer in the palm of his hand?

I was somewhere between handbags and silk scarves when the truth hit me: Nash wasn't the thief! It was Trip, his secret son, who had stolen the money!

I still wasn't sure what it all meant, but I felt a big part of the puzzle had finally been fitted into place.

# chapter 41

**B**ack at The Plaza I found three waiters and a maid cleaning up the remnants of an impromptu brunch for nine Jayne had thrown in our sitting room while I was gone. From the leftovers I observed being wheeled away on various room-service carts, I could see this had been no bran muffin affair.

"Pancakes?" I inquired ruefully.

"Crepes suzette," said my wife, "preceded by fresh strawberries and accompanied by California champagne."

"Hmph! What a moment I chose to go off detecting."

"You would have hated it, darling—just a bunch of women chatting away. I was only trying to cheer up poor Emily."

"How's Jasper? Have they let him out of the hospital yet?"

"Yes, this morning. Now he's terrified the newspapers will find out he has AIDS and his career will be over. That seems rather unfair, don't you think? After all, he picked up the disease from a blood transfusion in Africa—I should imagine the public would be sympathetic."

"Well, in post-Rock Hudson show biz, actresses want to be damned sure about who they're kissing on screen, but other than that, I'd think quite a few roles would still be open to Jasper if he wants them."

"Oh, he *does* want them," Jayne said. "Apparently now that he's aware of his own mortality, he thinks he must go out and make a bundle of money to leave Emily and the kids. It's absurd, of course. Emily is quite comfortable and she believes it's best for the children to make their own way."

"Money," I muttered gloomily, sitting down at the grand piano. I couldn't help but wonder how badly Jasper wanted money, what he would do, for example, to get his hands on seventy-five grand. It wasn't a cheerful thought.

"Who else did you have for brunch?" I inquired while playing.

"Oh, Audrey was here and Ann Jillian and a number of people you don't know. And, oh yes, Natasha."

"Sergeant Dimitriev again?"

"She was off duty, dear. She fit in rather well."

"Darling," I asked as patiently as possible, "do you really think Sergeant Dimitriev was *completely* off duty? She wasn't here possibly to keep an eye on us?"

"You sound paranoid."

"The sergeant grills you, doesn't she? Sneaky little questions—about our love life, and finances?"

"Well, she did ask if you had a violent streak, but I assured her you were a pussycat. Anyway, I'm certain I got much more information out of her than she got out of me."

"Like what?"

"Like the fact that the police have checked out every single person who was on that ship, and they haven't been able to find a soul who had reason to kill Bernie, except for your A list of suspects."

"Oh?"

"And here's something else. The police now have a theory that Bernie was stabbed and the bomb planted by not one person, but two people working together. Isn't that interesting?"

Normally I can play piano through the heaviest of conversations, but at this point my hands lost interest.

"Two people," I mused. "Working together . . . and one of those has got to be—"

"Trip Johnson," finished my wife.

We looked at each other. When you've been married as long as Jayne and I, a sort of semi-telepathy sometimes becomes part of a conversation. The idea of two people working together made sense.

"Then Trip was killed—"

"By his accomplice!" Jayne smiled triumphantly, then frowned slightly. "At least that's the latest theory, according to

Bobby and Natasha. Incidentally, darling, that relationship is going nowhere. Do you know he never even noticed the beige cashmere sweater from Bergdorf's that had cost the poor girl a very big chunk of her savings?"

I share many of my wife's interests, but the romantic future of Lieutenant Carlino and Sergeant Dimitriev was off my charts at the moment. My hands started playing again while my mind tried to assimilate the new information she had given me.

After a few minutes I said, "I think it's time we flushed out this damned killer!"

"And how do we do that, darling?"

"I want you to throw a small party. Today's Monday. . . . Let's make it Thursday night at seven . . . I think that will give me enough time. Just make it an intimate cocktail party here in the suite. Nothing fancy. I want you to invite Mimi, Clancy, Jack Wolfe, Nash Stuart, Zach, Suzanne, La Volpa, Annie Locks, and Jasper and Emily, of course.

"Your entire A list of suspects," Jayne remarked as she jotted down the guest list I had rattled off.

"Exactly. And when you invite them, I want you to pass on a little secret—pretend you're telling them for their ears alone—say that Steve has finally figured out who the killer is and that the real reason for the gathering is to announce the guilty party. Make it sound like a parlor game—remind them how I like to play amateur detective and that this is just the sort of denouement we amateur sleuths really like."

"A guilty party? But, darling, you don't really know who the killer is yet, do you?"

"Not now, but I will by Thursday night."

Jayne continued to make notes about the party, and I was glad that she was momentarily distracted by questions of etiquette so I didn't have to explain exactly what I had in mind to back up my pronouncement.

"Exactly what do people wear to a guilty party?" she mused.

"Oh, there's one more little thing . . ."

Jayne eyed me suspiciously as I plunged ahead in my most casual manner. "I want you to get us a room across the street at the Sherry Netherland. Do it discreetly, under your own name, and please, don't tell *anyone*. We'll leave our things here, but we'll sleep across the street. Won't that be fun? Beds on both sides of Fifth Avenue!"

"But why?" she asked, studying me even more intently.

I tried to look nonchalant and masculine and very much in charge. "Let's just say I don't want to find any more bodies in my piano."

"Steve, there's something that worries me about your little plan."

"Trust me," I told her with a smile any used car salesman would be proud to flash. "Have I ever led you astray?"

"Often," she said, and then went back to her party lists.

# chapter 42

**M**eanwhile the show went on—*Murder in Manhattan* that is. On Monday I had only been on standby, but Tuesday morning I had one brief scene to film, with Mimi, at the children's playground in Washington Square Park.

In the scene Mimi and I sat on the swings, deep in adult conversation, chasing away a precocious five-year-old who wished to have a turn. This was supposed to be a comedy of sorts, but no one was smiling. Trip's death had left a grim cast and crew who did their jobs as quickly and efficiently as possible and stopped neither to laugh nor socialize. Nash Stuart managed to direct the scene without once looking me in the eye. To give you an idea how grim things had become, Clancy was on the set—almost sober.

In fact, the only person among us who was at all her usual self was the grieving widow—Mimi Day. She was friendly. Too friendly. Every time I looked up, I found her smiling at me—a cozy little smile, as if we were sharing some intriguing secret.

I didn't like it, but what could I say? The poor lady seemed on such fragile emotional ground that I didn't want to be the one to rock her boat.

"Steve, you look pale," she told me, her voice full of concern. "Is Jayne feeding you properly?"

"A low cholesterol feast," I said. "We try to keep our weight down."

To my dismay, she took hold of my hand. "Everything in moderation," she said, "including moderation."

The situation made me very uncomfortable. Fortunately the work went quickly. If Barnes had been around, the scene might have taken all day, but Nash and his crew had it in the can within an hour. And so by eleven A.M. I had finished work and was sitting in the back of a limousine watching Fifth Avenue roll by outside the window as we headed toward The Plaza. It was a gray, messy-looking day, and all the people hurrying to and fro managed to look equally gray and exhausted. I could identify with the feeling.

When we finally stopped at the hotel, I stepped out of the limo and hesitated in indecision. If someone had been watching, they would have observed me starting to cross the street toward the east side of Fifth Avenue, change my mind, head up the steps into the hotel, change my mind again, and finally walk purposefully across the street to F.A.O. Schwarz.

I had decided that grim realities required a grim response. F.A.O. Schwarz, as you probably know, is one of the world's most expensive toy stores, but I was not there to play games. I walked past computerized teddy bears, kid-size Ferraris which really ran, a ten-foot-high stuffed giraffe, and a panda of almost King Kong proportions until I came to an object which caught my eye: an old-fashioned wooden baseball bat. I was surprised that F.A.O. Schwarz had something so marvelously simple.

I picked up the bat and felt its weight and balance. It would do. I went to the nearest cash register and said, "Gift-wrap this please."

"Shall I put it in a box?"

"No, just as is will be fine."

A few minutes later I carried a baseball bat wrapped in white paper with rocking horses of turquoise, red, purple, and yellow printed on it. On my way out of the store my eye was caught by one more object I thought might prove indispensable for a television personality turned detective—a toy gun. There were several to choose from, ranging in style from Buck Rogers to Wyatt Earp. After some thought I eventually singled out a black rubber snub-nosed revolver à la Dick Tracy which happened to be full of bubble bath. I suppose a bathroom toy like that could be useful to the mother of a dirty child who resisted hot water. I had another use in mind.

I slipped the bubble bath revolver into my trench coat and

with the gift-wrapped baseball bat propped jauntily against my shoulder crossed back to The Plaza, passed through the lobby, and took the elevator to my suite. Jayne was not there; she had followed my instructions and moved into the Sherry Netherland.

I leaned the bat within easy reach against the piano, sat down to do a little George Gershwin, and waited for someone to try to kill me.

# chapter 43

waited . . . and waited. I spent the afternoon writing a new song and almost forgot I was waiting for someone to attack me—until I noticed it was dark outside, and I was still alive.

Around six-thirty I phoned Jayne across the street.

"Hi, dear," I said. "How would you like to have a romantic dinner for two in your hotel room?"

"Is this a proposition?"

"You got it."

"You put it so sweetly, how can a lady resist? Maybe we can catch a play afterward and—"

"Not tonight," I interjected. "Tonight it's early to bed, early to rise." Then I added, hoping it sounded like an afterthought, "So, you contacted everyone on the list about the party?"

"Certainly. The party's set for seven, on Thursday."

"And you mentioned that I was going to produce the killer?"

"Darling, I made you sound like a cross between Hercule Poirot and Mickey Spillane. Everyone's expecting a scintillating scene—so don't disappoint them."

"Oh, ye of little faith . . . you're talking with a man who can deliver the goods."

"Hurry on over," Jayne said flirtatiously, hanging up the phone.

Despite the banter, I was worried. My brilliant plan to flush out the killer so far had resulted in nothing whatever. I decided to put the scheme out of my thoughts for the intermission with my wife.

I spent several nonfattening hours with Jayne and then returned to The Plaza by myself to spend the rest of the night—despite her objections. She suspected I was up to something, but I said I needed to tape a song at the piano and gave her a tender good-bye kiss.

Alone in the suite, I did everything I could to stay awake: finished composing the song, read a book—one of those mysteries guaranteed to keep you awake until dawn turning pages. Despite a breathlessly fast-moving plot, beautiful women, and ironic dialogue on every page, I found my eyes getting heavier. Shortly before midnight I stretched out on the sitting room couch with the bat by my side and the rubber revolver under my pillow, determined to close my eyes for only a few moments.

I don't know how much time passed. I was having a light-sleep dream that seemed entirely realistic. In the dream I was at the Shrine Auditorium in Los Angeles accepting a Grammy for a new song called "Murder in Manhattan." I was startled to discover, by my side onstage, my co-composer, Lieutenant Bobby Carlino, who hogged the mike and started telling the audience what a talented man Steve Allen had been and what a pity poor Steve had to go and get himself murdered while trying to solve a crime last year in New York City.

It was about this time I became aware that no one could see me waiting my turn at the microphone. To my horror, I caught sight of a television monitor and Lieutenant Carlino seemed to be all by himself up there.

So where was I?

The truth began to sink in: I was dead. A ghost.

I wasn't too sure what woke me. It took a moment to come out of dreamland and figure out where I was—in a darkened hotel suite, lying a bit uncomfortably on the sitting room couch—and I wasn't sorry to be back in reality.

Then I heard it again—the sound that had roused me—a scratching on the door to the hall. I sat bolt upright, reached for the bat, which I had unwrapped earlier, and rubber revolver, completely awake now and straining to hear the sound over the beating of my heart.

For a moment there was nothing. And then it came again.

This time it sounded like a soft knocking on the door.

"Open up!" came a hoarsely whispered voice from the hall. "I know you're in there!"

I stuck the gun in my pocket as I tiptoed to the side of the door. Then, holding it firmly with both hands, I raised the bat above my head.

"Steve, let me in," came the voice.

I watched the doorknob turn, and there was a cold, metallic taste of fear in my mouth. The door rattled in its frame, securely locked. I had to remind myself I wanted to catch the person on the other side—that's why I was alone and stiff from lying on the couch, that's why I was separated from Jayne, that's why I was brandishing these stupid toys.

"Who's there?" I called softly.

"Is that you, Steve?" came the hoarse whisper. "Let me in."

With an unsteady hand I reached over and pulled back the chain and the deadbolt and turned the butterfly screw of the lock. Then I stood back from the door.

"Come in, come in!" I invited, holding the baseball bat once again high over my head.

The doorknob turned, and the door creaked slowly open. Light spilled in from the hallway, casting a bulky shadow of a person onto the carpet of the darkened room.

"Where are you?" came the hoarse whisper.

I didn't move or speak. I heard footsteps move cautiously forward as the shadow drifted into my sitting room. Now I could make out the figure itself with its back to me. I raised the bat a little higher and started to bring it down hard.

"Steve!" A female voice screamed as the form spun around to face me. The light from the hall fell on the woman's face, and I diverted my swing just in time, pulling to the right so that the bat smashed an elegant little lamp into a dozen pieces and sent a small decorative table halfway across the room.

The lady screamed again. I'm not sure who was more surprised, she or I.

My late-night visitor was Mimi Day.

# chapter 44

I turned on the overhead light by the door. Mimi was dressed in a tan raincoat and I had the horrible suspicion that she didn't have anything on underneath.

"My God, Mimi! What in the world are you doing knocking on my door at this ungodly hour?"

She stood before me, looking very pale, staring at the shattered lamp on the carpet.

"You're a madman," she whispered, dazed.

"Mimi, it's two o'clock in the morning," I told her, peering at my wristwatch.

"I was having drinks at the Sherry Netherland," she said, trying to catch her breath. "I saw Jayne in the lobby. She's cheating on you, Steve!"

"Mimi, that's absurd."

"I mean it. I watched your darling Jayne go to the desk, pick up a room key, and then go up in the elevator to a room. What could that mean but a secret rendezvous?"

Suddenly this mix-up with Mimi struck me as absurdly funny.

"I thought you might need some consolation," she told me angrily. "I can see I was wrong."

"I'm sorry, I'm not laughing at *you.* Come in and have a drink?"

*"Don't come near me!"* Her voice was shrill, and she almost tripped backing away as I moved forward to close the door.

"Mimi . . ."

"You're a maniac! If you come one step closer, I'll make such a noise I'll wake this entire hotel. I swear to God!"

"Look, Mimi, I'm sorry I scared you, and I'm certainly not laughing at you. But you see . . ."

She didn't wait for me to finish but made a dash for the hallway, slamming the door behind her.

"Don't ever come near me again!" she cried, and then I heard her footsteps fade down the hall toward her room.

It was a rather terrible way to get rid of her, I supposed, but at least I had the consolation that Mimi Day would not be flirting with me again.

# chapter 45

**O**n Wednesday I spent most of the day on the set. We were filming at Rockefeller Center, once proud symbol of American capitalism, now owned by the Japanese. I thought I detected a few strange looks aimed my way: Jack Wolfe stroking his chin and regarding me with undisguised curiosity; Suzanne Tracy staring, then glancing away quickly when I met her eye; Nash Stuart almost openly hostile, glaring at me, then sighing.

Mimi was giving me a wide berth, but now it was La Volpa who seemed to be giving me the eye. To my surprise, every time we had occasion to pass within a few feet of each other, she smiled. Perhaps our encounter in the lingerie department of Saks had put us on a new intimate footing. Eventually she came slinking over.

"*Ciao,* Steve," she said, flashing her eyes. "Could I ask you something?"

"Sure."

"Why is eet you carry that be-eg stick?"

She was referring, of course, to the baseball bat, rewrapped in the slightly wrinkled paper, and children's ribbon and bow back in place. All day long the bat had left my side only when I was actually in front of the camera.

"It's a gift for someone I'm expecting," I said.

Around four o'clock, finished for the day, I walked the short distance from Rockefeller Center to The Plaza. The depressing prospect was beginning to cross my mind that all the suspects would gather for my cocktail party the following evening and I would be unable to pull off my little parlor trick—Detective Allen would be left with egg on his face!

I walked heavily up the steps to the hotel and stopped at the front desk to pick up messages before going upstairs to the suite. There were a few letters, two calls from my office in California, and a plain envelope without a stamp that had only STEVE ALLEN typed neatly across the face. I opened that envelope first, while riding the elevator to my floor.

Inside I found a printed claim check and a brief note typed in capital letters:

LOOKING FOR ME? USE THIS CLAIM CHECK AT SARDI'S AFTER TEN TONIGHT.

THE K

Adrenaline shot through my veins. The fish wasn't exactly on the hook, but he—or she—was circling with flashing teeth.

# chapter 46

**B**y eight o'clock a steady rain was falling, turning the city into an impressionist painting of umbrellas and red and white car lights reflected on the shiny streets and windshield wipers beating time. Jayne and I had a quiet dinner at The French Shack on 55th Street, and I made a noble effort to go easy on the calories and not look constantly at my watch.

"Steve, tell me the truth—do you have an appointment with someone tonight?" Jayne asked.

"Just business. I have to see a man about a book."

Jayne toyed with the filet of sole on her plate and gazed at me suspiciously. I hated lying to her, but if she knew what I was really up to, she would have had the silly idea it was too dangerous and wouldn't have let me go.

"No joke, I'm simply helping out a writer who's doing a book about the golden age of television."

"Does the writer play baseball too?" She looked at the gift-wrapped bat I had been carrying everywhere the past twenty-four hours.

"Ah," I said.

"Steve, you're up to something!"

I blinked innocently and commented on my grilled tuna.

A little before nine o'clock I walked Jayne back to the Sherry Netherland under the shelter of her huge umbrella and then had the doorman flag me a taxi. Jayne told me to be careful; she hadn't been fooled at all. After a touch of our lips, she went toward the elevators, and I slipped into the cab, feeling the comforting weight of my bubble bath revolver in my trench coat pocket.

Most of the time it's faster to walk in midtown Manhattan than to take a cab. We made our way slowly westward from the stately buildings of Fifth Avenue into the neon confusion of the theater district. Despite the rain, Broadway was thronged with pedestrians—the poor, the rich, and tourists drifting in and out of theaters and restaurants. Sardi's is on a narrow street between Seventh and Eighth avenues a little to the north of Times Square. My taxi driver got stuck behind a double-parked truck, and rather than listen to him honk his horn for another ten minutes, I got out and walked the last half block, arriving at the restaurant dripping wet, since I had refused the offer of Jayne's umbrella.

At Sardi's I was greeted by the warm combination of tempting aromas and the buzz of conversation that hits you as you step inside the crowded, old-fashioned restaurant. Even at nine-thirty, every booth and table was full, and there was still a line of diners waiting to be seated. At Sardi's even the walls are occupied—by the famous caricatures of all the Broadway personalities who have gone there over the years. I saw people I knew both on the walls and in the booths. I waved to comedian Martin Short and declined the invitation of a TV producer to join his party. I had not gone there to socialize.

Having time to kill, I made my way to the bar.

"What'll it be?"

"I'll have a Double Brontosaurus," I said.

"What the hell is that?"

"Actually, there is no such drink," I said. "I just said that to see if you were paying attention. I'll take a tomato juice."

I drank the juice and watched the clock on the wall slowly make its way to ten. As I watched a group of tourists from the Midwest trying to get a table without a reservation, I thought a little about "The K," trying to imagine his or her face. Tick . . . tock . . . time passes slowly when you watch the clock. To prove to myself I had tons of character, I waited until it was 10:05 before paying for my tomato juice and making my way to the cloakroom. I produced the claim check I had received in my hotel and was given an envelope by a pretty young girl who was perhaps hoping to use the Sardi's cloakroom as a springboard to stardom, or at least to a better class of friends. I gave her a couple dollars to help her on her way.

I took a few steps back toward the bar and opened the envelope with eager fingers. Inside was a single piece of paper with a message typed in uppercase letters:

ISN'T THIS FUN? NOW GO DIRECTLY TO THE FOUR SEASONS. DO NOT PASS GO! DO NOT PASS A PO-LICE STATION! SIT AT THE BAR, ORDER A SINGA-PORE SLING, AND LISTEN TO THE FAT LADY SING.

Damn! I folded the envelope, thrust it deep into my trench coat pocket, and headed back out into the wet streets. I was beginning to get the idea that this could be a very long night.

# chapter 47

The Four Seasons may be the most expensive restaurant in New York, a dubious distinction. Located in the Seagram Building on Park Avenue, it's an entirely different kind of place from Sardi's; it's cool and plush and modern, with high ceilings, enormous shimmering windows, and a decorative marble pool in the very center of the dining room. You might say Sardi's is of the West Side, old and traditional and steamy with life, while The Four Seasons is East Side, sleek and up-to-date and a little antiseptic.

I settled onto a comfortable stool at the bar. The room was dimly lit with small islands of light at the various tables. The bartender was an attractive young lady who came over with a good-egg smile.

"A Singapore Sling," I said.

"Up or blended?"

"Either way, as long as I get one of those paper umbrellas sticking out the top."

I looked around the room. There were two Japanese businessmen in dark blue suits seated near me at the bar, and several couples talking in muted voices at the dimly lit tables. This time of night the place was not crowded, and I saw no trace of any fat lady, singing or otherwise. I had no idea what might happen next. At this point I wasn't sure if I was on a treasure hunt or a wild-goose chase. And what, by the way, *is* a wild-goose chase?

My drink came in a tall glass. I ate the maraschino cherry and twirled the paper umbrella between my fingers, but left the drink itself alone. Time passed and not much happened. I found myself thinking about one aspect of the case that had been puzzling me for days: How had someone gained access to my hotel suite to dump the body of Trip Johnson into my piano? One would assume the locks at The Plaza would be solid and immune to amateur attempts to break in. In fact, I had learned from Lieutenant Carlino that the lock had not been forced. Someone had entered my room with a key.

It was puzzling all right. I also wondered how someone— the murderer presumably—had known exactly when Jayne and I would be out of the suite. I imagined the deed must have been done while we were spending money at Tiffany's, though that had been a trip made entirely on the spur of the moment.

So who had seen us leave? Who had been able to gain access to our key and hide Trip's body? I asked myself this question with the annoying feeling that deep inside my subconscious I somehow knew the answer. The brain itself is a great mystery. I felt the specific memory trying to force itself upward from the murky depths, but when I tried to reclaim it, it went away.

I was deep in these thoughts when I heard a low, husky voice near me at the bar.

"I'll have a Singapore Sling, darling. You can skip the umbrella, but go heavy on the booze."

I glanced up to see an enormous woman, at least three hundred pounds big, dressed in a gaudy red dress. She was smoking a cigarette in a long black holder and wearing jewelry that could make a down payment on the Seagram Building—an enormous diamond ring on the fourth finger of her left hand and a dazzling diamond choker around her neck. Perched on the barstool, she reminded me of a brightly colored parrot.

As I watched her, the fat lady began to sing, crooning softly to herself: " '*Falling in love again, what am I to do? . . . can't help it . . .*' "

She had a voice that sounded as if she'd been smoking cigarettes for a thousand years. I couldn't take my eyes off her, though she completely ignored me. She wore so much makeup—bright red lipstick and deep Pan-Cake powder—I could hardly guess her age. It could have been anywhere between the mid-thirties and the mid-sixties.

I waited, raised my Sling to my lips so she might see I was drinking what she was drinking—but still got no response from her. She continued to sing softly to herself, staring straight ahead. Occasionally she took a puff on her cigarette, and I almost expected the words of her song to appear outlined in smoke issuing from her mouth—like the caterpillar sitting with his hookah in *Alice in Wonderland.* In fact, this was seeming more and more a Lewis Carroll situation.

I summoned the bartendress. "Excuse me," I whispered. "Does that lady come here often?"

"I've never seen her before, sir."

"Would you please give her another drink? On my tab?"

The help at The Four Seasons are top-notch, of course, but I noticed a brief flash of surprise cross the young woman's face—apparently she thought I had tagged the fat lady for a romantic adventure.

I watched her make up a fresh Singapore Sling and deliver it to the enormous woman in red.

"This is from the gentleman down the bar," she said.

The fat lady gazed in my direction with imperious disdain.

"I beg your pardon, but do we know each other?" she asked, and then added immediately, "My goodness, sweetie, you bear an absolutely uncanny resemblance to Steve Allen."

"I hear that a lot," I said, picking up my drink and moving down the bar to her side. "Listen, this may sound a bit odd, but do you have a message for me by any chance?"

"A message? Do I look like a post office?"

"No, indeed not, but you see, I was told to keep an eye out for . . . well, for someone who would be singing at the bar."

"Hmmm . . . you are *the* Steve Allen?"

Actually I was beginning to get irritated at this strange charade. The fat woman gave me a long-lidded look.

"Hmmm," she said again. "Are you absolutely alone, sweetie?"

"Absolutely."

"You did not pass Go?"

"Nope. And I did not pass the police station either. Look, do you think we could hurry this along? It's after my bedtime."

The fat, painted woman looked me up and down. "I have to go to the little girls' room. Stay right here, Mr. Allen."

She left, and I stayed. After ten minutes she had still not returned, and I was not completely surprised. I took a sip on my drink and sighed gloomily. This night was turning into a real bust.

The phone rang behind the bar. The bartendress picked it up, listened, then raised an eyebrow in my direction.

"Mr. Allen?" she asked suspiciously.

"In person," I admitted. This was all getting to be a little ridiculous. She handed me the phone, and I heard what sounded like a cockney fishmonger—of what gender I could not particularly say.

"Eh, is this Mr. Allen, mate?" screeched the voice. I had to pull the phone back a few inches from my ear.

"Look, I'm getting a little tired of all this. . . ."

"No, you look 'ere, mate. You want to get to the bottom of this 'ere mystery, you do exactly like I tells you. You got that?"

I got it. I was told to leave The Four Seasons and take a cab to an address on Hudson Street in Greenwich Village. The voice, loud and insistent, disconnected before I could object. I paid my tab and walked out onto Park Avenue in a foul mood. It was nearly midnight by now, the rain was coming down hard, and I was very tempted to stop all this nonsense and hurry back to Jayne at the Sherry Netherland. I was able to flag a cab almost immediately, and it was on the tip of my tongue to tell him to head uptown, but I was stopped by my own damnable curiosity. Feeling every inch a fool, I gave the driver the address downtown.

We headed down Park Avenue, scurried around the Pan Am Building, and continued at almost sixty miles per hour all the way to 14th Street—where we headed west. At Seventh Avenue we ducked down to Sheridan Square and from there traveled into the far West Village—past the lovely old brownstones of Bank Street and into a lonely area of decrepit old brick warehouses near the river itself. The address on Hudson Street was a building that looked as if it might have once been a light factory, now reborn as an artist's loft. We stopped under the cone of light of a single streetlamp, but other than that I did not see another light or a single human being. It was not a comforting scene.

"Will you please wait for me?" I asked the driver. "I shouldn't be more than ten minutes."

The driver was an East Asian who didn't seem to speak much English. "So sorry, off duty now," he said.

"Wait for me and there'll be a big tip. Twenty dollars."

"No twenty dollar. No wait. Off duty, so sorry."

I pleaded, but it was no use. New York taxi drivers are a hard lot. I paid my fare, stepped out into the rain, and the taxi sped away, leaving me on a street as dark and inhospitable as the moon. A shiver ran up my spine. I heard a soft sound that made me jump; it was a cat leaping down from a garbage can. There seemed nothing else to do but go to the address I had been given on the phone.

I walked up the stoop into a dimly lit hallway. For an old building, the front door seemed new and expensive, and there was a single mailbox and gleaming brass doorbell to my left. As I stood observing this, a buzzer sounded by the front door. Someone was expecting me, perhaps watching my every movement. I turned the knob and the door swung open. I found myself facing a flight of stairs. I clutched the baseball bat in my right hand and the rubber pistol in my left, and climbed upward, listening to my footsteps reverberate in the silent hall. After a while I noticed another sound as well—the beating of my heart.

I walked up to the second floor landing and came face-to-face with an ornate wooden door. The stairs stopped at this point, and since I could continue no farther, I gave the door a knock with the back of my hand. From the other side I could hear footsteps coming toward me. Suddenly, to my horror, the lights in the hall went out, and I was left in total darkness.

And then the door began creaking slowly open, making a terrible sound like fingernails screeching across a blackboard. My breath seemed to catch in my throat. I tried to call out, but could make no sound.

Standing in the open doorway, lit by an eerie amber light, was a sight I had never expected to see again—Bernie Barnes, his eyes bulging in death, his mouth frozen in mute horror.

As I watched, the eyes relaxed and the mouth curled slowly into a smile and began to speak.

"Hey, Steverino! So glad you could make it!"

# chapter 48

**B**ernie roared with laughter at seeing the look on my face. He certainly was enjoying himself.

I patted my chest, glad I had a strong heart. "Whew! You're . . . you're . . ."

"Alive!" he agreed happily, clapping his hands together in delight.

My brain was working overtime, trying to take this all in. I'm not often at a loss for words, but in this case I was approaching incoherence.

"Didn't you love the fat lady?" he cried. "That was an old Broadway actress who owes me a few favors. Had you fooled pretty good, didn't I, Steverino?"

"You've had everyone fooled, Bernie!" I was beginning to get angry.

He began to sing to me in a smoky voice: " 'Falling in love again, what am I to do? . . . can't help it.' "

"Cut it out, Bernie, what's wrong with you anyway? Can't you see all the trouble you've caused? You've got police divers risking their lives searching for your body and a homicide squad trying to find your killer."

I went on a bit about how irresponsible he had been, but the more I scolded, the more Bernie seemed to be enjoying himself. I was beginning to understand a lot of what happened—including my treasure hunt tonight—in terms of his childish sense of the dramatic.

"But wasn't it a lovely treasure hunt? Come on, admit it, Steve-o. When Tripper told me you were all hot on playing amateur detective, I thought I'd make a fun evening for you—

notes and clues all over town. 'Fess up, Steve-er, you definitely weren't bored."

"I can't believe this" was all I could think of to say.

"Steve, you really must relax and enjoy yourself more. Life is a cinema, just a lot of flimflam, my friend, a shadow projected upon a screen! Some of us are bit players, some of us are stars. And others are directors of the whole splendid show. Like gods, we rearrange events and make them suit our purpose."

"You're mad."

"Am I? Why should life's exciting moments be caught only on two-dimensional pieces of film? I have an imagination that refuses limits. I am an *auteur,* Steve, a master of illusion."

My anger was being replaced by deep exhaustion. "Bernie, you risked everyone's life on that damned boat. It's a miracle nobody was killed when *Easy Money* went to the bottom of New York harbor."

Bernie shook his head. "Oh, that wasn't part of *my* illusion, Steve. Do you really think I would do something as crude as to sink a lovely yacht? Think about it, man."

"You didn't sink *Easy Money?* Then who the hell did?"

"Steve, you're upset. Why don't you let me fix you a drink—perhaps a nice, tall Singapore Sling, eh?"

Bernie slapped his thighs and started laughing all over again at the memory of the fun he'd had yanking me around Manhattan. I sat down on a cane-seated rocking chair and waited for him to stop. The room in which I found myself was a huge loft, a single open space with a living area on one side, a kind of open kitchen in the middle, and an elaborate round water bed toward the far end. Near the water bed was a big redwood barrel with a few wooden steps leading up to a surrounding deck. This seemed to be the hot tub.

"This is my secret spa and escape hatch from polite society," Bernie explained as I looked around. "I've kept it for years, since the days I was poor and used to make moronic little TV commercials for a living. Surprising how useful it's been. Sure you don't want a drink?"

"Bernie, how the hell did you get off that boat?"

"*Ship,* Steve . . . a one-hundred-and-fifty-foot yacht is a ship."

"So how'd you get off the damned ship?"

"Simple. I had a wet suit and scuba gear stashed away under the bed upon which I so conveniently 'died.' As soon as you left, I slipped into my gear and went out the stateroom window into the water."

"Wait a minute. As crazy as you are, I can't believe you'd try to swim underwater all the way to Manhattan."

"I wouldn't. This was a well-planned operation, amigo. There was a small speedboat *sans* running lights waiting for me a hundred yards off the starboard side of the yacht. I climbed in and we zipped up the Hudson almost to the door of my little Greenwich Village hideaway."

"And the explosion?"

"That was not my doing. You kidding? I just wanted to disappear and cause a little stir, not kill off my cast and crew, for chrissake! Don't you understand what this whole thing was for?"

"Publicity."

"Very good. My last two films didn't do so good and *Murder in Manhattan* was way over budget. I'm no fool. I knew if I was ever going to work again in pictures, this film had to be a big hit. And to have a hit, the public's gotta hear the title. Right? I was simply insuring a certain amount of notoriety to the production."

I shook my head disgustedly.

"Hey, listen, I planned to reappear in a few days with a small case of amnesia and some circumstantial evidence to indicate I'd simply fallen overboard. As for your story that I had been stabbed, I thought I'd leave that as a little dangling mystery to make people talk."

"You really thought you could get away with this?"

"It would have worked—if that damned kid hadn't taken it into his head to blow up the ship."

"Trip."

"He and his accomplice, of course. But we'll come to that part later. After the ship sank I knew I'd be charged with some pretty nasty stuff if I miraculously reappeared. So I had to lay low for a while and figure out my next move."

"Which is exactly what?"

"You, my friend, are going to clear me of any criminal charges so I can come to life again and finish my lovely film. It is absolutely *intolerable* that a gentrified idiot like Nashville Stuart should touch a single frame of my masterpiece."

"A-ha!" More pieces of the puzzle were falling into place, including the fact that Barnes was about as nuts as could be. Show biz people often live under a lot of strain and at the farthest edge of their imagination. In Bernie's case, he had stepped off the edge into empty space. There was no other way to account for someone who believed he could blackmail half the cast of his film, abandon ship off the shores of Manhattan in some crazy publicity stunt, and then calmly reappear to finish directing his work.

Bernie was flashing me a cagey smile. "You're going to help me, Steverino, and then I'm going to make you a much bigger star than you've ever been! Wha'd'ya say to that?"

There wasn't anything to say to that. I tried a new tack. I spoke in a gentle voice and looked at him with eyes full of friendship and understanding.

"Listen, Bernie, if I'm going to help you, I have to know what happened. Why did Trip plant the bomb?"

"Trying to cover his tracks."

"By blowing up the boat?"

"Ship, Steve. Exactly. He thought if he could stop the production with enough bang and smoke, no one would ever discover the— You know Tripper and company were also hoping yours truly might go down with *Easy Money*—then they really would have been off the hook."

"Because you found out they had been embezzling company funds?"

"Very good! Damn right! Seventy-five thousand dollars worth. Those bastards thought I was spending so much money, nobody would notice. What they didn't count on was the fact that old Bernie's got eyes in the back of his fuckin' head."

"So who—"

"Listen to me, pardner, I'm telling you the truth because

you're like a brother to me. From now on it's you and me, guy, against the whole friggin' planet!"

"I'm flattered, Bernie, but there's something I don't understand. Trip and his accomplice knew what you were planning to do, right? They knew about your scuba gear and your fake murder . . . so why did they imagine sinking *Easy Money* would kill you?"

"A-ha! It was a matter of timing, my friend, and I deliberately misled them by five crucial minutes, giving myself just enough time to get away."

"You knew they were going to bomb the boat?"

"What they didn't count on, of course, was the speedboat driver."

"For chrissake, Bernie, what are you talking about—the speedboat driver?"

"He came to me, that's what I'm talking about. He told me Trip and company paid him *not* to show up to rescue me. There could be only one reason for this—the bastards wanted to kill me. What they didn't know was I had already promised that particular young sailor a screen test for my next picture, so he naturally had a vested interest in my survival."

This was all too complicated—a double-cross within a double-cross—and I could see Bernie enjoyed the Machiavellian plotting the same way some people might enjoy crossword puzzles.

"I had been suspicious that they would try *something,*" Bernie went on. I would have done the same thing in their position. They thought they would take advantage of the situation and turn my fake murder into a real one—to protect their little hides. With me gone, no one could ever connect them to the missing seventy-five grand."

"But you were in touch with Trip after the sinking?"

"Naturally. But not his friend. Not directly at least."

"Why not?"

"Well, whatever nastiness Trip might plan, I always knew I could stay about ten steps ahead of him—hell, he was just a kid having his little rebellion against adult society. But the other one's a real killer. I couldn't trust that tricky bastard not to come at me again."

"And just who *is* this 'tricky bastard'?"

"Now, if I came out and told you, Steverino, you wouldn't have the fun of guessing for yourself, would you, my friend?"

"Is the accomplice Nash Stuart?"

Bernie flashed me a jagged smile. "Ah, we're playing Twenty Questions, are we? You know, of course, that this nasty accomplice murdered poor Tripper and stuffed him into your piano?"

"I know that. *So who is it?*"

Bernie's sense of the dramatic simply would not let him impart such climactic information without a buildup. Smiling in anticipation, he strolled over to what looked like an old-fashioned hot dog cart that stood in front of the enormous loft windows. The cart, like everything else around there, was something other than what it appeared—it was a bar.

"Hey, I'm going to have a drink to celebrate. Come on, Steve, what about you? I make a mean Sling."

"You can give me a Double Brontosaurus if it helps you tell me who the killer is."

"I guess I am keeping you in suspense, aren't I? Okay, Steve, I'll tell you. The accomplice is—"

The gunshots probably came from the rooftop across the street. They weren't loud, more like three firecrackers going off one after the other. Bernie stopped speaking in midsentence and staggered forward with a look of surprise on his face. He sank slowly onto his knees, and I noticed three small holes in the glass behind him. I flung myself on the floor, but there were no more shots. Bernie remained upright on his knees for several seconds, his eyes bulging in the same way I remembered from the . . . ship. This is when I realized I was being had—again.

I stood up grumpily and brushed myself off.

"Very funny!" I told Bernie. "Look, if you think you can fool me again with this same old trick . . ."

Bernie fell forward onto his face and lay still. I applauded sarcastically and went over to his side.

"Ha-ha-ha. Now tell me . . ."

I tugged on his arm, and this is when I noticed he had smashed his nose falling forward and there was blood on the back of his shirt. Rather a lot of blood, as a matter of fact, warm and bright, and—I touched it—with none of the consistency of catsup. This was more than clever acting. This time Bernard L. Barnes was really dead.

# chapter 49

I was staring at the body in horror when the lights in the building went off. I stood, trying to get my bearings in the almost total darkness, and smelled something that gave me new cause for alarm—wisps of smoke were drifting into the loft from the floor below.

I knew it wouldn't help to panic. Quite calmly I walked like a blind man—arms in front of me—to where I imagined I would find the front door. What I found was the cold exposed brick of the wall. Keeping my hand on the wall, I edged slowly to the left, thinking I would find the door in that direction. I eventually came to the hot tub and knew I was going wrong, so I reversed my way and edged slowly to the right. By this time smoke was pouring into the room in thick acrid clouds.

My hand touched the front door and turned the knob—but the door wouldn't open. Less calm with each passing moment, I began feeling wildly for the lock. I yanked open a deadbolt, threw back the heavy bar of a police lock, and found the door still would not budge. By now I could hear the crackle of fire and see dull orange flames shining at the window.

The flickering glow at least helped me see. I picked up a chair and threw it at the window. The glass shattered but, to my surprise, the chair bounced back at me. I soon discovered the reason—in the manner of paranoid New York, the window opening was protected by a lattice of decorative metal bars.

My plight stared me in the face: I was trapped in a burning building with no means of escape!

The heat became intolerable as flames swept into the room. For the second time since I had come to New York I had the awful, foreboding feeling that my time was finally up.

# chapter 50

**J**ayne likes to throw parties, whatever the excuse, though a party to flush out a killer may have been a first even for the most seasoned Hollywood hostess.

By six-thirty on Thursday night she had our Plaza suite decorated with flowers and laden with food and spirits. There were prawns on ice prettily arranged around a glass dish of cocktail sauce. There was smoked salmon on small squares of black bread, raw vegetables and dip for the more health conscious, and hot canapes as well—miniature, bite-size quiche waiting in a small room-service oven, kept warm by flaming cans of Sterno. To serve these delicacies, Jayne had borrowed a waiter and a bartender from downstairs.

The scene was set. Knowing Jayne, I doubt if any denouement had ever been prepared with more grace. Probably she let her party instincts carry her away, making her forget what this little gathering was all about. One way or another I must rely on her description of the evening's beginning, for I was not there.

She tells me Suzanne Tracy and Zach Holden were the first to arrive, at ten minutes past seven. They arrived together, and there was a subtle glow of newly found affection about them that Jayne noticed right away; she said she could sense it just in the way they sat on the sofa, but then Jayne is a romantic. For the next ten minutes there was that awkward period of dealing with the first guests at any party—a hostess actually has a chance at that stage to sit down and visit, but there is always that unspoken fear shared between guest and hostess: *What if nobody else comes?*

Jayne nursed a Perrier with a sliver of lime. Zach had a beer—he insisted on drinking it out of the bottle—and Suzanne sipped demurely from a glass of California chardonnay. And what do you imagine they talked about for ten minutes? The latest Hollywood gossip? Who was going to win what award or mount a hostile takeover against which major studio? No, Suzanne led a discussion about the destruction of the Brazilian rain forests and the greenhouse effect on the atmosphere. For ten minutes they talked about polar ice caps and Third World debt. Suzanne spoke eloquently about Hollywood's moral duty to speak out on important issues. Zach cagily suggested that as soon as *Murder in Manhattan* was finished, he and Suzanne might make a quick trip to Brazil to witness the rape of the land first-hand. He gave a good imitation of global consciousness, but Jayne says she could tell he was more interested in fun-in-the-sun with Suzanne.

Jayne tells me she thought Suzanne might be a little too serious for a party and that she was relieved when other guests began to arrive.

Nash Stuart and Annie Locks came in together, followed almost immediately by Jack Wolfe and Victoria La Volpa. A party atmosphere began to develop. Zach had another beer and began to talk sports with Nash, while Jack Wolfe drank scotch and told loud off-color stories to Victoria, who giggled at every naughty innuendo.

In any event, according to Jayne, this was not the best party or the worst ever thrown. She spent a few minutes discussing new Paris fashions with Annie while Suzanne joined Nash and Zach and managed to change the conversation from baseball to how there should be a total trade embargo with both Japan and Russia until those two countries stopped killing whales.

"I heard of a whale once with a fourteen-foot penis," said La Volpa, passing by on the way to the bar.

"Whales," said Suzanne sternly, "are probably more intelligent than some human beings. It's a scientific certainty that whale language is vastly more complex than ours, which implies a level of development that . . ."

Suzanne, I am told, spoke for some time on the subject, while everyone listened with polite smiles and glassy eyes. Five minutes later there was an uncomfortable lull in the conversation as Jasper North came in with his tall, regal, and very British wife, Emily. Everyone seemed to know at this point about Jasper and Annie, and there was a slight awkwardness about having them all in the same room. Still, there were no daggers drawn and the talk remained friendly. Jasper headed quickly to the bar for a gin and tonic, Zachary had another beer, La Volpa switched from vodka to champagne, and Jack had another scotch. The talk grew more animated as the level of the bottles went down, and the hors d'oeuvres were quickly gobbled. Like a good hostess, Jayne darted hither and thither, making sure everyone had everything they needed.

Nash eventually cornered her by the room-service oven as she checked on the quiche. "Where's Steve?" he asked.

"Oh, he'll be along," she said. "You know Steve—he probably made some new friends somewhere and forgot to look at the time."

"This is still on, then?" Nash continued, rather nervously according to my wife.

"Still on?"

"The, er . . . payoff?"

"Oh, of course, darling," Jayne said. "Steve wouldn't miss it for anything."

Clancy Donahue arrived with Mimi Day a little before eight o'clock, and it was obvious they had both been drinking heavily. Clancy was wearing a dinner jacket and black tie for some reason, but the tie was askew, and he had neglected to shave. Mimi wore a low-cut black cocktail dress, and she laughed too loudly at everything. The moment Clancy and Mimi walked in, they went straight to the bar.

And so the suspects were all there, except for me. As if on cue, there was a rap on the door and Lieutenant Carlino and Sergeant Dimitriev joined the group. They looked less like cops than ever tonight—Carlino in a cream-white double-breasted Italian suit, pink shirt and tie, and Natasha also in white, a short and slinky cocktail dress Jayne had helped her pick out at Bloomingdale's. The dress showed off the sergeant's stunning legs, and her makeup was applied and hair arranged carefully to accent her aquamarine eyes. Jayne, as you might assume, later

told me in great detail how pleased she was with the results of
her attention.

"What are the police doing here?" Jasper asked nervously,
coming up to Jayne.

"Bobby and Natasha? Honestly, Jasper, do they look as if
they're on duty? Steve should be here any minute to explain
everything."

Even though they looked as show biz as everyone else in the
room, the arrival of the NYPD seemed to remind everyone what
this party was about. Conversations faltered, and Jayne could
detect some sullen glances passing to and fro.

"Look, if Steve's not coming, I've really got to be on my
way," said Nash, approaching Jayne with an anxious look on his
face.

"Relax, Mr. Stuart," said Lieutenant Carlino, appearing
with a drink in his hand. "Knowing Steve Allen, I'm sure he'd
walk through a wall of fire to be here tonight."

Nash flashed the lieutenant a quick and mistrustful look, but
he seemed to have no further objections. In one corner of the
room a very drunk Clancy was on his knees comically singing an
Irish love song to La Volpa. Jayne sensed I'd better make my
appearance soon.

And I did. A few minutes past eight I came in the front door
of my suite in a sooty trench coat. All conversation stopped.
Every eye turned my way.

"Welcome, everyone, and thank you for coming," I said,
removing the coat to reveal a suit I had picked up at a vintage
clothing store in the Village: a square-cut fifties jacket and trousers with a white shirt and narrow tie that made me look like my
favorite alter ego—that dashing and bungling reporter of hidden steel, Clark Kent.

"Well, gang," I continued, "I think it's time to begin."

# chapter 51

"*Murder in Manhattan,*" I told the assembled group, "has more than lived up to its name. Personally, I've had some experiences the past few weeks I'd like never to repeat—I've been hurled off a sinking ship, left to swim for my life, rescued by a helicopter and flown through the air. I've been bullied, insulted, and been suspected of murder by the New York police. I've had bodies hidden in my piano, and I've been sung to by fat ladies who couldn't carry a tune . . . personally I've had enough."

"Hear! Hear!" I heard someone say—Jasper, I think.

"Would you like some sliced carrots and low-cal clam dip, dear?" asked Jayne, which goes to show no man is Superman to his wife. I responded to these interruptions with a patient smile.

"And for this reason," I continued, "I have invited you here tonight to solve this crime. Or, rather, I should say *series* of crimes, for we will soon see there is more than one criminal involved and certainly more than one crime."

I paused dramatically and looked around the room. I definitely had everyone's interest.

"I'm afraid I must begin by informing you that Bernie Barnes is really, truly dead."

"We *know* that, Steve," said Nash Stuart irritably.

"No, only *one* of you knows that for certain," I said ominously, waving a finger in the air. "You see, despite appearances, Bernie was not actually dead until last night, when he was shot in the back in his Greenwich Village loft. The first homicide was only a hoax."

I noticed a few puzzled faces around the room. Mimi Day,

the grieving widow, had gone very white.

"This is ridiculous!" growled Clancy, moving toward the bar for another drink.

"Is it?" I asked. "I doubt if you will say that once I tell you who the killer is."

All movement seemed to freeze. Even Clancy did not make it all the way to the bar, but turned to look at me in anticipation. Nash Stuart had been standing, but now quietly sank upon a chair as if his legs would no longer hold him. Lieutenant Carlino and his sultry sergeant stood grimly near the smoked salmon.

"Who ees thees nasty person?" asked La Volpa without apparent concern.

"Let's consider the possibilities. Perhaps it is you, my dear."

All eyes turned to La Volpa.

"How *dare* you accuse of sin the one radiantly innocent being in this filthy room?" shouted Clancy, staggering my way. "La Volpa may be a whore, but she is a *pure* whore! You are looking at a woman who would kill only for love . . . or maybe money . . ."

"How about a new fur coat?" muttered Jack Wolfe as an aside to Mimi Day, who howled with laughter. Unfortunately, Clancy heard the remark and was about to clobber the publicist when Lieutenant Carlino intervened.

"Sit down and behave yourself, Mr. Donahue," said the lieutenant. "Why don't we let Mr. Allen finish?"

So I continued:

"Miss La Volpa, you have the oldest motive of all. . . ."

". . . *And* the oldest profession," Mimi muttered under her breath. There was about to be a new ruckus, so I continued forcefully:

"You were being blackmailed. You had no desire to do this film at all, but Bernie Barnes learned a secret of your youth and threatened to expose you if you didn't do as he wished. I have no desire to tell the people in this room what that secret is. . . ."

"She is *not* a whore!" shouted Clancy suddenly, quite contrary to what he had cried out only moments before. Clancy was becoming a problem. He tore open his ruffled shirt with great passion, baring a somewhat hairy chest.

"*I* am the whore!" he bellowed. "*I* sold my soul to Hollywood, and now God looks at me and spits and turns away!"

"Clancy, your problem is you think about yourself too much," said a disenchanted Suzanne Tracy. "You need to do something useful—like save a Brazilian rain forest."

"You stupid, sexless schoolgirl!" snarled Clancy. "You idiot American yuppie jackass bitch!"

"Now, wait a damn minute!" said an angry Zach Holden— and for the second time blows might have been exchanged if the lieutenant had not stepped in. Clancy, unfortunately, was too drunk to leave ungagged—and that's eventually what Lieutenant Carlino actually had to do—handcuff the author to a chair and tie a bar towel around his mouth.

This was slow going. I had an iced prawn to keep up my strength, and then continued.

The room fell silent as I told how La Volpa's career would never have been safe with Bernie alive, and that murder might have seemed the only way to protect the secret of her past. La Volpa denied this vigorously, shouting some unseemly and operatic things at me in a mix of Italian and English. I gave her a disapproving look and proceeded to the other suspects in the room.

I tried to do things in a tidy way. I covered the blackmail victims first, moving from La Volpa to an embarrassed Zachary Holden. Zach bowed his head—and Suzanne glared at me fiercely—as I explained to the room how he also had been coerced by Bernie Barnes into appearing in *Murder in Manhattan.* I had no wish to stir up unnecessary muck, and I left Zach's secret undisclosed—though you could almost hear the click-clack of brains in motion, furiously trying to guess what dark deed had left Holden open to blackmail.

Jasper was the next on my list, and his situation was slightly different—he had been blackmailed not by Bernie, but by the second murder victim—or perhaps you'd have to say the first—Trip Johnson. Jasper listened to my account carefully, nodding from time to time. Eventually he politely raised his hand, as if we were in a classroom.

"Excuse me, Steve, but I'd like to add I was a *double* blackmail victim. Not only was that unfortunate youth after me about my medical history, but Bernie was having a go at me as well. Like Zach and Victoria, I had not been particularly keen on this project, but Bernie found out about my—er—relationship with Annie and suggested it would be to my advantage to sign on the dotted line. You see, Steve, Emily knows all about that now," he added, squeezing his wife's hand. "So I had a pretty fair motive to do away with both Bernie *and* Trip—wouldn't you say?"

"Thank you, Jasper," I said. The Britisher had a sense of fair play, but I let his double motive dangle and went on to some of the more complex passions around the room.

"Clancy—you had more than enough reason to wish Bernie dead—he destroyed your self-respect. He treated you like dirt and you blamed him for transforming you from a serious writer to a hack. But most of all, you hated him for defiling the woman you loved—Victoria La Volpa. I would almost certainly accuse you of being Bernie's killer, except for one thing—I can't quite see you shooting him in the back through a closed window. Your style would have been more to bash him over the head with a whiskey bottle."

Clancy, handcuffed to his chair and gagged, could only glare at me with red eyes. I turned to Suzanne.

"Suzanne, when I first came to New York you told me you were in love with Clancy. Now it seems your affections have turned toward Zach. Don't get me wrong, a young woman has the right to change her mind, and in this case you may have made a wise decision. I'm only pointing out that Bernie had been blackmailing the two men in your life, which might be considered a fair motive for murder."

"Barnes was a pig!" Suzanne said in a low voice.

"Yes, and I doubt if he gave a damn about whales or fur coats or rain forests either. So, if it weren't for the fact I have unearthed no motive for you to kill Trip Johnson, you would be high on my list of suspects."

I turned to Annie Locks.

"Annie, as costume designer, you were in a unique position to hear a good deal of gossip around the set. People tend to tell you their deep dark secrets as you measure their arms and legs and stick pins in pieces of material. I suspect you knew all the dirt, knew all the really nasty things Bernie had been doing, and Trip as well. In your case, you may have had no personal motive for murder, except to protect the man you have loved for nearly twenty-five years."

Little Annie stood up from her chair and faced me. "I would have been delighted to kill Bernie, *and* that parasite Johnson, for what they were doing to Jasper. It would have been a pleasure."

"Well, maybe you did . . . and maybe you didn't. But let's go on." I turned to Bernie's widow. "Mimi, you may have the most classic motive of all. You were married to a man who not only cheated on you but humiliated you in public. I'm not exactly sure why you'd kill Trip, but if you did murder your husband, Mimi, a good lawyer could probably get you a medal of commendation from a sympathetic jury."

"*If* I murdered my husband, I'd be bragging about it," Mimi said, stepping to the bar for another drink.

I turned to Nashville Stuart.

"And then there is you, Nash—in a very difficult situation indeed. You were producing a film with a mad director who was spending money like water. And you had personal problems too—an old secret, an illegitimate son whose sudden appearance threatened to destroy the security of your family. All in all, the two deaths benefited you a great deal, professionally and privately. You were even able to indulge a fantasy, to take over Bernie's job and direct the film yourself."

"This is a lie! Insanity!" cried Nash.

"Is it? You're a cool-headed executive accustomed to dealing with tricky situations. If there's one person in this room who could plan and carry out a double murder, I think that person is you, Nash."

Stuart's elegant facade failed him. He leaned forward in his armchair, sputtering for words. "That's . . . why, it's . . . I think I'm going to let my lawyer deal with these accusations."

"Why don't you just sit back and relax awhile, Mr. Stuart.

Enjoy the show," said Sergeant Dimitriev.

The producer seemed uncertain whether to call in his legal brigades or do what the sergeant suggested. With a long sigh he leaned back in his chair.

"So that's the lot," I said. "I've shown how each person in this room had a powerful reason to remove Bernie Barnes from his or her personal horizon, and how some of you even had a reason to murder Trip Johnson as well—"

"Hey, wait a second," interrupted a voice from near the bar. "Aren't you forgetting me?"

It was Jack Wolfe, our unit publicist. He laughed his nervous laugh, and glanced to the others in the room as through he would like to be included in this fun parlor game.

"Oh, I couldn't possibly forget you, Jack," I assured him. "After all, you're the murderer."

# chapter 52

There was a moment's silence as the terrible word *murderer* hung in the air. We all seemed frozen in an eerie tableau. Then Jayne, ever the proper hostess, went to the room-service cart and pulled out a fresh tray of hors d'oeuvres from the portable oven.

"Would you care for another egg roll, Mr. Wolfe?" she offered.

Jack didn't seem to see her. He looked around the room for support but was greeted only by the predatory stare of people who were all too happy to have someone in the hot seat other than themselves. Jack reached numbly into his shirt pocket for a cigarette.

"Mr. Wolfe, would you kindly not smoke in my sitting room," Jayne said politely but firmly.

He stared morosely at his unlit cigarette. For a moment I wasn't certain which was worse for him—being accused of a double murder or not being able to smoke.

"This is a joke, right?" Jack said nervously.

"It's no joke, Jack," I said. "You see, up to now I've talked only about motive, which encompasses pretty much everyone in the room. When we get to *opportunity*, however, it's quite another ball game."

"Look, maybe I'll zip downstairs to the bar for a quick smoke," said Jack optimistically. "Then I'll come back and you can make all the crazy accusations you want."

Lieutenant Carlino and Sergeant Dimitriev moved reluctantly from the smoked salmon and stepped up close behind where Jack was sitting.

"I'd stay right where I was if I were you," suggested the lieutenant softly.

"You see, Jack," I continued. "Once I realized Bernie's first death on the yacht was a hoax, I could forget about who might have had the opportunity to sneak off and stab him in the back—he arranged that himself for his own purposes. But there was still Trip to consider. I had to ask myself: Who in this select group had access to my room key and knew I had gone out at just that time so he could come in here and dump the body in the piano? And then I remembered something—"

"This is ridiculous!" cried Jack, standing up from his chair. Lieutenant Carlino put a hand on his shoulder, and Wolfe sank back.

"I remembered," I continued, "that you picked me up at the airport when I arrived in New York, and that *you* were the one who gave me my room key, not the front desk."

"Hey, I handled that kind of stuff as a convenience for you. So what? That was the only key I had."

"Was it?" I took a small spiral notebook from my coat pocket and flipped open a page. "Would it surprise you to know you've been identified at Ernie's Lock Shop on Sixth Avenue and 56th Street as the man who came into the store two days before I arrived in New York and had copies made of a number of keys? Ernie particularly remembers you because when he saw these were keys to hotel rooms you handed him three hundred-dollar bills to ensure his cooperation."

I had been busy that day doing my homework, and it was paying off. For the first time Jack looked at me with real fear in his eyes.

"Hey, look—sure I had the keys made, but there's an innocent reason, I swear to God. I mean, I've been in this business a long time. I know what it's like when a bunch of crazy actors go on location. They get drunk, they pass out, they get in all sorts of jams where they suddenly need my protection against bad publicity. You see what I mean? Having keys to your rooms was just a little insurance I could get in and *help* you in case you needed me fast. I did it for *you!*"

Jack Wolfe blinked and flashed us the most helpful smile of

which he was capable. No one was buying.

"And then I remembered something else," I went on. "On the day Trip was killed, you were in the lobby with Suzanne Tracy just as Jayne and I were going out. You had the key, and you knew my room was empty. From then on it was a simple matter to go upstairs and move Trip's body into my piano."

"But why?" he asked. "You think I'm crazy? If I kill someone, you think I'm going to start dragging the corpse all over some goddamn hotel?"

"You moved the body because you couldn't leave it where it was—in Victoria's room."

"What a crock."

"We now know Trip was strangled in Victoria's room because the police found fragments of her carpet beneath his fingernails. As it happens, Victoria's carpet is different from any other in the hotel; until recently that suite had been lived in by an eccentric artist who loved the color burgundy and redecorated the sitting room at his own expense."

Jack seemed stunned. He looked up at Lieutenant Carlino, who gazed back impassively. "But La Volpa . . ."

"Victoria wasn't there. She was on a picnic that afternoon with her chauffeur in Westport, Connecticut. You knew that and invited Trip up to her room for a little tête-à-tête. Trip, after all, was your partner in crime, and you were accustomed to finding discreet places to meet."

"This is like some kind of bad dream," said Jack. He was visibly sweating, but still trying to talk his way out. "But why? Why should I kill poor Tripper?"

"To cover your tracks, Jack. You and Trip had done something very foolish—you thought money was flying around so freely on this production you could steal seventy-five thousand dollars and no one would notice. I imagine this was Trip's idea, but you were happy to go along."

"That's a lie!"

"Jack," I said sadly, "we even know how you did it—you simply submitted false publicity expenses. A lot of them. Lunches you didn't go to, big cash tips you never really paid out, full-page ads in the trades that were never actually printed, even a computer you never bought. You were counting on the general chaos to not get caught, but Bernie was a little sharper than you'd imagined."

Jack sat silently, shaking his head.

"And so Bernie had you in his power—you and Trip. He said he wouldn't turn you in if you helped him set up his little publicity stunt where he was going to disappear for a few days under mysterious circumstances. You knew all the details, didn't you? Like about the speedboat that would pick him up from the water—only you tried to pay the driver *not* to come because you were planning for Bernie to really be dead by then."

Jack licked his lips and stared at me with slightly glazed eyes.

"Unfortunately for you, the speedboat driver told Bernie about your offer, so he knew you were going to try to kill him, or maybe let him drown. Your reasons were obvious—you figured with Bernie gone you'd be able to keep the seventy-five grand and be safe from him ever pointing the finger at you—isn't that so?"

Jack shook his head vigorously. "B.B. was like a father to me. I wouldn't hurt a hair on his head! Maybe Trip planned to kill him, but not me. I swear to God!"

"No, you thought up the murder, Jack, but Trip was the one who came up with the idea of planting the bomb. The idea was to get rid of Bernie and at the same time create so much chaos, no one would be able to figure out exactly what had happened. Trip knew a bit about explosives. Seems that the police investigation turned up the fact that before he came east he had a summer job in an old silver mine in California."

"That's right," Jack said eagerly. "See, Trip did it. He was nasty enough. He killed Bernie and sank that boat."

*"Ship,"* I told him. "You and Trip planned all this out together, but then, Jack, you got a little greedy. You figured, why split the money with Trip? With the kid dead, it would all be yours, not to mention you could now sleep easy at night. You never really trusted Trip, did you? He was young and flaky; you figured he'd probably get you arrested one day. Not only that,

but you were afraid he was working out some deal with Bernie behind your back."

"You can't prove any of this!" Jack sneered.

"Oh, no? After Bernie thwarted your plans and got away alive in the speedboat, he telephoned Trip, hoping to work out some deal so he could reappear and finish his film. He thought he could manipulate the kid—after all, Bernie had money and power and if he could come back from the dead, he could do a lot more for an ambitious young man than you ever could, Jack. This made you awfully nervous, the two of them talking behind your back—you thought you were being set up to be the fall guy. And that's the reason you killed Johnson."

"Do I have to listen to this crap?" Jack asked, looking up at New York's finest.

"I think so," said Carlino calmly.

I was able to continue:

"With Trip out of the way, you had only two people to worry about—Barnes and me. You knew I was asking a lot of questions, and you were afraid I might come up with some answers, so you kept an eye on me and waited for a chance to create a convenient accident. You followed me the night I went over to Nash's and tried to run me down in a limousine when I was walking home."

"You must be crazy!"

"Am I? I bet we'll find you signed out one of the company limos that night and let the driver off for a bite to eat while I was upstairs at Nash's. You thought you'd be safer with me out of the picture, but Bernie's death was absolutely essential—as long as he was alive, you'd never have a moment's peace. Unfortunately, you couldn't find him, could you? Even Trip didn't know where Bernie was—when Bernie wanted to contact Trip he always did it by phone. But then you got lucky.

"Yesterday afternoon you ran into an old Broadway actress at the Russian Tea Room by the name of Sally Malloy—she had played a small part in one of Bernie's movies three years ago that you had worked on as well. Imagine your surprise when she said she had just been talking with Bernie, whom the papers were reporting as dead! You bought her a drink, and she told you

Bernie was staying at his Greenwich Village loft on Hudson Street and that he had hired her to wear a red dress and meet me at The Four Seasons last night."

"No," said Jack in a strange whisper.

"Jack, Sally has given Sergeant Dimitriev a sworn statement. There's no doubt about this at all. Sally, by the way, thought she was hired only as part of some harmless practical joke Bernie was playing on me, but you immediately saw how you could kill two birds with one stone—get rid of Barnes and me at the same time.

"So you went to the loft and waited on the roof across the street. When I arrived, you shot Bernie in the back with a .22-caliber hunting rifle and then set fire to the building after barricading the front door of the loft. As it happens, Jack, the police are at this very minute using a search warrant to go through your apartment, and I have a feeling they're going to find your rifle and match it up with the bullet fired from the murder weapon. Don't you agree?"

Jack Wolfe sat with one shoulder raised, looking gnarled and tense. He kept sighing and shaking his head, and there was a funny half smile on his lips I didn't like at all.

Then, without warning, he made a dash for the door. Lieutenant Carlino reached out for him, but he was too late. Jack crossed the room in a blur, his eyes fastened on the door and his escape.

He might have made it, too, but Jayne quite calmly gave the room-service cart a push so that it rolled directly into Jack's path. Jack fell across the smoked salmon and knocked over the small portable oven with its cans of Sterno. He fell in a great clatter of plates and silverware and food, and ended up on the floor surrounded by tidbits of egg rolls and quiche.

"Oh, dear," said Jayne, "I just hate guests who are greedy about the hors d'oeuvres!"

# chapter 53

**T**he gala premiere of *Murder in Manhattan* took place at Radio City Music Hall a week before Christmas in the first snowstorm of the season. Despite the weather, it was a star-studded event with crowds of spectators pressing against the police lines outside the theater on Sixth Avenue and two huge searchlights scanning the snowy skies.

I sat through the movie with Jayne holding my hand, and when it was over, and the applause had died down, I walked with her back toward the lobby of the theater, where a champagne fountain had been set up beneath a huge crystal chandelier.

"It's a satiric masterpiece!" cried the reviewer from *The New York Times,* coming over to say hello.

"Bernard L. Barnes's final film is a work of genius," said the man from UPI.

"This is a film that's going to positively *make* the career of everyone connected with it!" enthused a columnist from the *Hollywood Reporter.* "Do you have any film plans for the future, Mr. Allen?"

"Not on the immediate horizon," I admitted with a wry smile.

Ah, there's nothing like success! For two weeks I had been seeing advance rave reviews for *Murder in Manhattan.* "Two thumbs-up!" said Siskel and Ebert. "Brutally funny," said *Newsweek.* "A decisive and important portrait of greed and snobbery among the upper echelons of New York society," said *Time.*

Theaters around the country were preparing for a record run, and the Museum of Modern Art was mounting a Bernard L. Barnes retrospective. Death certainly was treating Bernie kindly. I couldn't help but imagine him smirking with glee from his place beyond the river. As for his widow, Mimi Day, I had a glimpse of her still dressed in black—though it was a rather gorgeous gown—standing near the champagne fountain surrounded by a horde of respectful admirers. As a widow she was regal and quietly proud, and seemed to be enjoying her finest hour.

"Oh, look, there's Natasha and Bobby!" said Jayne. Lieutenant Carlino, in tux and black tie, was escorting a dazzling Sergeant Dimitriev, who was draped in a stunning white gown, looking more like a movie star than most of the actual stars there. We had sent them tickets to the premiere but had not seen them before the show.

"I can hardly believe it," said the lieutenant, shaking my hand. "The damned picture's actually good!"

"That's not a very complimentary way to put it, Bobby," Natasha said, giving me a sweet smile.

"That's quite all right," I told them. "This isn't the first movie that was murder to make but in the end, amazingly enough, all the hassles and conflicts of the production are forgotten, and all that's left is the magic on screen. By the way, you two look great."

The lieutenant and sergeant stood smiling at us with the secret inner glow of those in love. They were holding hands, which normally might be considered unbecoming behavior for NYPD officers, but they were off duty. We hadn't seen them for nearly five months, and we spent some time catching up.

"June," said Jayne with a sigh. "What a lovely month for a wedding."

"We're going to Paris for our honeymoon," said Natasha, beaming at us.

"And maybe take a week or so and drive around the wine country," said a smiling Bobby.

There had been some changes, all right. Jayne had long finished her makeover of Natasha and now the diamond in the rough was a diamond pure and simple. Bobby Carlino couldn't take his eyes off her. I couldn't help thinking that it isn't every murder case in which the cops get not only the killer, but each other as well.

Jasper and Emily North spied us and made their way through the crowded lobby to our sides. I hadn't seen Jasper since the film's wrap party, and he seemed thinner than I remembered him, but he was deeply tanned from some tropical idyll and appeared quite spry.

"I'm doing fine, Steve," he said with gentle humor, noticing how I looked him over. "I'm going to beat this disease—Emily and me together, that is."

Emily linked her arm through her husband's and gave him a supportive pat.

"A perfect Hollywood ending," said Jayne with a contented sigh, taking my hand in hers. "In the end everyone gets what they deserve—the bad go to prison and the good find love."

"You must excuse me," said Jasper. "I was rather unwell there for a while, and then I've been in Tahiti the last few months deliberately avoiding newspapers, but Jack Wolfe, is, er . . ."

"In prison," I told him. "Thirty years."

Jasper nodded, then scrutinized me closely. "You know, my dear chap, there are still a few things I never did quite understand. For instance, how did you find this Tommy person who made copies of the hotel keys?"

*"Ernie,"* said Carlino and I at the same time. We laughed, and he insisted I tell the story.

"Well, once I remembered it was Jack who had given me my room key when I first arrived, everything else seemed to fall into place. On the day before the cocktail party, Lieutenant Carlino sent a small army of investigators to every locksmith within a fifteen-block radius of The Plaza, hoping we'd get lucky and find Jack had indeed made a copy of the key. It was quite elementary, my dear Jasper."

"Was it now? And how, Mr. Holmes, did you learn Jack was padding his publicity expenses and putting in false claims?"

"That was a bit of luck," I admitted. "After I saw the company accountant, he made a complete review of all the expenditures on *Murder in Manhattan.* When he found the publicity budget was wildly bloated, he called the police right away. I suppose he wanted to distance himself from any crime—an accountant has to be careful in these matters."

"Steve and I spent the entire day before the party searching desperately for solid evidence," said the lieutenant. "Our big break was finding the actress Bernie had hired to lure Steve down to the Village. When he said she had run into Jack at the Russian Tea Room and told him where Bernie was hiding out, we knew we were getting close, but our case against Jack, legally speaking, was pretty thin. That's why I decided to let Steve go ahead with the party. It seemed best to bluff a little and hope Jack would do something foolish like confess."

"And did he finally?" asked Jasper.

"Once that guy started blabbing, the stenographer could hardly keep up with him," said Natasha.

"You see, Jack and Trip stole the seventy-five grand over a period of some weeks," I explained. "The money was supposed to go into an elaborate scheme: They were going to buy drugs, make a fast profit of about three hundred percent, and then return the original amount to the production budget before anyone became the wiser. Jack claims this was all Trip's idea—a scam too good to resist."

"Did they buy the drugs?"

"They never got that far," said the lieutenant. "Jack was taken in by his own greed and didn't realize Trip didn't have any kind of serious deal put together. My guess is Trip wanted to steal the money mostly as a way to get back at his father—he certainly didn't have the kind of big-time drug connections to turn seventy-five thousand into half a million, as he claimed to Jack."

"And when Jack realized this," I added, "he knew he was dealing with an unstable kid who might expose him anytime, accidentally or otherwise. This is when he decided Trip had to die."

"Well, I feel sorry for poor Trip," said Jayne. We were all silent for a moment, thinking about the dead young man as the din of the champagne reception went on around us. I felt sorry for Trip, too, but he'd had more opportunities than a lot of kids, and he had certainly made some wrong decisions.

I noticed a new look of puzzlement on Jasper's brow. "But why did Jack need to move the body from La Volpa's room to yours? Wouldn't it have been safer to leave it right where it was?" he asked.

"Naturally Jack had to get rid of the body *somewhere,*" said Natasha grimly. "Victoria knew he and Trip were using her room, and if she returned to discover the dead third assistant— well, she certainly would have been able to figure out who the killer was."

"But why would La Volpa be willing to let the two of them use her suite in the first place?" asked Jasper. "*I* certainly wouldn't have."

Natasha smiled. "You can't exactly accuse La Volpa of big brains. Besides, Trip kept her supplied with diet pills—speed really—and she thought he was cute. They were, uh, seeing each other, you know."

"Trip and Victoria?" I said. The officers had managed to surprise even me with that one.

"You see, Jack killed Trip in the heat of the moment," said Natasha. "If he had had a chance to plan it better, he probably wouldn't have done it in La Volpa's room. But that's the way it came down, and once it was done he had to make the best of it."

"They were arguing about the drug deal," put in Lieutenant Carlino. "When Trip still wanted to go ahead and use the money to buy cocaine, Jack knew he was in trouble. With Trip for a partner, they were both sure to get caught. So he strangled the kid and then was in a panic—until he remembered that Steve was a suspect in the first murder and that his suite was just down the hall. Not only could he get rid of the body, but he could even throw the suspicion onto someone else."

"Lucky I have a sense of humor," I said grimly.

"I have just one last question for you, Steve," Jasper said. "Unless you really *are* Superman under that mild-mannered exterior, how the hell did you get out of that burning building in Greenwich Village? I thought you said there were bars on the windows and the door was locked."

"Didn't I tell you how I got out?" I asked innocently.

"No, at the cocktail party you were damned secretive and just a little smug about that particular part of the story. So tell me, Clark Kent, how *did* you get out of there?"

"How does Clark Kent always get out? He finds himself a phone booth and changes into Superman."

"Steve, honesty, I want to know."

"I'm telling you the truth."

"There was . . . a phone booth?"

"No." I grinned. "But there was a telephone. I picked it up and simply dialed 911. You see, my friend, some mysteries aren't really that mysterious at all."